For Cookie –

A token of thanks for judging
our Public Speaking Competition 1995/ תשנ"ה !

Bialik High School

THE PRINCE *of* WEST END AVENUE

THE PRINCE of WEST END AVENUE

A Novel   **Alan Isler**

BRIDGE WORKS PUBLISHING CO.
Bridgehampton, New York

Library of Congress Cataloging-in-Publication Data

Isler, Alan, 1934–
    The prince of West End Avenue : a novel / Alan Isler
        p.   cm.
    ISBN 1-882593-04-9 (acid free paper)
    I. Title
    PS3559.S52   1994
    813'.54—dc20   93-35927
                                                     CIP

10   9   8   7   6   5   4   3   2   1

Book and jacket design by Edith Allard

Printed in the United States of America

First Edition

FOR ELLEN,
Without Whom Most Assuredly Not

The best actors in the world, either for tragedy, comedy, history, pastoral,
pastoral-comical, historical-pastoral, tragical-historical, tragical-comical-
historical-pastoral, scene individable, or poem unlimited.

Hamlet 2.2

THE PRINCE *of* WEST END AVENUE

HE LAST FEW WEEKS have not been easy for me. After an absence of sixty years, Magda Damrosch has reentered my life and my system is in turmoil. I cannot sleep and I am troubled by constipation. How ironic that the release of the psychological mechanism should be accompanied by stoppages in the physical! And of course there are the headaches, two points of pain that gather behind the temples and converge at the base of the skull. No cause for alarm, however. I shall not die at the Emma Lazarus for want of a laxative and an aspirin. Not for nothing does Benno Hamburger call our little home the Enema Lazarus. This witticism is still making the rounds. No doubt about it, he is our specialist in coprological humor, a man of unbounded cloacal enthusiasms.

But what sort of a way is this to begin, for heaven's sake? Even to talk of such things! I am ashamed of myself. First I should tell you who I am. My name is Otto Korner. Dropping the umlaut over the *o* was my first concession to America. Yesterday, September 13, 1978, I celebrated my eighty-third birthday at the aforementioned Emma Lazarus, a retirement home on West End Avenue in Manhattan. Eventually you'll find me just south of Mineola, Long Island, where I will be taking up permanent subterranean residence.

Quite a few of my friends are already buried there. Only last week Adolphe Sinsheimer led the motorcade. He was to have been our Hamlet. (Yes, we have our little theatrical society here. Nothing to boast of, I suppose, by the severe standards of Broadway, but good enough.) Adolphe alone of all of us could claim some professional experience. For reasons now buried with him, he was in Hollywood in the 1930s and, amazingly, found brief employment as a Ruritanian soldier in the movie *The Prisoner of Zenda*. This was, it is true, his sole public offering on the altar of Thespis, but such are the vagaries of fame that this happenstance has granted him a kind of celluloid and ghostly immortality. He always spoke fondly of Ronald Colman, the great English actor, on the anniversary of whose death he would wear a black armband. Well, Sinsheimer is gone, and it would be meanspirited to question the closeness of his friendship with "dear Ronnie," as he always called him. It appears Adolphe choked upon a lump of sugar he had hidden in his room against a midnight hunger pang, turned purple and died before he could summon help. Thus we can say that Sinsheimer, the first of us to become a supernumerary, discovered at the last how sweet it is to die.

But my subject is not amateur theatricals, it is art—or, more accurately, *anti*-art: in brief, Dada. I want to set the historical record straight. For sixty years I have been harboring the truth, a private possession, whether out of greed or modesty I cannot say. But Magda Damrosch has reappeared, and now the truth must out. It groans for expression. If, as a result, my part on the world's stage appears inflated, so be it.

I might as well tell you that I have been cast as the Ghost in *Hamlet*. There is an irony in that if one can but sniff it out. We produce only the classics at the Emma Lazarus. Of course, you have to make allowances. Last year, for example, our Juliet was eighty-three and our Romeo seventy-eight. But if you used your imagination, it was a smash hit. True, on opening night, when Romeo killed Tybalt, it was Romeo who fell down and had to be carried on a stretcher from the stage. Look for him now in Mineola.

Meanwhile, we've lost our Hamlet. Our little troupe is in disarray. We are to meet formally this afternoon to discuss what we are to do. But already cliques are forming. You cannot imagine the flutter in our dovecote. Some are talking of canceling the production, as a token of respect. Others say that if the play were a comedy, then yes, cancel it, no question; but since it is a tragedy . . . Tosca Dawidowicz, our Ophelia, flatly refuses to play opposite Freddy Blum, Sinsheimer's understudy, claiming that he lacks "stage presence," and besides, his halitosis would make her forget her lines. Actually, it is an open secret here that Blum wooed her, won her, and rejected her in the course of a single hectic weekend. La Dawidowicz has found an ally in Lottie Grabscheidt, our Gertrude, another Blum reject. As for me, I remain aloof from such childish squabbling and bickering. In principle, I believe that "the show must go on," but I should not be much put out were it called off. Sinsheimer, the cause of the tempest, is, needless to say, beyond caring. In the meantime, I hold my counsel. But at the meeting I intend to reveal that I have already mastered the Prince's role, and should I be asked to take the part, I will of course accept. Under those circumstances, Blum could become Osric, and Hamburger could be shifted from Osric to the Ghost. We shall see. "The readiness is all."

2

OR REASONS I AM not prepared to examine, it is difficult for me to write about Magda. Let me note only that in sixty years Magda Damrosch, miraculously, has not aged by so much as a single white hair. She looks exactly as she looked—unbearably beautiful!—when I last saw her in Zurich, in 1917. She holds herself with the same slender grace, the same quizzical tilt to her head, as then. Even now her smile, accompanied by a slight raising of her left brow, sends arrows directly to the heart. What is she doing here? Tristan Tzara used to say, only half joking, that she was a spy in the service of Franz Josef. But the Emperor is long gone. The only undercover work at the Emma Lazarus has to do with bedpans.

She joined the staff four weeks ago as a physical therapist. Dr. Comyns, who is an even bigger fool than he looks, accompanied her on a round of introductions. We were at rehearsal. Poor Sinsheimer, not yet a resident of Mineola, had just grasped Tosca Dawidowicz by a plump wrist and was saying, with heavy and deliberate sarcasm, "Nymph, in thy orisons be all my sins remember'd." He was sarcastic, I should explain, not because La Dawidowicz is eighty-two years of age, was wearing a gray Mickey Mouse sweatsuit and large, pink hair curlers, tips the scale at no less than 175 pounds, and has a chin that strains upward to meet an eagerly descending nose. Nor was he sarcastic because he recognized in his words a veiled, punning reference to himself. No, it was Sinsheimer's belief that Ophelia was a whore. His argument, I must say, was quite convincing. He had backed it up during auditions with pointed references to the text and a complete Stanislavskian disquisition on hidden motivations. For our little group, of course, there was an additional element of irony to be found in the fact of La Dawidowicz's in-house reputation.

At any rate, he spoke his line, turned from Ophelia with a sneer, and saw Dr. Comyns climb onto the stage with Magda Damrosch in tow. Sinsheimer was not one to miss a trick. "Here's metal more attractive!" he said. Still in character, he waved a regal hand in Magda's direction.

Comyns has a slight frame and is constantly on guard against overweight. His hair and voguish beard are of a deep, lustrous black. When he smiles, his fleshy lips reveal square white teeth, wantonly gapped. In fact, he is something of a dandy and even wears a silk handkerchief in the pocket of his physician's smock. On formal occasions such as this, he eschews brevity and embarks on serpentine sentences that loop and meander, coil in upon themselves, creep and digress, taking his auditors upon a harrowing journey through the language. "It gives me—how shall I put it? great pleasure?—yes, I am more than happy—in fact, Miss Dattner, I am delighted—to have you meet a gentleman who is not only the director of the Emma Lazarus Old Vic but also, and from this you can get some idea of his many talents, also, in short, the principal actor in the current production, which, as you can see, is even now in rehearsal, and thus he is one of our, if you will, celebrities." He ended triumphantly and mopped his brow with his silk handkerchief. "And how are we today, Adolphe?"

"I humbly thank you, well, well, well." Sinsheimer felt a touch of the antic disposition.

Comyns made the rest of the introductions and chose to express "in behalf of all of us here at the Emma Lazarus a warm welcome to Miss Mandy Dattner, the newest and youngest and—not a word beyond this friendly group!—surely the prettiest member of the staff."

There was polite applause. Magda—my Magda!—smiled and raised her left brow. I almost fell from the stage.

Lottie Grabscheidt, who sucks up to every new acquaintance, broke the silence: "I hope they've given you a nice office, darling." Dressed as always in black, La Grabscheidt was sporting for rehearsals a new pin: in silver filigree, a mask of comedy superimposed upon a mask of tragedy, a botched design that from the slightest distance looks like a grinning skull. This she fingered, as if to demonstrate her thespian credentials.

"Miss Dattner understands how cramped we are here," said Comyns. "She has agreed to share Mrs. Baum's office, right next to the staff dining room." He showed his teeth briefly and narrowed his eyes behind his spectacles: thus he signals that a witticism is on the way. "Next to the dining room, she'll easily be able to get her just desserts. I ask you, could we treat her better than that?"

"God's bodkin, man, much better!" said poor Sinsheimer angrily. He held his arms akimbo and stamped a petulant foot. "Use every man after his desert, and who shall 'scape whipping?" Say what you will about Sinsheimer, he knew the play inside and out.

What she said to me personally I was too agitated to take in. But by not so much as a blink did she betray that she knew me.

Later that day I found Comyns relaxing in the library. He was dreamily stimulating his inner ear with a stiff index finger. The pose quite suited him. Quickly I brought the conversation around to the new therapist. "She seems so young for so responsible a position," I suggested.

"Nonsense. She's been trained in Europe. All the latest techniques."

He thinks he knows us "Europophiles," as he calls us, forgetting what it was that brought so many of us here in the first place. Needless to say, it is Comyns who wags his tail, rolls over, and pants before the idol of Europe. His car, for example? A Mercedes Benz! "Europe!" I shook my head in wonder. "You don't say!"

Comyns showed his teeth and narrowed his eyes. "She's kind of sexy, too, eh? You old devils won't have any trouble getting your limbs in motion."

To this sally, of course, I made no reply. Better to suppose he confused me with Blum, the satyr. I nodded frostily and strode away. (No, no, Otto, only the truth: you winked in return and shuffled off.)

But I have other, more reliable sources of information. I waited patiently for two days and then visited Personnel—that is to say, Mrs. Selma Gross. Selma occupies an office that has a bulletproof window looking out into the lobby near the main entrance. Thus she doubles as portress. No wily Orpheus could tootle his Eurydice past her. In brief, we must check with her if we wish to go out. She has the daily list of "solo-ambulants."

Like Dr. Comyns, she is of native stock. To look at her, one would suppose her a resident rather than a member of the staff. But in fact there is a Mr. Gross: Bernie, a C.P.A., with whom she leads a full and active life far away from us—in Fresh Meadows, to be precise.

At any rate, I waved cheerily to her through the bulletproof glass and pointed at her bell. She buzzed me in.

"I kiss your hand, dear lady," I said, as breezily as if we had met at the Hotel Sacher. Selma loves such archaic formulations. "Pining for the sight of beauty, I thought immediately of you. And here, dear lady, I am."

Selma pursed her lips and patted her hair, a piled mass of

drab blond whose declivities give off a curious orange tinge. Her face was, as ever, a thick, grotesque mask of makeup, pure Dada. In such a way, no doubt, she keeps alive her Bernie's guttering flame of passion. "Going out, Mr Korner?" She reached for her list.

"No, I came only to see you. Ah, but I imagine you must be busy, what with new staff appointments, forms to fill out, red tape, heaven knows what. I must not selfishly keep you from your work."

"Oh, you mean Mandy Dattner, the new therapist." Selma patted a file on her desk. "That's all done."

"She's European, I understand."

Selma snorted. "If Cleveland is in Europe."

"But she was trained in Europe. Lausanne? Vienna?"

"Two years, Shaker Heights Community College, 1973 to 1975," Selma began, counting on her fingers. "Two years bumming around Europe, 1975 to '77; one year, Spenser School of Gymnastic Vigor, Wigan, England, 1976 to '77, graduated magna cum laude, Ph.Th.D."

I raised a puzzled brow.

"Physical Therapy Diploma."

"And now she graces our little community?"

Selma sniffed. "If you ask me, it's a scandal. But you know Dr. Weisskopf. One look at a body like hers and he's making a fool of himself. That's the only credential a woman needs around here."

Dr. Hugo Weisskopf is director of the Emma Lazarus, which he rules with an iron fist. One shake of his head and we're out of the play, erased from the list of solo-ambulants, put on a diet of fruit juice and porridge. He is not to be trifled with. Hence I have not as yet reported my insomnia and my constipation. Behind his back we call him the Kommandant: Hamburger, rhyming Teutonically, calls our distinguished director "Dr. Scheisskopf." For Hamburger, the shift from Weisskopf-Whitehead to Scheisskopf-Shithead was a matter of course.

The conversation, clearly, had taken a dangerous turn. Not wishing to speak words that might later be used against me, I rewarded Selma's confidence with a sympathetic smile. "I think, dear lady, that perhaps I will go out after all. A little fresh air before lunch."

Selma reached again for her list of solo-ambulants.

* * *

MANDY DATTNER, MAGDA DAMROSCH: the similarity is evident to the meanest understanding. But what does it mean? No, I am not senile, I am not mad. I know as well as you that this child from Cleveland is not—cannot be—the Magda Damrosch who broke my heart in Zurich all those years ago. *That* Magda Damrosch went up in smoke at Auschwitz in 1943. For this appalling piece of information I am indebted to Egon Selinger, who wrote from Tel Aviv in 1952, finding me heaven knows how. He was looking for other survivors. Not believing myself to be a survivor and having, besides, personal reasons enough for not corresponding with him, I never replied.

But in some sense this Mandy Dattner *is* that Magda Damrosch. Her arrival here cannot be accidental. Not that I think she knows more about her purpose here than I. But that we have been brought together for some purpose, I do not for a second doubt. Richard Huelsenbeck, one of the original gang of Dada nihilists, once mocked me as the typical German poet, "a dope who thinks that everything has to be as it is." (Years later he enlarged upon this idea of his in print. He had of course expunged any reference to me. They had long ago decided that I was a nonperson.) But one does not have to believe in Order or in Fate or in the God of our Fathers to believe in Purpose. When at a royal ball an aide whispered in Prince Metternich's ear that the Czar of all the Russias was dead, the Prince is reported to have mused, "I wonder what his purpose could have been." Sinsheimer, now in Mineola, perhaps knows.

3

WELL, WE'VE HAD our little meeting. The warring factions had apparently met in advance and ironed out their differences. The rest of us were presented with a fait accompli. Nahum Lipschitz was in the chair. He has a small head, thin and alert as a lizard's. "We asked ourselves," he told us, "what Adolphe would have wanted." Sinsheimer, it transpired, would have wanted none other than Lipschitz himself to replace him. But wait, there was more: Lipschitz looked at me and licked his lips. Sinsheimer would also have liked to see Freddy Blum as the Ghost. That left vacant the role formerly assigned to Lipschitz, the Gravedigger. It appeared that Sinsheimer would have wanted me to fill it.

Benno Hamburger, a true friend, came spiritedly to my defense. "What kind of nonsense is this? You think we're in Russia here? A ukase from the Supreme Soviet? To play the ghost of a former king of Denmark, you need talent and a certain natural majesty. To these qualities Korner can lay a decent claim. Let Freddy Blum play a small-town sponger, a schnorrer, which no doubt he is."

Lipschitz's bald head glistened. He blinked rapidly and turned to La Grabscheidt as if for succor. She did not fail him.

"That's some crust you got there, Benno Hamburger, some crust! I don't speak for Blum, God knows. I make no secret what I think of him." (Here Blum winced.) "But a little respect for Adolphe, may he rest in peace, wouldn't hurt. And a little consideration for Nahum wouldn't hurt either. He takes over from poor Adolphe not only the role of Prince but the role of director also. So maybe you should think twice before you open your mouth."

Hamburger shot Lottie a look of disgust. He would not deign to reply.

Lipschitz licked his lips. "Let me reason with him, Lottie. An objection is an objection. A director I may be, but a Stalin I'm not." And he embarked upon an apologia that wound its way like a wounded snake through intractable underbrush.

"Enough!" Hamburger held up his hand. "Dr. Comyns is on duty, Lipschitz. I diagnose an acute case of verbal diarrhea. Go see if he can give you something for it." He got up and made for the door, pausing only to point a pudgy finger at Lipschitz: "On the day of your birth, you were accurately named!" The door slammed behind him.

I, of course, adhering to my policy of aloofness from the fray, said nothing. Besides, I had experienced a sudden glimmering of understanding, like a small, dull light momentarily glimpsed through swirling mists. True, it was gone before I could locate it. But it left me convinced that there was purpose, too, in all my change of roles. Things were coming together. What things? We would see. I was to be the Gravedigger.

* * *

As a boy—a prepubescent, we would unblushingly say to-day—I was always losing parts of myself. Tonsils, an appendix: those, of course, were normal. But I also lost a little toe, my left earlobe, the tip of a finger. Nothing essential, you understand. And I can't say I remember any pain associated with "Otto's accidents," no lasting traumata. "He'll grow out of it, Frieda, don't make such a fuss," Manya, my maiden aunt, told my mother firmly. "I only hope," moaned my mother, "there'll still be something left of him."

I was reminded of these boyhood misfortunes by a devastating discovery this morning: my letter from Rilke has disappeared! Rilke, the most sublime of German poets! I've looked everywhere, turned my room upside down. Lost and Found knows nothing of it. The maids, if in fact they understand my rusty Castilian, claim not to have seen it. Naturally, for so important a loss—a theft?—I went to the Kommandant's office, pushing my way past his receptionist. In vain. The Kommandant was unmoved, impenetrable, a Philistine. Why was I making such a brouhaha? He was sure the letter would turn up. I grew incoherent. To my shame, I wept, I could not stop myself. The Kommandant grew severe. If I allowed myself to become so upset over nothing—*nothing!*—I would soon be unable to continue in rehearsals. He gave me a sedative and ordered me to go and lie down. He would look in on me later.

The pill seems to have worked.

* * *

TWO WEEKS HAVE PASSED since I wrote that last sentence. I have been ill, bedridden. The headaches persisted and the constipation gave way to painful stomach cramps. There were other complications: for example, a heavy numbness in my left arm. But all that is over, and I am happy to report that I am now convalescent. What remains is a slight dizziness and a new weakness in the legs.

Hamburger has been in to see me. Also Lipschitz. He was very decent, assuring me that the role of the Gravedigger remains mine. Ordinarily, removal from the list of solo-ambulants means automatic removal from the play. But he had spoken on my behalf, he said, with the Kommandant and had managed to secure my place. He brought with him a bouquet of flowers and the good wishes of the cast.

My letter has still not "turned up."

What a catastrophe of a life! To have started at the pinnacle, an established man of letters before one's career had properly begun, at nineteen a book of poems already published, *Days of Darkness, Nights of Light,* an article in the cultural section of the *Nürnberger Freie Presse!*

I came across an English translation of one of my poems in a secondhand bookshop some years ago. It was in a volume with the doomed title *Silver Poets of Germany, 1870–1914: A Pre-War Anthology* (London, 1922). Obviously I had scrambled through just under the wire. The book was thick with dust and falling apart; for twenty-five cents it was mine. Here is a sample of what a German Silver Poet sounds like in translation:

> The roots dig deep,
> Thrust through the shattered skull,
> Drink water from the rock,
> Embrace the shards of lost millennia. . . .

"But what does it mean, Otto?" I hear my father, the bourgeois literalist, asking doubtfully. To be honest, I'm not sure I myself knew; certainly I've no idea today what it meant. My poems were the vague gropings and premonitions of a very young man, expressions of feeling and thought utterly divorced from experience in the world.

But I tell you I can still feel something of the Wunderkind's exultation as I held tremulously my first published offspring, buckram the color of dark moss, and gold-stamped. Its crisp freshness is still in my nostrils, the riffle of its pages in my ears.

The reviewers were generous. A bright future was forecast for me. Kapsreiter proclaimed me a "bold new voice in a sluggish season"; Drobil welcomed me to the Groves of Parnassus—something of a witticism since this was the name of a coffee shop in Berlin frequented by writers and poets, where he himself held a regular table. But to me most exciting of all was the letter from Rilke, a poet of infinite subtlety and

sensibility, offering warm praise for my "precocious talent."
No, I did not lack for encouragement.

Even so, to have immediately submitted an article on
poetry to the cultural editor of the *Nürnberger Freie Presse*
required a wayward impudence, a youthful hubris, a chutzpah
that still leaves me breathless! The *NFP*, after all, spoke with an
authority in Europe in those days matched only by the *Times* of
London. To appear in the cultural section was to etch one's
words in adamantine rock. Max Frankenthaler, the editor then,
was a man of colossal energy and integrity, and of extraordinary
intellectual rigor. His contributors were the giant voices of
Europe: Zola, yes, but also Shaw, Gide, Ibsen. In the *NFP* my
parents' generation found those opinions they could with confidence adopt as their own: liberal enlightenment in the van,
comfortably supported by the massed troops of conservatism in
the rear. A young writer of quite exceptional talent might
reasonably hope to appear in the literary pages at the back of
the *NFP*, but in the cultural section, the feuilleton, the bottom
half of the front page, separated from the ephemeral political
twaddle of the day by a thick black line that ran from margin to
margin? And yet Frankenthaler accepted my article. I was
nineteen, for heaven's sake!

The moment in the breakfast room that morning was
surely the happiest of my life. We sit around the table, Mother,
Aunt Manya, my sister Lola, my father, chatting of this and
that. Polished wood, white linen, gleaming silverware, a warm
breeze fluttering the curtains at the window. The breakfast
smells mingle with the aroma of my father's cigar. In comes the
maid with the morning's letters and the *NFP*; she places them
on the table at my father's left hand. I feel my knees begin to
tremble. "A little more coffee, Käti, if you please," says Mother.
Aunt Manya tells Lola that she will meet her after school for a
visit to the dentist. Lola makes a face. Father glances at the front
page of his paper. Consternation! I laugh out loud. There

before him is the name of his own son, a boy whose opinions until this moment have been automatically dismissed. The phone begins to ring: our friends and relatives have also been looking at the *NFP*. For months my mother was to carry that article with her in her purse, showing it to anyone she could buttonhole.

The descent from the heights was almost immediate. There were to be no more volumes of poetry, no more articles in the *NFP*. The feuilleton that had emblazoned my name among the worthies appeared on the edge of the abyss, a bare fortnight before the events of Sarajevo hurled us all into the darkness. My fate too, it seems, was bound up with that of the Austrian archduke.

The letter from Rilke, retained under glass first in my father's study and then in my own, miraculously preserved even in the concentration camps, yellowed and almost indecipherable along its creases, a spot of warmth between my bones and my rags, that letter is now gone, swallowed up in the maw of the Emma Lazarus.

4

EWS FROM THE OUTSIDE occasionally reaches the convalescent. For example, the "Perlmutter Seminar" has had another of its ad hoc meetings in the residents' lounge. This is a loose grouping with only Hermione Perlmutter and Hamburger as its constants. It is otherwise made up of whoever cannot escape in time. La Perlmutter seizes her moments cunningly, usually after dinner, when a somnolence descends and no one has yet poked the television into life. The chatter grows desultory, then ceases altogether, and suddenly, with girlish insouciance, she drops a question like a small explosive among us. "What *is* ethnicity?" "What *is* a pseudointellectual?" "What is a *Jewish* artist?" Then she looks around with the eager air of a bright child hoping for new knowledge. Of course, her opinion has already been formed. At any rate, somebody offers an answer. Someone else refines it, Hamburger weighs in—and the seminar is already launched. "Why don't we draw our chairs into a circle," says La Perlmutter winningly, "and really thrash this one out."

Blum, who came to see me in my illness and brought with him a small box of chocolates (which, incidentally, he consumed during his visit), reported on last night's seminar, "What is the role of the poet in a time of national strife?" He stayed, he told me, only because Hermione has "great boobs." He is talking, please understand, about a short, dumpy woman with the little arms and hands of a chipmunk, who dresses like

Shirley Temple, in waistless frocks cinctured with satin sashes, shiny-black Mary Janes and cotton anklets. Her long, frizzy hair she ties back from her moon-round face with a velvet ribbon. In these seminars, she likes to take on the role of the martyr, receiving with painful joy the exasperated and sometimes heated responses she invites us to batter her with. She will make some outrageous, indefensible comment, and when she is challenged ("But what about *x* and *y*, to say nothing of *z*?"), she will assert in a high-pitched squeak, "I know *nothing* about *that,* and I don't think I *need* to. My *bubba* used to say . . ." At times she is driven to tear at her hair with her tiny claws, throw her round head back, and implore the ceiling, high above which no doubt her gnomic *bubba* is looking down, "Why must they twist everything I say?"

Once I found myself telling Hermione that her intellectual pretensions were placing my entire alimentary system at risk—that, in short, she was a pain. *Her* pain, however, seemed to me at the time transmuted into excruciating pleasure. "Oh, oh, oh," she said. Still, I don't think she likes me.

But last night's topic was, for reasons I have yet to divulge, of considerable interest to me. I am sorry I missed it. Blum's attention, of course, had been on Hermione's "boobs."

How I long to find myself enrolled once more on the list of solo-ambulants!

5

OME OF MY FRIENDS here are amused by my industry. They see me bent over my table, scraps of rejected manuscript, crushed spheres of thought, scattered around me. I must be writing a modern *War and Peace,* they say. Hamburger, with telling insight, assumes it's an autobiography. "Excellent," he says. "Get all that shit out of your system. The pipes have been clogged long enough. It's time to flush the toilet." (There you have the essential Hamburger!) But once it is out of my system, what will remain? My system is a shell, a hollow cave in which what's left of my life flaps about like a bat with a broken wing.

Meanwhile, events here have not stood still. All during my illness and convalescence, they have been creeping forward. For example, a new easy chair has appeared in the residents' lounge; Emma Rothschild has emerged as third-floor chess champion, a triumph for the nascent feminists among us; costumes for the play are nearing completion: Lipschitz, with studied nonchalance, appeared in my room the other day in a black shirt, black leotards, and a princely crown tilted at a rakish angle. "My customary suit of solemn black," he said apologetically. And of course old liaisons have been breaking up, new ones forming.

When Dr. Comyns arrived on his morning tour of inspection, he brought Magda with him. At first I pretended to be asleep. This little subterfuge was meant to suggest to the doctor that sleeping pills should no longer be a necessary part of my regimen. The fact is, I can't sleep without them, but with them my bad dreams have returned, after all these years. What they contain, I have never known; I know only that I awaken from them in terror, my heart shuddering against my rib cage, gasping for air. The bed is soaked, not alone from the sweat that has been wrung from my withered flesh. Terror gives way to shame: the price for a few hours of drugged sleep is too high.

At any rate, I continued my little deception for a few moments and secretly watched them. Events had indeed been moving forward at the Emma Lazarus. They stood side by side, hovering over me, holding hands and gazing not at the poor convalescent but into one another's eyes. She was caressing his hip with hers, a slow, exquisitely erotic motion. From where I lay, I could not help noticing the effect she was having on him. The foolish jealousy I felt at that moment was scarcely diluted by my certainty of the outcome of this affair: she would break his heart, or what passed in him for such an organ, as she had broken mine, and the hearts of who knew how many others. Ah, Magda, Magda! Meanwhile, well within arm's reach above my bed were her fine breasts, pushing against the material of her dress. Between the buttons and the straining cloth I swear I saw a triangle of warm, dark, swelling flesh! It would have been so easy, so very easy, simply to put up my hand. I longed to join the lovers in their ecstasy. I wanted to plug into them as into an electric circuit. Instead, I coughed and opened my eyes wide. They sprang apart.

Comyns had, at least, the grace to blush. Not so my Magda, who smiled and raised her left brow. "Well, young man," she said, "and how are we this morning?"

Just like that: "Well, young man"! I almost fainted; I don't know what I stuttered in reply. You see, that was what she used to call me all those years ago! Just so: "*junger Mann*," in her delightful Hungarian accent. "Talk only when you're spoken to, *junger Mann*"; "Ach, *junger Mann*, how boring you are!" Tell me, how did this child from Cleveland know that?

Comyns used his stethoscope and felt my pulse. His fingers were as cold as the metal disk. "You're as healthy as I am," he said. "All you need is a little exercise."

"Ah, but I'll still need my sleeping pills," I said cunningly. "Please, doctor, I'll still need them."

"Not on your life. No more goldbricking." He wagged a finger at me in mock admonition. "You some kind of junkie?"

Success!

Meanwhile, I am to avoid all excitement—what idiocy!—and to do as I am ordered by my therapist, a specialist in whom—here Comyns blushed once more—he has the greatest confidence.

Now it was Magda's turn. She pulled back the covers before I could stop her and revealed my shame. "Tsk, tsk." I closed my eyes. "Let's see now." She bent my arms, raised them, squeezed the muscles; she did the same with my legs. One would have sworn she knew what she was doing. "All right, now let's see what *you* can do." And I was made to walk around my room, a performing animal, stand in place and bend my legs, swing my arms like a drum majorette, arch my back. At the end of this demonstration of my limberness, the room was spinning. I tried to mask the rising nausea by leaning casually, unconcernedly, against the bureau. She turned to Comyns and they nodded at one another, two specialists of one mind.

"Okay," said the doctor, "tomorrow, you're a solo-ambulant. Congratulations. You can be real proud of yourself. Today, you go for a walk with Miss Dattner." He showed his teeth and narrowed his eyes. "You're on your honor, now: keep your hands to yourself."

"We've got a date," she said. "Eleven sharp, in the lobby. We'll take a stroll along Riverside Drive, look at the birds and the bees, see if they're up to their old tricks." She and the doctor were in lockstep.

"Watch out for him, now, Miss Dattner," said Comyns. "I'm told he's pretty hot stuff."

She winked at me. "Remember, eleven sharp."

"In the lobby," I said.

I watched them contrive to rub against one another as they left my room. How hateful they were! Rage boiled within me. How defenseless we are, we "old folk," in a world of the young. To them I was not a man, equipped with intelligence and feeling. I was a "character," a caricature; more accurately, perhaps, I was a child, incapable of following fully an adult conversation whose nuances were deemed to be well beyond my supposedly immature understanding.

* * *

FOR OUR RENDEZVOUS I dressed with care, hoping to erase the image Magda must be carrying of me, wasted limbs and sodden nightshirt. The mirror was not flattering: I had achieved only modest success. My good gray suit hung shapelessly on me; like my nose, it has grown in proportion as my flesh has withered. On the other hand, a blue polka-dot silk tie, neatly fixed with a pin, and a pocket handkerchief, generously flounced, were after all interesting foci. And so was my boutonniere, a Shasta daisy I had removed from the breakfast room. I examined myself this way and that. No use, no use. As Prufrock puts it, "I am not Prince Hamlet, nor was meant to be." Fortunately, I still hold myself erect.

Precisely as the eleventh hour registered on the clock above Selma's bulletproof window, I entered the lobby. Magda Damrosch—no, henceforth I shall call her by her new name,

Mandy Dattner—Miss Dattner was not there. I felt like a rejected swain. Thus cavalierly had Magda herself always treated me. I sat down in a lobby chair and waited. Selma waved to me through the glass. I pretended not to notice.

6

HE REAL MAGDA DAMROSCH entered my life for the first time shortly after the train left the German border station and crossed into Switzerland. I was twenty, alone, and on my way to Zurich. It was September 12, 1915. She tore open the door of my compartment with such zest that it slammed against its frame. I sprang to my feet in alarm, no doubt cutting a ridiculous figure. Indeed, I have often thought that this first impression she had of me must have determined how she would regard me for ever after. There she stood, a young woman of about my own age, the most beautiful woman I had ever seen.

"So sorry to disturb you," she said, "but has the ticket inspector been here yet?"

She was Hungarian; her charming accent gave her away immediately. She was, moreover, clearly a young woman of means, not simply because she stood at the door of a first-class carriage but because she carried herself with a certain hauteur, and her travel suit, of a delightful and subtle blue, bespoke her breeding. (How odd such words and concepts sound today: *breeding,* for heaven's sake! Still, it is true that in those days one could place a person on the social ladder with a single glance. A mere gesture could tell the whole story.)

I was already caught in her net; I wanted her to stay in my compartment. Wanted? I longed, I passionately burned for her to stay.

"Ah, but you have missed him, *liebes Fräulein*. He was here with the customs officer and the other officials when we stopped at the border. Do please allow me to find him for you."

She closed the door and sat down. "But that is exactly what I *don't* want you to do."

"But . . . ?"

"With me it's a matter of principle," she said. "Do sit down, young man."

I obeyed. "But what, if I may ask, *is* the principle?"

She smiled and raised her left brow. The arrow of Cupid lodged itself firmly in my heart. "I cannot be expected to discuss my principles with a young man to whom I have not yet been introduced, a young man who, for all I know, may himself be unprincipled."

We got along famously after that, chattering our way into Zurich. Still, it must be admitted that she revealed little of herself. While she did not scruple to ask me the most outrageously personal questions, she somehow, without actually saying so, made it clear that any personal question of mine would bring our friendly conversation to an immediate halt, a delicate bud blasted by my clumsiness, my bad manners. Was I still a virgin, she wanted to know, or had I freed myself from Mama's apron strings? Such a question in 1915 from a young lady to a gentleman stranger! It was unheard-of. It was also exhilarating, captivating. I *was* in fact still a virgin, but I did not know whether experience or inexperience would prove the more appealing to her. On the whole, it seemed better to emphasize my independence and let her think what she would. "You see me here without Mama," I said. Then why was I not laying down my life for the Kaiser? This was a sore point. I actually believed at that time all that dangerous, disgusting rubbish about *Kaiser, Vaterland,* and *Kameradschaft*. Yes, I really did. I had longed to become a war hero; to my shame, I still wove fantasies of my exploits at the front:

A bullet came a-flying:
"Is it meant for me or thee?"
Him did it tear away,
Him at my feet did lay,
As 'twere a piece of me.

(Excuse the poor translation of Uhland's poem. I've grown rusty.) It was always my comrade-in-arms who received the bullet. As for me, I wiped away a manly tear and went on to living glory. My God, can you imagine!

But in the early heady days of mobilization, when there were not uniforms enough to put on the backs of all the eager volunteers, I had been pronounced unfit for military service, my missing parts denying me access to the Kaiser's sausage grinder. ("So you see, Frieda," Aunt Manya had said, "it all turned out for the best.") There was nothing for it in that sun-bright carriage but to hint at some mysterious war-related mission: "There is more than one way to serve the Kaiser." I suppose I blushed.

"Reasons of state!" She laughed, delighted. "Well, I must not ask you to reveal state secrets, secrets upon which the fate of all Europe no doubt depends."

I squirmed.

"Tell me instead," she went on, "what your prewar occupation was."

I toyed for a moment with several possibilities but saw her mocking smile. "I was—I am—a poet."

"Wonderful! Say something in poetry."

"*Kennst du das Land, wo die Zitronen blühn—*"

"Not that Goethe rubbish, something of your own."

Goethe rubbish! Good heavens! I began to intone my

favorite poem from *Days of Darkness, Nights of Light.* In it a young man caught in the coils of a femme fatale expresses his wretchedness.

"Rubbish!"

She had allowed me no more than half a dozen lines. I knew in my soul that hers was the first word of honest criticism my poetry had ever received.

As the train pulled into the *Bahnhof* at Zurich, she gave me my instructions. We were to walk together along the platform toward the ticket collector, obviously companions. About fifteen paces from the wicket, I was to put down my bags and begin worriedly to feel in my pockets. I had mislaid something, something important, perhaps left it on the train. Meanwhile, she would herself walk on through the wicket and stop just beyond it, indicating to the collector with a nod of her head that she was waiting for me. Perhaps she would stamp her foot impatiently. I was to open one of my bags, obviously looking for the lost item. But I should contrive to keep an eye on her. When I saw that she had successfully mingled with the crowd departing the *Bahnhof*, I was to give a cry of relief—I had found it!—do up my bag, and go and hand in my ticket to the collector. Should I be asked for *her* ticket, I had only to tell the truth: I had met the lady that afternoon on the train; only in that sense had we been traveling together.

There, that was easy enough, wasn't it? Did I understand what I was to do? "We'll make something of you yet, young man."

The plan terrified me. She was asking me to abet her in the commission of a crime. My bourgeois soul rebelled against the very idea. If she found herself temporarily embarrassed, I told her as delicately as I could, I would be honored to furnish her with the money for a ticket.

"What a silly mama's boy you are!"

As it turned out, her plan worked like magic. When, with a pounding heart, I handed my ticket to the collector, he merely took it and reached past me for the next. He had forgotten all about her.

Too late I realized that I had no idea where I might find her. All Zurich yawned before me. My eyes smarted, and I cursed my stupidity.

7

HE LOBBY OF THE EMMA LAZARUS, a cool marble vault of graceful arches and slender pillars, still retains some of the grandeur of an earlier era. In some ways this is the hub of our little community, and many of our residents like to spend the day here, watching, gossiping, reminiscing. Solo-ambulants and staff come and go, bestowing on the sedentary a gratuitous whiff of the great world beyond our doors, pausing for a friendly word. To the left of Selma's bulletproof window is the bulletin board, detailing the daily and projected events of our home, prayer schedules, group and club activities, and, with Selma's official stamp of approval, private notices and messages. Among these last this morning was the following: "Hannah: Goldstein's. 10:30: Benno."

Meanwhile, I sat apart, waiting for Mandy Dattner, for Magda Damrosch, past and present mingling, time dissolving, between hope and despair. The Kommandant entered the building, with Jorge, his chauffeur, smartly opening the massive door for him and touching his cap respectfully. He rapped sharply on the bulletproof glass en passant, signaling to Selma that he, the chief, was once more in residence, and paused before me— "So, Korner, up and about again? Good. Remember, I warned you: *Du calme, du calme, soyez tranquille*"—then continued on his way, magisterial, dignified, in a fine gray suit, heavy silk tie, Italian shoes, deep in medical and administrative thought about the welfare of his charges, a latter-day Atlas confidently carrying the weight of our world on his shoulders, the sedentary sitting up alertly on both sides as he passed, smiling at him, "Good morning, Dr Weisskopf," solo-ambulant material all. The great man continued on his way.

Three of the four members of I Solisti di Morrisania, our string quartet, scurried across the lobby on their way out, prompting speculation among the sedentary that the group was breaking up, that Menasha Futterman, the missing cellist, was seriously ill, was perhaps already dead. Then Futterman emerged from the cloakroom, rosy-cheeked, buttoning up. "How you doing, Menasha? Feeling okay?" To which, Futterman, alarmed: "Sure I'm okay. What you think? I don't look okay?" And he hurried to join his mates, a hand over his heart. "That's not a well man," the sedentary agreed with satisfaction.

Hermione Perlmutter skipped in from the street, her Mary Janes twinkling, scanned the bulletin board, found her message, glanced at her watch, stamped a frustrated foot, and turned to skip out again, merely waving at Selma, throwing the solo-ambulant bookkeeping into disarray. For me, La Perlmutter did not spare even a glance, a rudeness duly noted by the sedentary, who nodded to one another very wisely. As I have hinted, she does not much like me.

Hermione and I arrived here in the same week, she a widow of some years' standing and I once more a widower. These circumstances threw us together, for we were both feeling our way into a new community. Perhaps I misunderstood her overtures. It seemed to me that she was after more than friendship. My experience with the Contessa, my second wife, had made me wary. La Perlmutter would often sit and stare at me with a very strange smile on her lips. She was always at my elbow—in the dining room, in the library, on my walks. "Hermione is a bit of a mouthful," she said. "Why not call me Hannah?"

Over the course of those first few weeks, I learned quite a

lot about her. She was born into London's East End, a teeming Jewish community, daughter to a tailor and his seamstress wife, turn-of-the-century Russian emigrants who had stopped off in England on their way to America and settled there. She was the last of seven children, "the baby, everyone's pet," she said, placing a finger upon her chin, a gesture of a faraway time. "As soon as they'd scraped together a little money, Daddy sent for Mummy's parents. Times were hard, but one thing we had in plenty was love. I would sit for hours on my granny's lap, smothered in kisses. She was something of a philosopher, as a young woman an active socialist, later disillusioned. No remark was permitted to stray past her unexamined. 'The Bolsheviks are transforming Russia,' Grandfather might say innocently. 'Wait a minute, smarty,' my granny would interrupt him, 'a Bolshevik is different from a Cossack? A Russian is a Russian. Tell me, what *is* a Bolshevik?' And they were off on an hourlong discussion. That was my milieu."

The brightest of her siblings, Hermione completed grammar school and afterward found employment in the Whitechapel Public Library, a social advancement that awed her family. "I loved books," she confessed, "loved the look of them, the feel of them. There was no appeasing an appetite like mine. I swallowed a whole library." Here she made a self-deprecating gesture, as if to suggest that her gluttony for books explained her current rotundity. "My daughter's the writer of the family, but all my life I've tried my hand—secretly, of course." On that occasion we were sitting in the Emma Lazarus library, and so she was whispering. "Perhaps one day, if you'll let me, I'll show you some of my stuff, awful though it is." I was noncommittal.

She met Milton Perlmutter, her future husband, in 1944. She was then in her early thirties and "something of a wallflower." He was an officer in the judge advocate general's corps, on special mission in England to represent American servicemen accused of paternity by Englishwomen they had (or had not) "knocked up." They sat across from one another at a seder table in Hendon; with each of the four glasses of wine he impiously but romantically toasted her. Later he took her home. "He might have been from another planet. I was swept off my feet: lunch at the Savoy, a *thé dansant* at the Dorchester, a blissful weekend in Brighton"—she blushed—"flowers, chocolates, nylon stockings, a bottle of slivovitz for Daddy. I was overwhelmed. He showered me with prewar pleasures I had never known. Not in the East End." By the time she disembarked in New York in 1946, a war bride, she was already six months pregnant.

"But you've told me next to nothing about yourself," she said accurately.

"My dear lady, there is next to nothing to tell."

"I already know something," she said coyly.

I must have looked startled.

"You're very shy with the ladies. I like that."

After the war, Milton Perlmutter prospered, first in practice alone, later in a successful partnership. "Years ago he represented the Emma Lazarus in a million-dollar suit. It made all the papers. One of the doctors was accused of indelicacy with a female resident, and her family held the home responsible. Totally false, of course. The wretched woman broke down and confessed the truth under Milton's cross-examination. Her family had put her up to it. That was when I first heard about the Emma Lazarus. Who'd have thought then that I'd end up here? Well, of course, ours is not any ordinary home, more of a luxury residential hotel. We're not exactly paupers here." I winced at this, but she merely patted me on the hand, as if to help me past a painful bubble of gas. "You think we have class now? You should have seen the Emma Lazarus in those days. *Class* isn't the word. No need for bulletproof glass then. The riffraff wouldn't have dared poke a nose through the door. Why, the doorman dressed like a five-star general."

"Your grandfather might not have been comfortable here," I murmured.

She seemed not to understand. "He died in England, my granny too, may they rest in peace. *Frosch versus the Emma Lazarus* was Milton's first big case. He sent me to NYU, bless him, with the proceeds. I majored in English and minored in German literature."

At that time, we were walking on Broadway. She had invited herself along. I had some errands in the neighborhood. She put her hand on my arm, stopping me in my tracks. "I know something else about you."

"I'm really a very uninteresting person."

"You're a poet. I remembered just the other day. I *knew* the name was familiar. Then it came to me: the stacks at NYU, your book of poems on the shelf."

"That was another Otto Korner. With an umlaut. An understandable mistake."

I could see she didn't believe me.

"I suppose you could call it a comfortable marriage, no strains, none but the usual." Perlmutter had doted on her. "But it wasn't a perfect union." It had taken her eight years of widowhood to pinpoint the fault: "He lacked a spiritual dimension." For all the refinement of his education, he was too worldly, too much the lawyer, impatient of those immaterial truths with which literature deals. "There was no poetry in his soul, only torts and class reunions." But of course there was their daughter, Lucille, to link them in love—Lucille herself a mature woman now and, since her "sticky" divorce, "something of a spearhead in the women's movement," writing, lecturing, traveling all over the country.

One day I returned to my room for the siesta hour and, to my horror, found her sitting demurely and plumply on my straight-back chair. Her feet, crossed at the ankles, did not quite reach the floor. She was wearing the navy-blue tunic of the

English schoolgirl over a severe white blouse. Her hair was tied in a velvet ribbon. She was not in the least flustered.

"Forgive me," she said, "but the door was unlocked. In my view, you don't really know a person until you know the things he surrounds himself with. Don't you agree?" She touched her chin with her finger and smiled, dimpling. "You look so silly with your mouth open. Do sit down."

This was an insufferable impertinence! "Madam," I said, "I am still in mourning for my wife. Do me the kindness to leave at once."

Her round face crumpled, like that of a baby with colic. "Oh, oh, oh," she moaned, "how could you, you beast!" And she ran from my room.

8

ERE AT LAST CAME Miss Dattner, a mere fifteen minutes late, fetchingly got up in blue jeans and a gray sweatshirt, with the words *Coca-Cola* in scarlet Hebrew letters undulating across her bosom. She offered me no apology and barely hinted at an explanation.

"Let's go, young man, we're running late. There was an emergency."

From her flushed face I deduced that the emergency had taken place in the office of Dr. Comyns. Obviously this was to be no promenade but rather a therapy session—as of course I had known it would be. Feeling the crushing burden of my age and the unutterable folly of my boutonniere, I struggled to my feet.

The day was mild for late October, with just a pleasant hint of autumn in the air. Overhead a few white clouds chased one another across a pale-blue sky. It was a day for a picnic—to the charming little town of Küssnacht, perhaps, where once in the spring I took Magda, beguiled by the name of the place (Kiss-Night!) into vain dreams of amorous delight; or by boat to Rapperswil, at the far end of Lake Zurich, where she teased me beyond bearing, now leaning toward me, offering her lips, now pulling away, pouting, pretending indignation, while the sun warmed the wine and the ants marched over the white linen and bore off our crumbs. Yes, just such a day. . . .

We turned the corner of the Emma Lazarus, making for

Riverside Drive, Miss Dattner setting a pace irritatingly faster than I found natural or comfortable.

"Will you look at that!" she said angrily. The lower wall was adorned with graffiti, variously colored, largely illegible. New since my recent illness was an ill-formed swastika in bright yellow. Piles of garbage in bursting black plastic bags left only a narrow path for the pedestrian. I murmured something about this being New York, promising her that soon she, like the rest of us, would no longer notice.

"No, *that*," she said, and pointed: " 'Led Zeppelin sucks'! What kind of crap is that?"

I said I didn't understand why that particular graffito should offend.

"They're just the best there is, that's all. The greatest. They blow my mind. Shit."

We walked on, she in moody silence, I in silent perplexity.

Riverside Drive has fallen on evil times since my arrival in New York, thirty years ago. Neglect, decay, and vandalism have done their work here too. The grand promenade above the park, itself a victim, is covered now with sooty dust, through which desultory weeds have thrust their way, pushing aside the patterned, half-hidden paving stones. In 1978 litter is ubiquitous—paper, broken glass, empty cans, animal feces. ("A dog too has the right to comment on our civilization"— Hamburger.) Graffiti, graffiti everywhere. Few of the benches retain their slats. On one a derelict was stretched out supine, asleep or dead, his round white belly naked to the sun. Children broke branches from a tree. A man urinated against the wall, the sunlight glinting off his forceful stream. Some old people, out like me with their keepers, sat in the shade or tottered along. Still, through the leafy branches of the trees in the park below, one could catch a glimpse of the majestic river and of the Palisades beyond, so beautiful in the hazy distance—

as beautiful, no doubt, as the river and Manhattan must appear from the other shore. The breeze was gentle, the sun warm. They lightened Miss Dattner's mood and made possible conversation.

What little I learned of her in this therapy session was not enchanting. In intellect, in culture, in spirit, she is as far removed from Magda Damrosch as it is possible to be. Miss Dattner doesn't read much, hasn't the time, isn't into it, a couple of novels by Vonnegut, a great fat book called *Lord of the Rings,* she couldn't remember for the moment by whom. (No, nothing to do with Wagner; it was about elves, and like that.) She likes McKuen, he was cool—deep, y'know? Of what might reasonably be called music she knows nothing at all. Of art, of the theater, nothing. For relaxation she likes the movies, especially the creepy ones: she is a "creep freak." Also she is into discos. She shares a "pad" with two other girls over on the East Side, where they frequent Second Avenue bars. And she likes to work out, mostly at the Y but also in bed. (Here she laughed at her own naughtiness and winked.)

We had arrived by now at the exit from the parkway. The light was against us. Glancing at her watch, Miss Dattner announced that it was time to turn back. I must not overdo. In any case, I would not wish to be late for lunch, would I? We began to retrace our steps. I did not protest. The truth is, I was tired, not so much from the exercise as from sheer boredom. How dull she is! As empty-headed, as solipsistic, as unreflective as all her generation, of which she might serve as the signal example. I longed for a nap. For all her resemblance to Magda, I could find in her inanities no clue to that Purpose for which I had supposed us to have been thrown together. I had almost despaired of her, was ready to embrace the heresy of Coincidence, when she spoke those words that confirmed me in my faith. She had been telling me of her family: her father a stockbroker in Cleveland, her mother a musicologist in a local institute, its name unfamiliar to me. She despised what she called their "life-style." They despised hers. There were terrible fights at home. At last she left, heading for Europe. There she traveled for a while, sometimes alone, sometimes with "some guy or other" she had met. Illumination came to her in England, a bolt from the blue. She realized there and then that she might use her body and her gymnastic talent for the benefit of mankind. She had a mission. She had "gotten her act together."

"Either you become a lawyer or a doctor, or like that, or else you just marry some nice Jewish guy who *is* a lawyer or a doctor. That's what *they* think." She meant her parents. "Okay, so I didn't get the greatest grades in school. So what do they do? Get this: they start bringing home these guys from the Community Center—you know, at the temple?—on Friday nights, every Friday a new guy. D'you believe this? Weird! I mean, wee-urd! Little Mandy got the hell out of there. Sheesh! Let me tell you something: I'm no dummy, no matter what they think. I've got a head on my shoulders."

Poor parents! Perhaps they could take comfort in their daughter's Ph.Th.D., to say nothing of her newly minted romantic alliance with Dr. Comyns.

But that *she* should have said to me, "I'm no dummy . . . I've got a head on my shoulders"—those were her very words!—that she should have expressed her anger to *me,* as if I were somehow to blame (as in a sense I am), who after that would not believe in Purpose?

Yes, yes, I know how innocent of significance those words must seem—perfectly ordinary words, quite unworthy of note. Be patient, please. Soon enough you will understand their relationship to the historical moment I propose to reveal, the nexus in Time of Magda Damrosch and Dada and me.

Meanwhile, the sun had disappeared behind the clouds.

The day became gray. I felt an autumnal chill and shivered. Therapist and convalescent returned to the Emma Lazarus.

She left me in the lobby, where she had found me, casually, almost callously, certainly abruptly. "Okay, you did fine. You're on your own."

I was. Indeed, I am.

9

HIS AFTERNOON I returned to rehearsals. What a
fiasco! Only now do I appreciate the true greatness, the genius, of poor Sinsheimer: his dedication to the text, his sure
dramatic instinct; above all, his dignified authority.

The warmth with which the players greeted me put me off
my guard. They applauded as I walked onstage, shook me by
the hand, slapped me on the back. Blum tinkled "For He's a
Jolly Good Fellow" on the piano. La Grabscheidt, a glass of
seltzer and a twist of lemon in hand, offered a toast: "Ladies and
gentlemen, I give you the prince of Gravediggers, our good
friend Otto Korner!" It was an emotional moment.

Lipschitz brought us to order with a clap of his hands. "To
work, friends," he said. "Clear the stage. Enough socializing."

"Never enough," said little Poliakov tartly. The Gravedigger's Assistant in our production, Lazar Poliakov is an old-time
Bolshevik who came to this country in the twenties and made a
fortune in scrap metal. Despite his millions, he remains an
ardent communist and hence a sworn enemy of Lipschitz, the
old-time Zionist. He is known affectionately among us here as
the Red Dwarf.

We all moved to the wings, leaving Lipschitz and La
Dawidowicz in the center apron. She held the prompter's copy.

"Act five, scene one," announced Lipschitz. "Enter the
Gravedigger and his Assistant. Silence."

The Red Dwarf and I entered.

"Poliakov," said Lipschitz, "that pick's heavy, it weighs you down."

"I ain't got no pick."

"You will have." Lipschitz emitted an elaborate sigh. "Meanwhile, make like you do. Go back and try again."

We did as we were told. This time the Red Dwarf staggered on stage as if bearing the weight of an elephant on his shoulder. He grinned triumphantly at Lipschitz.

Lipschitz shook his head in disbelief but gave up. "*Nu?*" he said to me.

I peered down at my Assistant. "Is she to be buried in Christian burial?"

"Stop! Stop!" screamed La Dawidowicz.

Lipschitz struck his forehead with the palm of his hand. "Oy, nobody told him. You've got the old script, Otto. We've made some changes in the scene."

"What changes?" said Hamburger, coming out of the wings. "Nobody told me about any changes, either. You're improving on Shakespeare now, mastermind?"

The cabal had been at work again!

"It was felt," said Lipschitz, licking his lips, "that all these references to 'Christian burial' might offend some people. After all, many members of our audience are orthodox, not to say fanatic. How does it look? So we thought, what difference we get rid of a few words, make substitutions."

"Well, what is my line now?"

"Simple. You say, 'Is she to be buried in Mineola?' This same word you substitute in the other places."

"Wonderful!" said Hamburger. "Brilliant! Mineola, as everyone knows, is just south of Elsinore."

"*That's* what you want me to say? 'Is she to be buried in Mineola?' "

"Perfect. You got it. A little more emphasis on the *she*, but otherwise, perfect."

"I won't do it."

"That's it, don't knuckle under to the fascists." The Red Dwarf executed a defiant little jig.

Lipschitz dismissed him with a wave of the hand. "Why not?"

"Because I'd be a laughingstock. They'd hoot me from the stage."

"Mineola is funny?" said La Dawidowicz.

"Please, Tosca, let me reason with him." Lipschitz turned back to me. "Okay, let's just say for the sake of argument—mind you, I admit nothing—but for the sake of argument, okay? Okay, it's funny. So what? You remember dear Adolphe, may he rest in peace, what he said: 'Act five'—these are his own words, I quote—'Act five opens in the comic mode.' So people laugh. Good, I say. This was Adolphe's conception of the scene. Otto, I beg you, do it for his sake."

"I also remember what Sinsheimer had to say about the integrity of the text. For him Shakespeare's words were sacred."

"*Touché!*" The Red Dwarf produced another jig.

"Tosca," said Lipschitz, "I think you'd better tell him."

And then it came out, the whole shameful business. La Dawidowicz's son and daughter-in-law were coming to the play. The son had married a gentile. Hence her palpitations for the past twenty-five years; hence the tears with which she nightly besprinkled her pillow. God had cursed them with barrenness; they, in turn, had cursed her with a Vietnamese grandchild. "It's me they're giving a Christian burial—me, Ophelia. Not on your life. I wouldn't give that shiksa, that Muriel, the satisfaction. Forget it."

"In Act three we have Claudius on his knees praying," I said. "Perhaps we should equip him with a tallis and tephillin?"

"Not such a bad idea," said Lipschitz, scratching his chin musingly. "It has possibilities. Of course, Jews don't kneel."

"You're mad!" said Hamburger.

"You, Hamburger," said Lipschitz, "have nothing to say."

"Oh yes I do," said Hamburger. "I have this to say: I quit this farce. As of now." And he stalked out, after managing a very smart turn on the heel for a man of his age.

"Otto?" Lipschitz's voice was icy.

"I shall have to think very seriously about this, very seriously indeed." With as much dignity as I could muster, I followed Hamburger offstage.

10

HY, WITH A LIFE so stuffed with change, I should object so strenuously to a few alterations in the text of *Hamlet,* I do not know. If mutability is a condition of human existence, my life has been exemplary. The trick is not to confuse Change with Chance (a great temptation), but to allow the individual thread to merge into the varicolored fabric, where it takes its place in the harmony of the whole. Yes, I am once more talking about Purpose. Perhaps my objection to Lipschitz's mutilations has to do with the fact that in the Prince of Denmark I see much of myself. It is not to Hamlet's nobility of mind that I refer, not to the "courtier's, soldier's, scholar's, eye, tongue, sword" or to "the glass of fashion and the mould of form," but to his hesitations, his vacillations, above all his egregious eagerness to play the antic. In *this* mirror that he holds up to nature, I see my own reflection. And of course, like me, Hamlet recognizes Purpose (which he, in a Christian century, calls Providence) even in the "fall of a sparrow."

There is another point of similarity. No one would want to argue that Hamlet was good for women, whether the young Ophelia or the matronly Gertrude: one way or another, their deaths were on his head. As for me, both my wives were cremated, only one of them, the Contessa, by her own request. Of my first wife, poor Meta, I cannot yet write. The Contessa is another matter.

Whether Hamlet was capable of loving *any* woman, we

cannot know; on this subject the Bard is silent, no doubt sensibly so. *Love*, I need hardly say, is a notoriously shapeless term, a slippery abstraction. But even if we limit its meaning to a passionate regard for the well-being of another and a warm responsiveness to that other's offered warmth and evident need, a mutual concern and a shared denial of self, then we must admit that Hamlet was an utter failure, a zero, strictly from hunger. For him, Ophelia and Gertrude had no human reality; they did not palpitate with lively blood. They were instead private symbols for all he despised in this world, vessels into which he could pour all his bile, and he lashed them mercilessly with his acidulous tongue. For both of them death was a benediction. Well, of course, I was not quite so bad. I *have* loved, if only once (and with bathetic stupidity!) in my life. As for my wives, I was always superficially courteous to them, if not always decently kind. Considering the milieu and the time in which I grew up, it could hardly have been otherwise. But eventually you will be able to decide for yourself the exact degree of my responsibility for their deaths.

* * *

YOU MUST BY NOW have noticed my command of the English language, of which I am not unreasonably proud. I use it with a certain flair, I think, a certain panache that is distinctively my own. It is, of course, very un-English "to blow one's own horn," but as a wag once put it, "what else is a horn for?" The first few years after my arrival here I devoted to perfecting what was already a very sound ability in the tongue, thanks not only to my English governess, Miss Dalrymple, my years at the Gymnasium, where I was actually more solidly schooled in Greek and Latin, and my visits to England between the wars, but also and most especially to my love of English literature, a lifelong passion.

Certainly I have an ear for nuance that is often lacking

even in the native speaker. For example, in the English version of my poem that appears in *Silver Poets of Germany, 1870–1914,* I would have translated the phrase *zerschellte Schädel* as "shivered skull," not "shattered skull," trying for a play on words in the adjective, having been denied it in the noun. But perhaps the translator, Wilfred Ormsby-Gore, O.B.E., was not sufficiently sensitive to the original play on *Schädel,* which of course means "skull," but which suggests to the thoughtful the word *Schaden* ("loss," "hurt," "wound") or even *Schade!* ("what a pity!") for both of which *Schädel* seems a diminutive form. In fact, I wrote to the publishers, Leith & Sons, Ltd., about this, only to discover that Ormsby-Gore had died in the London blitz in 1941, that there had not been much demand for his little book despite their faith in its excellence, and that there was no immediate prospect of a second edition. Nevertheless, they were delighted to hear from me and wished to commend to my kind attention *Silver Poets of the Australian Outback,* which was still in print and enjoyed a lively, if rather selective, interest.

N 1947 KENNETH (NÉ KURT) HIMMELFARB, my brother-in-law, found me in a Displaced Persons camp on Cyprus. There I had already enjoyed for three months the several courtesies of the British authorities, who, to be fair, were wholly admirable when compared with those under whose aegis I had spent the war years. They had to do something with me, having found me in the company of two thousand other desperadoes aboard a rusty, leaking vessel within sight of Palestine, at dawn no more than a dark, uneven line of dune against the rising sun. By then our pumps had failed; our engines had coughed and spluttered, died, and returned to life again. Drinking water was down to half a cup a day. It was an open question whether we could reach the shore. When His Majesty's gunboats appeared, bristling with righteous indignation, our ship, renamed before the voyage *Ha-ma'avak,* gave up without a struggle. Of course, His Majesty's servants were humanitarians, decent chaps all. Although we were dirty, stinking wretches, defiant of the Crown, impudent threats to the final solution of the Palestine problem, they nevertheless offered us protection. "You'll like Cyprus," a British officer said to me. "It's like a holiday camp."

Enter Kenneth Himmelfarb. First came a letter of inquiry, however, followed by forms to be filled out, delays, more correspondence, more delays; then at last my brother-in-law himself appeared, burly, well fed, the true image of life, shouldering his way into the compound, sweating like an ox, equipped with documents, passports, visas, and a box of Hershey's chocolate bars melting in the Mediterranean sun. I must have looked a sight; he had tears in his eyes.

What a change had overtaken my brother-in-law in the thirteen years since last I saw him! How he had flourished in America! It was hard to believe. He and Lola had left Germany in 1934, shortly after the New Order relieved him of his position at the university. There he had been a specialist in medieval German literature, not in the first rank, perhaps, but able to produce abstruse monographs on minuscule topics as successfully as the best of them. Suddenly he found himself out on the street. A slight figure at that time, diffident, pale, blinking behind round spectacles, afraid of his shadow, he developed a nervous tic that produced every few minutes a dry, disconcerting grin. He could not grasp what had happened to him. It was far easier for him to deal with Wolfram von Eschenbach and Walther von der Vogelweide than with the modern avatars of German culture. He sat all day in his study staring silently at his books. We could do nothing for him. In desperation Lola wrote to his two brothers, Nathan and Edmond, who twenty years before had emigrated to New York. Their response was heartwarming: "Pack him up at once, him and his books, and get out of there, come to America." If an academic post could not be secured for Kurt, a position in the firm—a partnership, even—would be given him.

By 1947 German Kurt had been transformed into American Kenneth, a human dynamo. He knew what he wanted, and he expected immediate results. Impatient with the lackadaisical British officer in charge, who seemed unimpressed by the mound of documents thrust beneath his disapproving nose,

Kenneth banged on the desk, growled, and swore he would create an "international incident." The officer would be drummed out of his regiment, his medals stripped from him. "Oh, I say," said the officer, "steady on." Kenneth insisted upon phoning the American military attaché at the consulate and telling him that he had better come over right away, as the British were trying to frustrate the clear intentions of the State Department. Another imperious phone call summoned the chief local representative of the International Red Cross. "Now we will see," said Kenneth. And see we did. Within two hours I was given a cursory medical examination, all the appropriate papers were signed and stamped, and we were on our way. "Lousy bums," muttered Kenneth. "Lousy, inefficient, arrogant bastards."

Ten days later we were in Cherbourg, and two days after that we were aboard the *Ile de France*, en route to New York. In the meantime Kenneth had had me outfitted in the best that postwar Paris could provide, had personally directed the finer points of an elegant haircut at the Georges V, and had stuffed me with food of a delicacy I had forgotten existed. He seemed oblivious to the shock he had given me. Once more my world had turned upside down. I do not think I had spoken a dozen words to him; it seems to me that I giggled a lot, wept a lot, but was otherwise silent, "recalled to life" but not yet certain I was not dead.

In the taxi from the pier Kenneth's tic of 1934 returned. "Otto," he said with a sudden dry grin, "this is a joyous day, nothing must spoil it." He fell silent for a moment. "There," he said, as the taxi climbed to the West Side Highway, "that's the Hudson River again. Over there, New Jersey, as I told you. Higher up, the Palisades. Wonderful, yes?" Like a seeping mist, the misery in the taxi wiped out the sunshine. "Yes, we're all together again." He slapped me on the thigh. "All of us, at last. I mean, that is, we, the three of us, we . . ." Again silence. The taxi took the Boat Basin exit. Kenneth grinned twice in rapid succession. "You must not be surprised by Lola. It's been a long time. Very hard for her. She was so full of hope, she couldn't believe . . . and then the, um, the *events,* yes, the *events* in Europe, so horrible, shattering, for her, for all of us. Still she hoped . . . and then the search, and then to find out . . . But thank God, you're here, and that's . . . that's . . . she was so . . . it will be a wonderful moment for her." The taxi pulled up at an apartment building on Central Park West. "This is a joyous day."

We entered the apartment, Kenneth bounding through the door crying, "Lola, Lola, we're here! Otto's with me!" Silence, nothing but silence. The cork had not popped; his champagne was flat. The rooms were dim, the drawn Venetian blinds admitting only a few brilliant beads of sunlight. There was a faint aroma of mimosa in the air.

"She must be at the store, perhaps the beauty parlor. Remember, I sent cablegrams. We're expected. Wait, I'll open the windows."

The room was spacious, a recreation of their house in Nuremberg. I recognized the solid polished furniture, the books, the paintings, all disposed now as then.

"Sit down, Otto, sit down, be comfortable." The tic again. "What would you like, a beer? I'll get it for you, sit." And off he went, desperately striving to overcome his disappointment.

From what I took to be the kitchen there came a sudden, ghastly shriek, "No! no! no!" A loud clump, then again the silence.

What had he done to himself? I got up and ran after him.

There on the white linoleum floor was Kenneth, on his knees, crouched over, his arms protecting his head, shuddering.

From the exposed hot-water pipe that, just below the ceiling, ran the length of the kitchen, hung my sister, Lola, her dead eyes glaring. Her upper teeth must have shifted; she appeared to be chewing them. Almost she had not succeeded: her toes were within an inch of the linoleum. On her breast was neatly pinned a little note, a note that for pathetic modesty can scarcely be matched: "Otto, Kurt: a pity, Lola."

I lacked the strength to cut her down alone. First I had to unroll her sobbing husband. Between us we managed to lay her on the kitchen floor, but not before Kenneth, blindly stumbling, had banged her poor skull on the corner of the gas stove. What a howl he sent up then! "Sorry, so sorry, my darling! Forgive me, so sorry!" I did not have the heart to remind him that she was past pain. You must understand that he was unaccustomed to such horror.

As for me, I was numb, dazed, perhaps not quite sane. What had just passed as external reality scarcely ruffled my consciousness. I responded to Lola's death as to one for which I had long since grieved, a painful memory, vivid still, without any longer the power to shock. Remember, I had not yet fully left Necropolis; I still dwelled in the City of the Dead. Having clawed my way out of Europe's bloody pit only to find my sister dead, I nevertheless made an irrational effort to go on breathing.

Besides, there were things to be done, authorities to be informed. As in a dream, I phoned the police, my first phone call in America, conscious only of the miracle of my voice talking calmly into the receiver. Then I joined Kenneth on the kitchen floor next to Lola's body.

Poor Kenneth! He blamed himself for Lola's death, misconstruing the truth. The truth was quite simple: in the end my own sister could not bear to look at me. I cannot say I blamed her.

It was then that I stuffed Lola's memory high on the closet shelf with the rest of my past and closed the door tightly. (In unguarded moments, the door opens a crack, and I hear again the pitiful voices. But quick as a wink, to preserve my sanity, I snap the door shut again.)

12

Y LETTER FROM RILKE was stolen, not lost or mislaid! Of that there is no longer any doubt. But the elation that comes with sure knowledge is all too frequently dampened by the kind of knowledge gained. The poet Milton understood: like Adam and Eve, knowing, I am left naked and vulnerable, puzzled and afraid.

This is what has happened: I am the recipient of poison-pen mail. Well, perhaps "poison pen" is not quite accurate in this case; after all, the ostensible aim of the communication is to guide me to the thief. But its effect has been to cause me considerable anxiety, for it is unsigned, written in featureless block capitals, and hints only obliquely at the thief's name. Thus I am a double victim: of the thief and of his betrayer, who "could an if he would" speak openly but chooses (out of malice?) not to do so. In this they are in collusion, the one silent for obvious reasons, the second obscurantist for reasons that are darker, impenetrable, and hence frightening.

The note arrived today, slipped under my door between breakfast and lunch, while I was in Revolutionary Council at Goldstein's Dairy Restaurant. (Of that momentous meeting, more later.) It is a riddle in verse, what is called an enigma or (more properly, in the original sense) a charade. I reproduce it here:

A thief, unknown, lives free of any stigma,
Denounce him, after solving this enigma.

Ike's letters are not useful to our riddle;
The key's the end (less wise), not in the middle.
Whoever tries to mouth the culprit's name
Must end in ordure to assign the blame.

Now, for all my linguistic ability, I admit I have never been very good at this sort of thing. It is not that I lack ingenuity, but rather that the specific ingenuity needed to solve a charade, it seems to me, is the peculiar property of the riddler himself. *His* verbal associations, *his* mental synapses, so to speak, are unlikely to be another's. How to get into the mind of the riddler? Aye, there's the rub. Still, the first couplet is patent: it alludes to a thief and a theft, and it implies that the cause of justice is mine. So far, so good. The second couplet is more troublesome. Theseus in the labyrinth at least had help; how am I to find the minotaur? Well, I shan't bother to record the many false starts, the hours of perplexity, the culs-de-sac encountered along the way, but shall instead proceed immediately to the solution. Ike, of course, was the popular name of the late President Eisenhower, in my opinion a much underrated man, whose initials are D.D.E. *But,* says the couplet, these letters are "useless" to our RIDDLE. Very well, get rid of them! RIDDLE minus DDE equals RIL. The answer is already obvious. Put KEY'S at the "end" and *violà!* RILKEY'S. But we are to use KEY'S "less" WISE—that is, minus WISE, or Y's. And there you have it: RILKE!

So that's how I know my letter from Rilke was stolen, not accidentally thrown out or mislaid.

The third couplet, of course, conceals the name of the thief. But with the sort of irony that typifies my life, it is in a code that I am unable to crack. As yet.

* * *

THE REVOLUTIONARY COUNCIL, to which I earlier alluded, has begun its deliberations. I was sitting quietly in the library reading in the *Times* its leisurely accounts of daily outrages when the Red Dwarf peered round the door, spotted me, and sidled in. He leaned over me and whispered in my ear, "Comrade, we've nothing to lose but our chains." Glancing furtively around the room, he placed a finger to his lips. "Ssh." We were alone in the library. "There's to be a meeting of the Central Committee at Goldstein's, comrade. Ten-thirty sharp. Be there." And then, perhaps because he saw the expression on my face, he pulled an imaginary forelock: "The favor of your honored presence, noble sir, would be gratefully appreciated."

As it happened, I had other plans for the morning— little tasks, accumulated odds and ends, shopping in the neighborhood, and so forth—and was about to tell him so when the door opened again and in came La Dawidowicz. She ignored us, of course. The Red Dwarf's finger flew once more to his lips. "Ssh." Then, in a loud voice, effecting casualness, he said, "I see by the papers, the obituaries, that fourteen corpses are to be given Christian burial." La Dawidowicz sniffed. The Red Dwarf chortled and bounded for the door. There he danced his little jig. "Mum's the word," he said, winking knowingly, and vanished. Where at his age does he find his energy?

Goldstein's Dairy Restaurant, located on Broadway, is only a short walk from the Emma Lazarus and hence very popular with many of our residents. Here one can drink coffee or tea, play dominoes, devour such forbidden dainties as blintzes or apple fritters with sour cream, and, most important, on occasion see faces other than those encountered daily in the residents' lounge. I have been going there for years, well before I entered the Emma Lazarus, before I met the Contessa even. Bruce Goldstein, the proprietor, is a florid, portly man now in his late fifties, young by my standards, and a bit of a dandy. He is the only man on the West Side, for instance, whom I have ever seen wearing a mink overcoat, and his suits are always impeccably cut to his plump frame. Silk ties and pocket handkerchiefs are with him a matter of course. Because of his passion for the drama, the walls of the restaurant are decorated with old theater posters, and his various dishes bear the names of famous actors. Thus, for example, the Tony Curtis is a mound of chopped herring on a bed of red onion slices, topped with a tasteful arrangement of black olives; the Lee J. Cobb, a patriotic trio of blintzes, cherry, blueberry, and cheese, the whole sprinkled with powdered sugar. My own favorite is the Paul Newman: *gefüllte Fisch,* breaded and deep fried, garnished with the house's special horseradish sauce (a secret recipe, well guarded).

As is my custom when I have a rendezvous or appointment, I arrived ten minutes early. Goldstein, dressed in a neat, dark-blue pin-stripe suit, pearl-gray waistcoat, and maroon polka-dot tie, was leaning against a central pillar, on which he was scratching his back. He greeted me warmly: "Korner."

"Goldstein." I sat at my usual table.

Goldstein made rapid finger signals to Joe, the oldest of his four elderly waiters, which, translated, told him to bring over with all possible speed a cup of coffee, black. I have yet to hear Goldstein actually address his waiters vocally. He has an elaborate system of signals rather like those of a bookie or tout at an English racecourse. Goldstein sauntered over. "So?" he said.

"The Red Dwarf is joining me, and possibly some others."

Joe put down a cup of coffee before me. Goldstein made some signals. Joe picked up the cup and wiped the saucer with a cloth he carried over his shoulder for such purposes.

Goldstein went back to the pillar to scratch his back. At precisely ten-thirty Hamburger came in. Of course, I did not yet know whether Hamburger was a party to the Red Dwarf's shenanigans, but he put me immediately at ease. "The Red Dwarf not here yet?"

From his pillar Goldstein signaled to Joe, who brought Hamburger a cup of coffee upon which floated a dollop of whipped cream.

"How are the bunions, Joe?" Hamburger evinced real interest.

"Don't ask." Joe shuffled off.

"What's this Central Committee nonsense?"

"Not such nonsense," said Hamburger darkly. "Wait till the Red Dwarf gets here."

At the window, peering through cupped hands into the restaurant, was the Red Dwarf himself. Seeing us, he gave a clenched-fist salute and hurried in. He was wearing a cracked leather cap and a denim windbreaker. Goldstein made some signals, and by the time the Red Dwarf was seated, Joe was shambling over with a glass of steaming tea, a slice of lemon, and three lumps of sugar. The Red Dwarf took the tea from Joe's trembling hand and waved him off impatiently.

"Well, what has he told you?" he asked me.

"Nothing," said Hamburger. "I was waiting for you."

"All right, fine," said the Red Dwarf. "Let's get straight to the point. Some of us here"—he indicated Hamburger and himself—"some of us are losing our patience. The imperialists are stomping on our backs. We intend to topple the fascist hyenas from their thrones, in particular that people's traitor Lipschitz, the Zionist expansionist, and his lick-spittle running-dog Dawidowicz, and transform the Emma Lazarus Old Vic into an organization run on sound democratic socialist principles and answerable to the people."

"To begin with, you mix your metaphors," I said.

The Red Dwarf bared his teeth; a gold one glinted dully.

"Don't be superficial, Korner," said Hamburger. "We are

dealing with serious matters here. No one denied Sinsheimer his authority, never mind he alternated between diarrhea and constipation. After all, he knew something about Shakespeare, about acting, about directing. But what does Lipschitz know? He knows that Dawidowicz doesn't want to give any satisfaction to her daughter-in-law, he knows that the orthodox might be offended by certain lines in the play, he knows that he wants to get under Dawidowicz's skirts. That's what he knows. He knows crap."

I could scarcely argue with him.

"What can we do? The company goes along with him."

"I'll tell you what we can do," said the Red Dwarf. "We can secure the costumes, the makeup, the paints, the scenery. Then we can march onto the stage and announce the revolution of the proletariat. The people will flock to us. We will strike off their chains."

"Not so fast, Poliakov," said Hamburger. "You think Lipschitz and Dawidowicz will take this lying down? They will go to the Kommandant. No, better we go to the Kommandant first, the three of us. Scheisskopf, after all, is the ultimate authority. We put before him our grievances, the high-handed manner in which the production was taken over, the arbitrary reassignment of roles, the alterations in the text, and so forth. Our plea is a simple one: Justice. Korner here should be our director, that's obvious, and according to tradition already established, the director also plays the principal role, in this case Hamlet. What Scheisskopf wants is peace and quiet, cooperation and harmony. How can he refuse us? With Scheisskopf on our side, the assumption of power is automatic."

"Menshevik," muttered the Red Dwarf.

I began to warm to the idea. "Before we go to the Kommandant," I said, "we should sound out the other members of the cast. After all, what if we are the sole dissidents? With numbers there is strength. Our purpose is to strike a blow for freedom, yes, certainly, but also for art. First, however, we must know where we stand with the others. If, as I suspect, they are dissatisfied with the current state of affairs, and if we can impress this dissatisfaction upon the Kommandant, we will carry the day. What do you think?"

"Trotskyite," muttered the Red Dwarf.

We argued the matter back and forth, sometimes with acrimony, but at last decided upon a compromise. We would *all* sound out the other players. Meanwhile, the Red Dwarf would attend to logistics—that is, the most efficient means of securing the costumes, the makeup, the paints, the scenery. Hamburger would draw up a list of grievances for presentation to the Kommandant. And I? Why, I would reassign roles, not forgetful of poor Sinsheimer's conception of the play but prepared to superimpose my own vision on it.

This was the point the Revolutionary Council had reached when Blum entered Goldstein's Dairy Restaurant. Seeing us together, he naturally came over and sat down.

"What do you want?" said the Red Dwarf irritably.

"The Lee J. Cobb," said Blum.

Goldstein, who had overheard him, made signals to Joe.

"Things aren't working out," said Blum.

We three revolutionaries looked at one another significantly.

But of course Blum, being Blum, was talking about sexual conquest. Lately he had been laying siege for the heart (and other parts) of Hermione Perlmutter, but without success. He had invested, he wanted us to know, ten dollars in flowers and more than five in chocolates. "No dice": La Perlmutter remained coy. How much time could he afford to waste? "Now there, gentlemen," he said sadly, "is a sweet nooky."

"Because of the ordure, Blum, that in you passes for a brain," said Hamburger, "no one can blame you for what is engendered there. But in common decency you can keep such thoughts to yourself."

"Here, here," I said.

Blum sighed. "Anyone want to play dominoes?"

"Tell me, Blum," said the Red Dwarf. "You like being the Ghost?"

"Korner was better at it. To tell you the truth, I've always seen myself as Horatio: steadfast, loyal, true."

"And if I told you you could be Horatio?"

"Well, you know how it is. Lipschitz is in charge. What he says goes. It's not up to you."

"Gentlemen," said the Red Dwarf to Hamburger and me, "I know you have many things to do. Busy is busy. Don't hang around on our account. Blum here and me, we're going to play dominoes."

Hamburger and I rose to our feet. Goldstein, ever attentive, signaled to Joe.

"Blum is treating," said the Red Dwarf.

* * *

A SECOND CHARADE has arrived. I found it folded in my napkin at my place in the dining room. The only person to precede me to breakfast was Isabella Krauskopf y Guzman, who sat over her porridge. It is inconceivable that Señora Krauskopf y Guzman, long our oldest resident, could have secreted the missive or had anything to do with it. The señora has been off the list of solo-ambulants for more than twenty years. The tenacity with which she holds on to life is the wonder of the Emma Lazarus. The direct descendent of revolutionaries who fled from Bohemia to Chile in 1848, "Doña Isabella," as the domestic staff fondly call her, might have been a Spanish grandee of the purest blood. Frail though she is, she still holds her back proudly erect; her eyes, sunk deep in a face wizened like a bleached prune, still flash disdain and hauteur. What blue-black hair she has retained is drawn back into a severe bun.

The aristocratic effect was somewhat marred this morning by blobs of porridge that stuck to her cheeks and dribbled down her chin, for the señora sometimes has trouble locating her mouth. Although obviously not guilty herself, she might nevertheless have seen someone placing the charade in my napkin. Accordingly, and as neutrally as I could, I pointed to the note and asked whether she knew how it came to be there.

One difficulty in talking to the señora is that she all too often responds with a remark culled from another conversation going on at the same time in her own head. Her eyes flashed beneath hooded lids. "In Patagonia," she said, "there you feel free. I read, much of the night, and go north in the winter."

The staff of the residents' dining room, of course, knew nothing and wanted to know less.

The text of the charade follows:

To give my first is sure to give offence,
But may create a smile (in other sense).
Who does my second doubtless finds his ease,
But even if a czar must bend his knees.
Together, I have proved to be quite deft
At usurpation and at simple theft.

Well, I have not solved this one, either. But at last I have a way into the labyrinth, a modus operandi for finding the minotaur. The charade makes it plain that the name of the thief is composed of two elements, each of which has an independent meaning. Thus, for example, the name Krauskopf is composed of *kraus* ("curly") and *Kopf* ("head"). So a charade based on the señora's name might divide its clues accordingly.

As for my modus operandi, I shall wheedle out of Selma in Personnel a complete list of all residents and staff at the Emma Lazarus. To attempt to assemble such a list myself is to run the risk of omissions. From Selma's list I shall produce one of my own, containing all those names that have two meaningful elements. And these names I shall test against the clues in the second charade, confirming what I shall surely discover against the unsolved riddle of the first. "The game's afoot!"

13

CONSIDERATION OF BLUM'S SEXUAL ESCAPADES has put me in mind of my marriage to the Contessa. Blum struts around the Emma Lazarus like a bantam cock, his beady eyes ever on the lookout for a new conquest. The stories of his successes are legion; in corners the ladies whisper about his prowess. Who will be next? They giggle over the alleged dimensions and extraordinary potency of his *membrum virile*. Blum himself is not reticent. But all this leaves me with a faint disgust. Not that I am a prude, I hasten to add: I have lived my life, after all, in the twentieth century, familiar with the works of Freud, Krafft-Ebing, Havelock Ellis; the decadent twenties were the years of my youth. No, in this respect I am not easily shocked. My libido, moreover, so well as one can judge such things, has always been quite normal—though also, of course, always appropriate to my age. For example, I shall admit that some of the lingerie advertisements in the *New York Times Magazine* are still capable of stirring me. But Blum is seventy-seven years of age, for heaven's sake! For Hermione Perlmutter I have a new respect.

In 1957 I retired from the New York Public Library, where, within a year of my arrival in America, my brother-in-law, Kenneth, had found me employment. One could only admire the speed with which he bounced back from the tragedy of Lola's suicide; understandably, I was a reminder of the past. It was important to my well-being, he said, that I stand on my own feet, particularly in America. And so he found a small apartment for me on West Eighty-second Street, between Central Park West and Columbus Avenue, and he furnished it from his own home, with the old, well-preserved pieces from Nuremberg, now for him too painfully evocative. A poker-playing friend of his was on the board of trustees at the library. For the next nine years I worked in the Searching Section of the Preparation Division, where I was in charge of a mountainous backlog of materials published in Germany between 1939 and 1945—yes, I am also aware of the irony! Meanwhile, with exquisite tact, Kenneth had settled a small annuity on me, my sister's private funds, he pretended, the income from which, he assured me, would in a few years provide the means for a modestly comfortable retirement. In this last, he told the truth. In 1949 I received a card from him postmarked Saint-Tropez. He was on his honeymoon. He hoped, he wrote, that I would continue to think well of him. (I did. I do.) And with that he disappeared from my life.

The Contessa was born Alice Krebs, third daughter of Shmuel and Reisele Krebs, proprietors of Krebs Famous Strictly-Kosher Meats and Poultry, on Avenue B, the Lower East Side, in 1898. She was the first of their eleven children to be born into the New World. In 1916, a year in which with romantic ardor I, in Zurich, pursued, and pursued in vain, the devastatingly beautiful Magda Damrosch, a year in which my passionate young heart throbbed upon the altar of love, in that very year Alice Krebs married Morris Gitlitz, ten years her senior, ritual slaughterer and, according to the Contessa, already a "world-class" Talmudic student. "A *mitzvah* a day keeps the Torah okay" was his cheery watchword.

It was an arranged marriage but successful for all that: "My father was no dope," the Contessa confided to me. In Morris (she pronounced the name "Meurice") "Poppa outdid himself: in him he found for me a saint." Perhaps Shmuel Krebs had intuited that Meurice would shift by a kind of natural affinity from the profession of ritual slaughterer to the more rarefied profession of ritual circumciser. Such, at any rate, was Meurice's ascent. And since in those years, and in their crowd, large families were a cause for congratulation, not for disapprobation, and since, too, boy babies appeared with much the same frequency as girls, the Gitlitzes prospered. In 1922 they moved to the Bronx, the Grand Concourse, painting their apartment "passionate puce," in that year the color of the smart set.

But there was a single large and lowering cloud ever on the horizon of their marital bliss. *Adonai elohenu* had not blessed them with offspring, not even one, despite Meurice Gitlitz's frequent and enthusiastic efforts. They did not go to a doctor, neither wishing to be able to accuse the other of sterility. The Gitlitz line—he had only sisters—was doomed. Poor Alice Gitlitz! Where was she to direct her burgeoning creative energies? She wanted respect, and this, for a barren woman in her circle, was hard to come by. That was why she changed her name, Contessa being her second choice. Her first had been Principessa, but she was afraid that no one would pronounce it properly (except perhaps the Italian shoemaker on Fordham Road, but with him she was not on a first-name basis). So Contessa Gitlitz she became, legally: she had the paper to prove it. And soon after that she began to call Morris by the "classier" name, Meurice.

By 1953 Meurice had reached his sixty-fifth year. His hand-eye coordination was not what it had been. No longer was he the "Paganini of the Scalpel." There was talk of botched jobs, ugly rumors. It was time to retire. Financially secure, the Gitlitzes traveled south and moved into the Versailles, a condominium in Miami. Alas, Meurice's retirement was short-lived. In 1957 disaster struck: one morning before breakfast Meurice executed a perfect dive into the Versailles' "Olympic-size" swimming pool, stayed underwater rather longer than usual, and eventually surfaced as a corpse. The Contessa, for forty years a wife, had become a widow.

I have given this account of the Contessa up until the time of her widowhood only because I want you to have something to put into the balance when I come to tell my own side of things. That is only just. Still, any reasonable person would think it unlikely that our paths, the Contessa's and mine, should ever cross, much less result in matrimony. Such a mismatching strains the credulity of even the most credulous. But note, please, the following: on the afternoon of June 30, 1957, I was given a small retirement party by some colleagues in the *Preparation* Division; on the morning of July 1, 1957, Meurice Gitlitz took his classic dive into Eternity. *My first day of retirement was his last day of life!* Coincidence or Purpose? The question answers itself. The stage had been cleared; a new act was about to begin.

I met the Contessa in Central Park, a fine spring morning in 1960. We shared a bench by the *Alice in Wonderland* statue. In the three years since my retirement I had continued to live, modestly and quietly, on West Eighty-second Street; in the three years since her widowhood the Contessa had acquired an apartment in Flushing ("a toehold," she said, "in the Big Apple") and now spent only the winter months in Miami. She needed, she said, the stimulation of the city. Besides, she had been born here; New York would always be her home. It was pleasant to sit in the sunshine and hear her babble on. We agreed to meet again, weather permitting, on the following day. I found her plumply attractive, a welcome point of focus for otherwise indistinguishable days. In the weeks that followed we attended matinees, went to concerts, movies. She began to cook for me. I enjoyed being reintroduced to kosher food, seeing again the candles lit on Friday night. She said I provided what was missing from her life: culture and refinement. Of the saintly Meurice she had nothing but good to say, though she was forced to admit that in the "culture and refinement department" he had rather fallen short. "Your experience is different," she would muse. "You're European." I had for her "Continental charm," which is to say, simple politeness. Occasionally, the hour being late, she would spend the night at West Eighty-second Street, on the couch, of course. It was during this period of what I suppose I should call our courtship that I gained most of my knowledge about her past.

By August she was calling me Otto and I was calling her Contessa. In September she pointed out how foolish it was for two elderly people to be traveling almost every day between Flushing and Manhattan. (In point of fact, I had been to her apartment in Flushing only once. How shall I describe her building? There fat young women in large pink hair curlers ascended and descended in the elevator at all hours, always in the company of large mounds of laundry.) We got on well together, she added. She liked me, very much; she was sure I liked her. These were our "twilight years." Why should we not get married? Life would be simpler then.

The thought had not occurred to me. Still, as an idea it seemed to have its merits. She would make all the arrangements. Whom would I like to invite? No fuss, I insisted. Just the two of us. We would slip into marriage as into an old, comfortable shoe. Accordingly, we were married quietly in the study of Rabbi Ted Kaplan, spiritual leader of the Congregation Bnei Akiva, on West Ninety-eighth Street. Under the marriage canopy the Contessa smiled dreamily; I placed the ring on her finger without qualms.

We left immediately for Miami and her apartment in the Versailles ("very tasteful, every luxury"). I had never been to Florida before and was curious. We were greeted at the airport by some of her friends. A woman whose apartment was next door to the Contessa's expressed the hope that we would not keep her up too late; a man in houndstooth shorts and a horizontally striped shirt told me lugubriously that I would have a hard time filling the shoes of the dead Meurice—"A hard time, get it?"—giving me a wink and a sharp nudge in the ribs.

The embarrassing fact is that I had given no thought whatever to this aspect of married life. Yes, I had supposed we would share a bed, but we were, after all, already in our sixties, I the precise age of Meurice at his retirement. Certainly the Contessa had not aroused in me even a faint sexual stirring. But there was my new wife, blushing and simpering, holding on to me tightly and saying things like, "We'll see what we will see" and "I only hope I have the strength."

Accuse me of ungallantry if you will, but I am bound to the truth. Undressed, the Contessa was a piece of grotesquerie. Like her rich blond curls, her teeth were not her own. Her breasts, once full, depended flatly, wanly, from her pronounced clavicles. Flaps of flesh hung, pitted, from her upper arms. She wore her stomach around her middle like an apron, beneath the bottom edge of which the few straggly white hairs of her pudenda sought not very successfully to assert themselves. Her every natural part yearned toward the ground as if exhausted from the struggle with gravity.

But it is unfair to go on in this way, unseemly. Poor soul, she is not to be blamed for time's wintry attack upon the summer bloom of her lost youth. Do not for a moment suppose that I am proud of what I am writing here. The Contessa, I insist, was a decent, loving woman, a good wife. Nor, to go further, was I such a bargain in the Adonis department. At age 65, a natural decrepitude had made its depressing and relentless advances. We were well matched, I assure you. But before the Contessa, my last personal experience of woman had been of my first wife, Meta, still young and achingly lovely. "Look first upon this picture, and on this." Ach, it is impossible to say just what I mean.

Had I grown old along with her, as had her saintly Meurice, such details might not have pricked the bubble of contentment. Disfigurements accumulated slowly over years might have proved invisible; after all, "Love sees not with the eyes." But to have these deplorable mysteries displayed before him of a sudden, swaying sickeningly above him—thrust upon him, so to speak, by an aging woman insistent upon her nuptial rights—this is for an aging man to suffer the hell of instant emasculation. I shall say nothing of the seductive maneuvers wherewith she tried to recall to life my shattered libido, the sights and the sounds, the desperate encouragements. For a full week she persisted in her efforts:

> Nay, but to live
> In the rank sweat of an enseamed bed,
> Stew'd in corruption, honeying and making love
> Over the nasty sty!

After the first week she gave up, sobbing pitifully by my side while I pretended sleep.

One learns in time to *submit* oneself to Purpose, not to question it. Yet would it not have been better all around if the Plan had called for Freddy Blum, not me, to meet her at the *Alice in Wonderland* statue?

My fingers grow cramped from grasping the pen. Of our life together and of her death, more anon.

14

HE THIRD CHARADE has turned up in my jacket pocket!

How it got there I am beyond speculating. Such an invasion of my privacy leaves me aghast. Rather than helped, I begin to feel persecuted. The jacket was out of my sight for only a moment, when I hung it on a hook in the small cloakroom downstairs. How long does it take, after all, to wash and dry one's hands? I put the jacket on again, patted the pockets—an automatic, utterly meaningless gesture, I assure you—and discovered the piece of paper. My persecutor must have been following me around, lurking, watching, waiting for an opportunity. There is malice here, directed not merely against the thief but against me also!

Meanwhile, my plan to acquire a list from Selma in Personnel has been thwarted. Bernie Gross is in Queens General Hospital undergoing a multiple hernia operation—for Hamburger a rich source of comic material—and his faithful Selma is by his side, no doubt wringing her hands, and on indefinite leave. Her place behind the bulletproof glass has been taken by an "office temporary" with instructions to sit tight ("Bernie's problem"—Hamburger), to say nothing, to do no more than sign the solo-ambulants out and in.

My persecutor is growing impatient. The third charade has only two couplets, the second of which is devoted to an attack on me, sarcastic, mocking, deliberately goading:

The gap that stands in view 'twixt hip and tits
Can soon be closed in rhyme by clever wits.
How curious that a self-styled intellectual
In following clues should prove so ineffectual!

How now to proceed? I sense that I am being manipulated for ends other than my own. Suppose I solved the riddles: what then? Am I to confront the person thus accused? And if he denies the charge? And if he sues me for defamation of character, for slander?

My thoughts turn more and more frequently to the author of the charades. These thoughts are becoming obsessive, a condition I must guard against. It seems to me my current persecutor should be easier to discover than the thief. He has, despite his cleverness, left certain clues behind. I know, for example, that he is a man, which fact eliminates at a stroke half the population of the Emma Lazarus. How do I know? No one but a man would have followed me into the *men's* downstairs cloakroom to drop the third charade into my jacket pocket! I know other details about the would-be mystifier. He is a man adept at word-games, scrabble, perhaps: we have an annual tournament; crossword puzzles surely, particularly of the English kind. He is probably, although not certainly, native-born: witness his ability to compress his thought into idiomatic cum formally "poetic" English. This last point suggests he knows of my early years, he has done his research: why else should he choose verse for his medium? I have told only the Kommandant and (necessarily) the domestic staff of my loss. Of course, in a community as close as ours the news would soon circulate. Nevertheless, one must know something of the importance of Rilke for the letter itself to have any significance. This man must *know*.

To be honest, I have suspected Hamburger as the author of the charades. The word *ordure* in the first of them, for example, and the vulgarity of the third point to my friend. But for Hamburger, vulgarity is not inborn. It is rather a mask he put on years ago to protect himself from who knows what dangers and that has now grown into his flesh. It is clear that Hamburger is motivated by integrity, not malice. Besides, he is *not* native born, and he has never shown any interest in word-games, let alone poetic composition. Another point: he was with me when the first charade was slipped under my door. And besides all this, I like him.

No. I quit the search. If I recover the letter, so; if not, so. *Hic arma repono.*

15

 BROUHAHA AT GOLDSTEIN'S this morning: voices raised, insults hurled, Hamburger waving his fist under Blum's nose, the Red Dwarf muttering darkly, Lipschitz sneering, Goldstein himself livid. Korner alone a voice of quiet reason. What started it? Such things are not born of themselves. Petty resentments, slights imagined or real, accumulate over months and even over years, seething like molten matter within the bowels of the earth, gathering strength for the moment of eruption. But I imagine the proximate cause to be last night's ad hoc Perlmutter Seminar, from which fortunately I was absent, on the subject "What is male chauvinism?" The discussion, it seems, became heated, with La Perlmutter under heavy attack from a trio of male voices—Blum, Lipschitz, and the Red Dwarf—but championed, as always, by Hamburger ("I beg to remind you, gentlemen, that you had mothers"), and Tosca Dawidowicz treacherously condemning intellect in woman as a curse about which the less said the better, leaning the while toward Lipschitz, who sat beside her on a loveseat, and voluptuously stroking his upper thigh ("What matters is a man should be a good provider, in bed and out"), until, reeling from blows on all sides, ecstatic, weeping, Hermione Perlmutter fled the room ("Oh, oh, oh"), her defeated champion running after her to offer comfort.

Business in the restaurant was slow, as it invariably is in the hour before lunch on Tuesday mornings, so Goldstein was sitting with us when Hamburger came in and joined us at the table. Lipschitz was there, too. What were we doing, you will ask, sitting with Lipschitz in the first place? A matter of simple courtesy, a token of civilization. When Blum, the Red Dwarf, and I arrived, Lipschitz was already at the big table, alone, with not one of his toadies in evidence. He looked at us, we looked at him: a standoff. He indicated his table. Naturally, we joined him.

Goldstein signaled to Joe, who shuffled over with Hamburger's regular, coffee with a dollop of whipped cream.

"The Barbra Streisand, Joe, heavy on the sauce."

"Come again?"

"You heard."

"You got it."

There were raised eyebrows. The Barbra Streisand is a mixture of finely chopped raw pike and carp, delicately seasoned and artistically pressed into the shape of a fish. A pimiento-stuffed green olive serves as the eye, a wavy sliver of green pepper as the gills. The sauce combines crushed cucumber, yoghurt, and a dash of English mustard. So far, so good. But Goldstein, for whatever reason, has listed this dish on his menu, along with the Elizabeth Taylor and the Shelley Winters, under the heading "Diva Delights."

"So, Hamburger," sneered Lipschitz, "you've gone completely over to the other side?" He flicked his tongue between his lips, darting his reptilian eyes at us for approval.

Blum tittered.

"Meaning?" said Hamburger ominously.

"Every day is ladies' day for you?"

"Food is a matter of gender now, bubble-brain?"

"Bravo!" said the Red Dwarf. "Stick it to them, the lick-spittle Zionist hypocrites." He turned to Lipschitz. "On your kibbutz a woman can't eat a Tony Curtis?"

"From what I know of Tony Curtis," said Blum, "many of them did."

"For God's sake, Blum," I said.

Lipschitz, sensing that he was in the minority, licked his lips nervously and said nothing.

The tension was broken by the arrival of the Barbra Streisand. We all stared at it.

"Beautiful," said Goldstein. And in fact, so it was. But honesty compels me to record that there was something inexplicably outré about it, something frivolous and unmanly. Ridiculous, of course, but the Barbra Streisand is to the Tony Curtis what a snifter of crème de menthe is to a glass of vodka. "So eat," said Goldstein. "Enjoy." We watched Hamburger in a silence broken only by the click-clack of his knife and fork, until the fish shape was no longer recognizable.

"Well?" Goldstein wanted to know.

"Not bad, Goldstein, not bad."

A flurry of signals to Joe and our cups were refilled.

"Talking of fish reminds me of a story," said Goldstein. "A Jew goes to his rabbi, it's just before Purim. He says, 'Rabbi, what am I to do? My wife refuses now to keep kosher. You want kosher, she tells me, you got to get yourself a new wife.' Wait, this one's a scream."

"How many times, Goldstein?" said Hamburger wearily. "How many times?"

Goldstein sighed.

We watched Hamburger until he was finished, his knife and fork neatly lined up on an empty plate. He wiped his lips fastidiously with his napkin, looking up at us under angry brows. "Well, what are you waiting for? You expect me to go to the powder room?"

Goldstein, knowing nothing of recent events at the Emma Lazarus Old Vic, and anxious, no doubt, to achieve a mood of bonhomie, turned to Lipschitz. "So tell me, Nahum, how's the play coming along?"

"We're managing," said Lipschitz curtly.

"He needs a couple gravediggers," said the Red Dwarf.

"And a Fortinbras," said Hamburger.

"Maybe a couple other players," said the Red Dwarf.

" 'Why, this it is, when men are rul'd by women,' " I said half to myself.

Lipschitz heard me. "Speak up, Korner. You got something to say, we should all get the benefit." He darted his head at me, his cheeks an angry red.

"Gentlemen, gentlemen," said Goldstein pacifically, "forget I said anything. Is it *my* business? A friendly question, was all."

"They put you up to it."

"As God is my witness, Nahum."

"Sure, sure."

"I don't even know what we're talking about."

"We're talking *Hamlet*," said the Red Dwarf. "We're talking Tosca Dawidowicz, we're talking Mineola."

"Take it from me, Nahum," said Blum. "I've been there. Such a good lay you should sell your soul she's not."

"Whatever she is, Blum," said Hamburger, "she's also a lady. For that reason alone you should watch your tongue."

"Lady *shmady*, in that department I think I know what I'm talking. Look at you, sniffing after Hermione Perlmutter. What do you smell? You think it's incense? Lift both their skirts, you'll find the same thing."

Hamburger turned purple. With his fist clenched, he lunged at Blum, who ducked back, knocking his cup to the floor, where it shattered.

"For God's sake!" said Goldstein, signaling to Joe. "Are we savages?" There was a sudden silence in the restaurant as the few diners at the other tables looked at us in alarm. "You want to fight, you go outside."

"You shut your mouth, Blum, or I shut it for you!"

"Ignore him," I told Hamburger. "You know what he is. Calm down, you'll do yourself a mischief."

Blum, considerably cowed, bit his lip and lapsed into silence.

"Tosca has nothing to do with it," said Lipschitz. "I stand behind every one of the changes."

"What changes?" said Goldstein.

Briefly, I told him.

"That's ridiculous," said Goldstein.

"Listen who's talking ridiculous," sneered Lipschitz. "You know how to run a restaurant. How to put on a play, thank you very much, *I* know."

"I've devoted my life to the stage!" Goldstein gestured to the walls covered with theater posters and photographs, many of them signed, of theatrical personalities. "You think these mean nothing? The Adlers themselves were not so high and mighty they wouldn't listen to my advice." His voice rose, trembling with fury. "I've forgotten more about the theater than any of you clowns will ever know."

"Get stuffed, Goldstein," said Lipschitz.

Goldstein sprang to his feet. "Out of my restaurant, all of you!" he screamed. "Get out!"

"Lipschitz will apologize," I said. "He got carried away. Calm down."

"Why should we get out?" said Lipschitz. "This is a public restaurant."

"You want to see how public?" screamed Goldstein, livid, the veins in his temples throbbing. "You want to find out? Stay there. I'm going to phone the police, they'll tell you." He tripped over Joe, who was picking up the shards of Blum's coffee cup, and fell to the floor. I offered him a hand, which he struck aside. There were tears in his eyes. "Get out!"

There was nothing for it. We left the restaurant and scattered.

* * *

LIPSCHITZ MUST HAVE GOTTEN WIND of our little enterprise. Well, that is not in itself surprising, what with the many wagging tongues of the Emma Lazarus. And I do not imagine that Hamburger—let alone the Red Dwarf!—has approached his quota of players with the degree of tact and discretion that so delicate a subject calls for. At any rate, Lipschitz stopped me in the hall this evening, right after *Kiddush,* the blessing over the wine. "So, friend," he said, "when do the gravediggers return to work?"

The hall, which runs from the lounge to the dining room, is wide and well lighted. On its walls are displayed various pictures on Jewish themes, the work of residents past and present: a haunting photograph of the Vilna ghetto, a weak watercolor of the Wailing Wall in Jerusalem, a mosaic made up of tiny pieces cut from matzo boxes depicting a Middle European seder. Certainly it is impossible to hold a conversation there and expect not to be seen. This Lipschitz must have known.

"As for me, I have not yet made up my mind," I said, pulling away from his slimy grasp, anxious to be gone. "You will kindly remember, I agreed to play in Shakespeare's *Hamlet,* not in Tosca Dawidowicz's. Not even in yours. There are questions of literary integrity here that I, for one, take very seriously. As for the Red Dwarf, he must speak for himself."

As it happened, the Red Dwarf was hurrying past at that moment. Friday is boiled chicken night, and he dearly loves a drumstick. He eyed us with grave suspicion.

Lipschitz waved his hand airily, dismissing him. "Poliakov is no loss."

The Red Dwarf grinned nastily. "Cossack!" he hissed at me, and hurried on, food for thought being no substitute for the real thing.

Lipschitz drew me aside. "Listen, a little goodwill on your side, a little on mine, we can iron out our differences. What's so important it should come before the production? Cooperation is what I'm talking about; personalities, we don't need. If this one plows the field and that one makes the dinner, another keeps the accounts and still another stands with his rifle in the watchtower, each is working for the good of all. No big, no small. Any other way, the Arabs will be raping our women and cutting off our balls."

"On this particular kibbutz," I told him, "equality is achieved in other ways."

"All right," he said, "let's talk candidly." Lipschitz's lizard head darted this way and that. His tongue flicked his lips. "What I was thinking was this: a man like you, Korner, is valuable to the production. Such a man should be second only to me myself in authority. Here's what I'm offering: return to rehearsals, and you're my understudy. If anything, God forbid, happens to me, you're Hamlet! This I shall announce to the entire company."

He was trying to bribe me! My cheeks burned with shame.

"Wait," he went on. "That's not all. Come back to us and I'll make you my codirector. This, too, I shall announce. Think about it, don't answer right away. God forbid anything happens to me, you sit in the director's chair, no questions asked." He paused; his tongue flicked his lips. "That's my best offer."

One does not have to do with such a man. I turned on my heel and walked away. Still, I can only admire his cunning: we had been seen in private conversation by many of the residents on their way to dinner. The possible political implications of this meeting would set beaks atwitter all around the Emma Lazarus, the factions shifting and realigning: "Just a parley before the first salvo." "Obviously the putsch has collapsed." "It's Chamberlain at Munich all over again." "Rapprochement." "War by other means." "Zionist encirclement and annexation." In this war of nerves, Lipschitz had made an impressive first move.

Later Hamburger and the Red Dwarf came to my room. The Red Dwarf rudely pushed past me and climbed into the easy chair, almost disappearing in its embrace. For Hamburger he left the straight-back chair at my desk. They looked at me silently for a moment. I closed the door.

The Red Dwarf's gold tooth glinted. "So, comrade, you have chosen a life for the czar?"

Naturally I said nothing. To such sarcasm there is nothing to say. But since, standing there, I felt a little like the accused before his judges, I went and sat on the bed.

"What did Lipschitz want?" asked Hamburger.

"Perhaps you should ask," said the Red Dwarf, "what did Korner want?"

"For God's sake, Poliakov," said Hamburger. "Korner is no traitor. What nonsense is this? Apologize to him, or I quit this whole business."

"No offense, comrade," said the Red Dwarf smoothly.

I told them what Lipschitz had said.

"So Lipschitz knows," said Hamburger woefully.

"This is what we get for pussyfooting around," the Red Dwarf snarled. "If you'd listened to me, Lipschitz and his lackeys would be already groveling at our feet, whining for mercy. 'Let's sound the others out,' says Kerensky over here. 'Let's hear from Pinsky and Minsky and Stinksky.' Let me tell you something: if you want the people to march on the Winter Palace, you have to *shtup* them in their backs with a rifle butt and fire a few bullets into the air." He crossed his legs under him on the easy chair and began to sway back and forth, his eyes closed, as if in silent prayer or ill with stomachache.

"Perhaps if we'd gone right away to Scheisskopf," said Hamburger. He pulled at a long earlobe and slowly shook his head. His thin white face, gloomy at the best of times, was heavy with despair. "You don't happen to have a cookie, Korner? Perhaps a little schnapps?"

"Wodka," said the Red Dwarf.

I took some bottles and glasses from the cabinet and put out the gingersnaps.

"With such an attitude at Valley Forge," I said, "today we would be saluting the Union Jack and singing 'God Save the Queen.' "

"*Some* of us would," said the Red Dwarf.

"I have always admired," said Hamburger, "the British sense of fair play." He bit into a gingersnap musingly.

"Pip-pip," said the Red Dwarf. He put a hand behind his head before throwing it smartly back. Down his gullet went a half-tumbler of vodka.

We were in obvious disarray.

We pooled the results of our researches. Blum is with us in exchange for the role of Horatio. Salo Wittkower, our Claudius, is with us if we agree to play Elgar's "Pomp and Circumstance" for all his exits and his entrances—"a kind of leitmotiv," he says. (A small price to pay, even though the composition, I believe, was written for Edward VII.) Also Emma Rothschild, our costume designer (and third-floor chess champion), is with us, admirably, out of simple loyalty to Sinsheimer, whom Lipschitz, in her view, mocks by his directorship. Reynaldo and Polonius are undecided. The rest of the cast will accept whatever is decided for them.

Neither hopeful nor hopeless: there is no consensus.

"What is to be done?" asked Hamburger.

"Chernyshevsky," said the Red Dwarf dreamily, round-shouldered, rocking back and forth.

"Work more vigorously with the dramatis personae," I

suggested. "Exploit their dissatisfactions. Reason with them. Try to bring together a majority."

"It may yet not be too late," said the Red Dwarf, snapping upright. "But let me give you a warning in the form of a quotation: 'The great questions of the day are decided not by the votes and resolutions of majorities, but by blood and iron'—Comrade Lenin, 1916."

"Bismarck," I said.

"Lenin!"

"Hamburger?"

"Bismarck," said Hamburger wearily.

"What difference?" said the Red Dwarf, and then, as if to cover his heresy, he took a quick drink of vodka, hand behind his head as before. "The revolutionary takes from the Black Hundred whatever is useful for the liberation of the masses."

What would he say, this disciple of Lenin, if I told him that I met his hero in Zurich in 1916? Not even the Red Dwarf would have been impressed by him then. The champion of the people was far too busy trying to make his centimes last through the week.

"It's late," I said.

"What have we decided?" asked the Red Dwarf, now on his third half-tumbler of vodka and as a consequence growing teary-eyed.

I glanced at Hamburger. He nodded. "Let's go, Poliakov. We don't have to decide anything tonight."

The Red Dwarf sprang to the floor. "I've got it!" he announced, and stumbled through a little jig.

"Tomorrow you'll tell us," said Hamburger.

"It's simple, that's the beauty of it! You, Korner, you accept Lipschitz's offer. He makes the announcement: if anything happens to him, you become the director."

"You don't know what you're saying," said Hamburger.

"No, wait, listen. Once he makes the announcement, we take care of him!"

"For God's sake, Poliakov!"

"Don't you see?" said the Red Dwarf. Tears ran down his cheeks. "It's simple!"

Hamburger took him firmly by the arm. "Tomorrow. Meanwhile, we'll think about it." He led the Red Dwarf, weeping, to the door. "Good night, Korner."

"G'night," sobbed the Red Dwarf.

16

Y THE TIME THE GREAT WAR, as it was already being called, had completed its first year, it was no longer comfortable for a young man to be seen in Germany out of uniform. I could scarcely be expected to produce my official document of disability to counter every look of disapproval, or even of disgust, that met me on the street! This was particularly galling for me since, as I have already said, I longed to join the slaughter. One even heard, or thought he heard, anti-Semitic remarks about the laziness, the cynical war-profiteering, the lack of patriotism of the Jews. Recently, for example, a cartoon had appeared in *Simplicissimus* that typified the burgeoning attitude. In it an officer is facing a row of recruits, all but one of them seated, the standing recruit quite clearly a Jew. (I say "quite clearly" because he possessed all the grotesque, stereotypical features that within a dozen years the Nazis would so enthusiastically exploit.) It is the Jewish recruit whom the officer is addressing. "Tell me, Bacherach," he asks, "why a soldier should cheerfully sacrifice his life for the Kaiser?" "You are right, Lieutenant," says the Jew Bacherach. "Why *should* he sacrifice it?" (My cousin Joachim was to give a leg and an eye for the Kaiser, receiving in return an Iron Cross and a small pension. The Nazis, when they came to power, took back both, and then took the rest of him.)

The ugly event that galvanized my father into action was a note wrapped around a stone that crashed through the window of our dining room one warm summer night and landed at my mother's feet. The note said simply: "Cowards should be shot." Father and I rushed to the window, but there was nothing to see.

"You are a danger to us all, not just to yourself!" my father began to shout, his eyes bulging, the veins at his temples throbbing. "You must leave Germany right away, immediately!"

"But Ludwig—" began my mother.

"Frieda, leave this to me. He must get out of here." He began to pace up and down. "Intolerable!" he said. "Intolerable!" But whether the word was directed at me or at the note that he still held in his hand, it was impossible to say.

"But where will he go?" asked my mother.

"Switzerland," said Aunt Manya.

They were talking now as if I were not there to hear them. My sister, Lola, sat on the sofa, silent, frightened, staring wide-eyed at her adored brother, who seemed to have done something truly shameful, unmentionable.

"Don't you think, Father—" I began.

"Silence!" he screamed. "You have nothing of any interest to say. You will go to Switzerland. But not to moon about with the other loafers, the good-for-nothings sitting out the war. No more poetry rubbish, thank you! You will study something that might be of use to you in a future career, useful eventually to the firm, useful perhaps in time even to the Fatherland."

"But Ludwig, Otto is a *good* boy, never a day's trouble from him. Why are you so angry with him? He can't help it that he can't fight. What has *he* done?"

My mother's tearful rebuke brought my father up short. In a softer tone he said, "Some good may come of this. In Switzerland he can also act as the firm's agent with America and the other nonbelligerents. That should count for something, cut through some of the red tape." He ran from the room and locked himself in his study.

I do not condemn my poor father for his outburst. He was distraught, fearful for his womenfolk—the stone through the window had terrified my mother—fearful for his standing in the community, fearful even for me. Perhaps, too, he had had some glimmering of the truth: the weakness of the foundation upon which he had built his trust in the Enlightenment and the Emancipation, the bacillus of anti-Semitism bred in the very marrow of the *Volk*, the essential capriciousness of German toleration. Like all the impotent, he vented his frustration on the innocent.

Later he knocked very softly on the door to my room. "It's not your fault, Otto," he said, reaching up to pat me on the head. "Never mind, my boy. Soon the war will be over, and you will return to us." He meant to be kind, of course; this was as close as he had ever come to an apology. In the order of things, parents do not apologize to their children. But his words stung just the same. Far better, it seemed to me then, to be unjustly accused of cowardice than to be treated as a child.

* * *

As a small boy I once watched a beetle trying to climb out of a glass bowl: up the slippery walls he went, up, up, and then— hoppla!—down he fell on his shiny back, his little legs waving frantically in the air. Turn him over and he would start again, up, up, and then hoppla! How he wanted to get out!

The Contessa would not have liked Zurich. This was no place for a claustrophobe. In Zurich, surrounded by the oppressive mountains, the Contessa would have felt like that beetle. But during the Great War this claustrophobic atmosphere was much increased. There was a tension almost palpable in the air. One lived in the eye of the storm, the peaceful dead center, while all around the battle raged, the guns thundered, the mines blew young limbs to bloody shreds, and a world, a way of life, was dying.

I arrived in Zurich (as I have elsewhere noted) in mid-September 1915, a month before the university term was to begin, time enough to get settled, to find my bearings. The city was bursting with refugees and exiles, with speculators and spies, with artists, political misfits, and literati, all beached, as it were, on the shores of the lake, all in the service of a Greater Purpose, in a city best praised for its cleanliness and parsimony. Nevertheless, in spite of myself—in spite, that is, of my stupidly "heroic" self-disgust—here in Zurich, independent, after a fashion, for the first time in my life (thanks to a generous letter of credit from my father), here, in this tiny spot in the mountains, to borrow from the cryptic remark of Señora Krauskopf y Guzman, here I felt free.

My father had determined that I would study political economy under the world-famous Professor Dr. Max Winkel-Ecke, a scholar who might, if any could, transform an idle dreamer into a useful, functioning member of bourgeois society. In the unlikely event that the war should outlast the completion of my course of studies, said my father, perhaps I should move on to commercial law. We would see. He would in any case, purely as a matter of precaution, make suitable inquiries about the law faculty at the university.

My protests were halfhearted and anyway hopeless: I was, after all, a dutiful son. Besides, I did not seem able to write anymore; the flame of inspiration had been quenched. Oh, yes, I had the occasional "poetic moment," a phrase, an image, a thought that pleased me. But I could bring nothing together. The world's events marched gloriously by, and I stood on the curbside, not even waving a flag. I became a diligent student. The wonder is that despite the unutterable boredom of my studies and the abandonment of my youthful expectations of literary achievement, already chained, as it seemed to me, to the dull grind of a duller future, I still retained a heady sense of freedom.

No, I had not forgotten Magda Damrosch. All that autumn and into the following winter I combed Zurich looking for her, her image ever before me. Through jostling streets and lonely alleys, in the marketplaces, the shops and tearooms, in the theaters and concert halls I searched, and searched in vain. I filled my empty nights with thoughts of her, ran through my mind again and again the words we had spoken to one another, now magical in memory, and tossed on my narrow bed in lustful imaginings: "Magda, Magda." By the end of February 1916 I had given up hope of ever finding her. My wanderings through Zurich were now habitual, not purposeful. For all I knew, she had long since left Switzerland.

And then I met Lenin. It was late afternoon, already dark outside. I was sitting in the overheated reading room of the cantonal library, plowing my way, with heavy lids, through yet another of those vast (and vastly dreary) tomes required by my studies, when Lenin appeared beside me. Of course, I did not know who he was, though I had seen him often before in the library. Neither he nor I nor anyone else knew yet what he would become. There is no need to describe him; all the world knows what he looked like. Still, there was nothing there of the fiery zealot who is the central figure of countless historical scenes painted in the tiresome school of Soviet socialist realism, nothing of the awesome, brooding face with its piercing eyes that hangs on giant banners in Red Square on May Day, along with the faces of Karl Marx and whoever rules the Kremlin at the moment. What I saw was a balding, middle-aged man of middle height, sweating slightly in a heavy, worn suit of some dull brown stuff. He looked like a petit bourgeois down on his luck, a minor civil servant who had recently been given the sack, someone battered by circumstances but gamely not complaining, though perhaps a little bewildered.

He asked if he might have temporary use of the journals

stacked at my elbow, since I did not seem to be needing them at the moment. I told him he was welcome to them (not mentioning that in fact they were not mine), and supposed that was that. But when, an hour or so later, weary beyond reckoning, I got up to leave, he scampered after me into the hall. His name, he said, was Vladimir Ilyich Ulyanov. He hoped he had not interfered too severely with my studies. Not in the least, I assured him. Dare he invite me, he asked, to a lecture he was to give at the Volkhaus the following evening? In view of my youth and my evident interests, I might find it worthwhile. After the lecture perhaps we would have a drink together. I thanked him and said I hoped I would be able to attend. A mildly ironic smile played on his lips. Perhaps he knew I had no intention of going to hear him.

I went, of course. (There is a universally acknowledged truth enshrined in the proverbs of the folk: Man proposes, but God disposes.) It was an evening of bone-chilling damp. The Volkhaus is a pseudo-Gothic building, then the headquarters of the Swiss Socialist party, ill lighted and drafty. On the other side of the street paced a portly policeman flapping his arms across his chest to keep warm. The lecture was sparsely attended; only about thirty-five or forty seats in the cavernous hall were taken, a polite audience of young Swiss workers. Lenin spoke of the lessons to be learned from the revolution of 1905. He spoke fluently and softly, only occasionally glancing at his notes. The Russian revolution of 1905, he said, was to be regarded as a dress rehearsal for the European revolution that still lay years in the future. He did not expect to witness it; he spoke, rather, as one who was ready to hand on the torch to the next generation, which might, with luck and determination, live to see the victory of socialism in Europe. There was scattered applause.

I met him afterward, in the lobby, and congratulated him on an interesting lecture. The same ironic smile played on his lips. We would have our drink at the Café Odeon, he said; it was on his way home.

What did we talk about, Lenin and I? Not about political economy or the rights of the proletariat. You will scarcely believe me if I tell you that we spoke of love—or, rather, that I spoke of it. What possessed me I cannot say, but I poured out all my youthful longing into the ears of this unlikely father-confessor, this middle-aged and disappointed little socialist revolutionary with the unsightly nicotine stains on his teeth. (Of course, I knew nothing then of the illicit and intensely passionate affair he had conducted with the beautiful Inessa Armand in Paris some years before; in some ways, he was uniquely qualified to hear my confession.) Even when we left the warmth of the café and hurried along the narrow stone streets, the cold wind numbing our ears and bringing tears to our eyes, still I talked on. He must have thought he would never be rid of me. We were in Niederdorf, a somewhat seedy quarter. We stopped before Spiegelgasse 14, an old stone building with a low lintel over a peeling door.

"I would like to invite you up for some tea," said Lenin, "but the hour is late, and I'm afraid my wife may be asleep. We have only one room"

I apologized for having bored him with my problems. Utter hypocrisy: I imagined that anyone would be fascinated by what I had to say.

"You have been frank with me. Let me be frank with you," said Lenin. "There is important work in the world for a young man like you, work that your studies should well prepare you for. Take my advice, Mr. Körner: go over there"—he pointed diagonally across Spiegelgasse to a *Bierstube* called Meierei, which boasted the Cabaret Voltaire; one could hear the tinny tinkling of a piano and the distant sound of laughter—"go over there and find yourself a pretty girl. There you will find your cure. And then, only then, you will be able to divert your abundant energies outward into the world, where—who knows?—you may do some good. Good night, Mr. Körner."

The insult was like a slap across the face. It left me speechless. But since Lenin had by now disappeared into the house, that scarcely mattered. More than anything else, I felt a fool. And I suddenly became aware of the bitter cold. Before the long walk home, I thought, I had better fortify myself with a hot drink. It was in the Cabaret Voltaire, of course, that I found Magda Damrosch again.

Do I suppose that Lenin was in Zurich solely to point out to me the Cabaret Voltaire? Of course not. He was to serve the Greater Purpose on the world-historical stage. But how can I doubt that at that moment our separate purposes were interlinked? "Find yourself a pretty girl," said Lenin, not knowing the Purpose; and I, not knowing the Purpose, entered the Cabaret Voltaire.

Allow me to illustrate the point in another way. One evening some months later I was dining with Magda in the Restaurant zum Weissen Kreuz. The evening was not going well. She had found many things to complain of: my punctiliousness, my devotion to order. Even my suit was not to her taste: her grandfather might have worn it. That was how she used to torment me. Our attention was diverted to another table, where sat a group of men in jolly camaraderie, laughing, telling jokes in French, Italian, German, and Latin, singing songs, and all at a pitch inconsiderate of the other diners, or so it seemed to me. One in particular I took to be the "ringleader," and certainly he was the loudest: a cadaverous man about ten years my senior, with a long, half-moon face, wearing thick glasses and a mustache. None of the languages was native to him, but he spoke them all fluently and with a single, unidentifiable lilt. When he laughed, as he did often, he threw back his head and opened his mouth wide. There was something of the down-at-heels dandy about him, as if he were a gigolo at a lower-class holiday resort. He sat with his thin legs elegantly crossed, and I could clearly see the large hole in the sole of his shoe. At one point he sang, to much laughter, a risqué French song in a pleasant, if rather thin, voice. True, there were no ladies at his table, but there were ladies elsewhere in the restaurant. No one else seemed to mind, however, least of all my Magda, who laughed shamelessly and even lifted her glass to toast him. I thought him an unmannered oaf.

A lifetime later, leafing through the photographs in Ellman's classic biography, I discovered to my surprise and embarrassment that this "unmannered oaf" had been the great Irish writer James Joyce, even then, in 1916, at work on his incomparable *Ulysses*. Considerations of Magda Damrosch aside, would I not greatly have preferred to meet James Joyce than Vladimir Ilyich Ulyanov? To have numbered in Joyce's circle in Zurich! A genius may be permitted his idiosyncracies. But obviously—alas!—there was no Purpose in our meeting.

17

ISTENING TO MOZART earlier this evening, the "Linz" symphony, I was reminded quite suddenly of the Contessa. To be precise, it was during the slow movement, with its bittersweet flavor and beautiful precision, that she popped into my head, or, rather, not she but a clear image of the small urn that contains her ashes. Not so strange perhaps: I had been thinking of the circumstances of the work's composition, Mozart's reception by young Count Thun in Linz, a moment in joyous contrast to the misery of his recent visit to Salzburg. There he had failed yet again to win his father's approval of his marriage to Constanze Weber. My chain of associations is clear enough: "Linz"-Mozart-Salzburg-Constanze-Contessa. The similarity of the ladies' names explains all.

After the unfortunate contretemps in the Versailles, the Contessa and I returned to New York and West Eighty-second Street, taking up a life in keeping with our age and circumstances. At first she had wanted us to move to her apartment in Flushing, which, she claimed, was much more spacious than mine. She needed air to breathe, room to move about in. Hers was a restless spirit not to be confined. Besides, the West Side was on a downhill skid, filling up with "undesirables," drug addicts, who knew what? One scarcely could see a white face anymore, "let alone a Jew." It was dangerous to walk the streets. But I explained to her that Flushing was out of the question for me: my way of life was bound to the city. Had not she herself remarked on the great inconvenience of commuting? Was it not to avoid that very travail that we had married? No, if we went to Flushing, we would stay there: it was a bourn from which no traveler returned. Accordingly, she moved her belongings to West Eighty-second Street—as many of them, that is, as would fit into my already crowded apartment.

We made for ourselves, I think, a good life, comfortable, relaxed, companionable, our days filled with small matters, a rhythm that pleased us. Of course, we never referred to our "honeymoon"; that frenzy had left her. I became accustomed to her body beside me in the bed, began even to be glad of it as a source of warmth and quiet friendliness. At the beginning of each December, after a pro forma pleading with me to accompany her, she would fly south alone to Florida, leaving me a bachelor again until the end of the following February. She telephoned me daily, as soon as the cheaper evening rates went into effect, to "fill me in" on her activities and those of her friends, to inquire after my doings and ask whether I was looking after myself. By the end of February I was always glad of her return, my "half-life" at an end. Were we happy? Yes, I would say so. But I would also have to say that since our marriage and the Versailles, the Contessa had lost some of her earlier ebullience. She had become a trifle subdued, sometimes a trifle wistful.

As I have told you before, the Contessa was claustrophobic. This was often a great inconvenience for her. For example, she would trudge up the stairs to our apartment with a full load of groceries in her arms, rather than take the building's small elevator; she would not get on a crowded bus, and would get off one that had become crowded, no matter how far from her destination or how inclement the weather; never mind what Paris dictated, she could not wear a dress or a blouse that closed at the throat. All that was bad enough. But while still among the living, she carried her phobia with her in thought into the Next World. She could not bear to think of being sealed in a coffin and buried beneath the earth. The very idea of it terrified her. She had the most frightful imaginings: what if it should turn out that she was not dead after all, God forbid? What if she should awaken in that confined space, that airless darkness where one could not even move the elbows, scarcely a pinkie, the lid an inch above the nose, where one's screams would go unheard? Such things had happened, God forbid.

"When?" I asked.

They had happened. Oy, oy, oy, the thought alone could drive a person mad. She wanted me to promise her, honest Injun, on my word of honor, that I would have her cremated.

"Jews mustn't be cremated," I told her, adding, after a moment, "not voluntarily."

In contrast to my tenuous hold, the Contessa grasped her own Judaism with talons of steel: she was, after all, the daughter of a kosher butcher, the widow of a ritual circumciser and onetime world-class Talmudic student. But she was also resourceful. She always took her questions of ritual and observance to a rabbi, either Orthodox, Conservative, or Reform, depending on what kind of answer she wanted. On the question of cremation she had already gone to Rabbi Millard Matlaw, Reform spiritual leader of Congregation Beit Sefer ha-Adom ha-Katan in Greenwich Village. His credentials aside, he was a humane man, a mensch, who felt along his own nerves another Jew's anguish. "This is the twentieth century," he told her, "and we're into a different kind of bag. Go with whatever makes you feel good."

Would I, therefore, promise? Very well, I would promise.

"You mean it?"

"I mean it."

Her gratitude was poignant, touching. How else to describe it? For a little while the old Contessa reappeared. "Let's celebrate!" she said, and she put a noodle pudding on the coffee table, with cups and plates and forks. Her eyes sparkled. "How about some whipped cream? How long since dinner?" And then she went and dug out of the trunk that contained her personal items her urn. "What do you think of it?" she asked, holding it up triumphantly. I had never seen an urn like it, and I said so. It was in the shape of a Torah scroll, molded in copper. She demonstrated how it opened, unscrewed, on the tops of the opposite sides. "Half of me here, half of me here," she explained gaily. "Here, have some whipped cream on the pudding. Don't worry, enough time has passed." She raised her coffee cup to me. "Here's to us," she said. "L'chayim."

But then a cloud appeared on her horizon, appeared and grew.

"What's the matter?"

"Tell me," she said, biting her lip. "Will you want the ashes?"

How does one answer such a question? Of course I didn't want the ashes. Who wants ashes? On the other hand, would it not seem callous, would I not seem indifferent to her memory, if I refused them, if I did not say, unequivocally and firmly, that I wanted them with me always? I tried diplomacy: "What I want is that you should live long and be well. Why should we talk of ashes? Besides, I will be gone long before you. You'll see, you'll have to make other arrangements."

The cloud was not dissipated; the sun did not shine. "No," she said, "I've had a premonition. You know my premonitions."

True, I did. In the time I had known her she had batted a thousand. It was uncanny.

"Of course, I don't want to offend you," she said. "Naturally, you have a claim on the ashes, my husband, after all, my second." She raised her head and took a deep breath. "It's like this. When poor sainted Meurice died, I didn't expect to marry again. Who could have known? Such luck, to meet a person like you, who could have expected? So I designed for him a stone, not too showy, but respectable: he was, after all, a circumciser of the first rank and, besides, a good Jew, a loving husband, a good provider. And in this stone, this monument, is a niche. And in this niche is a Torah scroll, just exactly like this, a twin, you couldn't tell them apart. My idea was, when I died, and, please God, I should happen to be cremated, that Torah scroll, in the niche, should be unscrewed, and this Torah scroll, with me in it, should be screwed in instead. That way Meurice and I, without having to go through Central Inquiry in the Next World, would easily find one another. That was my idea. And Rabbi Matlaw, the direct descendent of the 16th Century Sage of Prague, he okayed my idea. 'Listen,' he said, 'who knows? And if that's what turns you on, well, hey.' So that's how it stands. But now I have a new husband. You have a claim, no question, and it's only fair I should hear from you on this."

Naturally, I told her, I would want her ashes, but I recognized—anyone would—that Meurice had a prior claim. Rabbi Matlaw would tell us that this was a fundamental principle of Jewish law. She need not worry, I would see to it that her Torah scroll would find eternal rest in the predetermined niche, united once more with her first husband: if the direct lineal descendant of the Sage of Prague had approved such a course, who was I to object?

We were married for almost ten years. One day she complained of a blinding headache; the next, she was in the hospital. Why go into the details: a blood clot in the brain. Mercifully, her suffering did not last long. Her last words to me were, "Remember, you promised. Best avoid trouble, go there at lunchtime when nobody's around. It's an Orthodox cemetery, there might be problems otherwise. Besides, who knows what the legalities are? Take a screwdriver." She sighed, weak and wan, but managed to smile. "Thanks, Otto."

And so, in fact, in spite of myself, I went to Florida again. It all went off without a hitch. I remembered the screwdriver.

I missed her, the Contessa. Ah, you will say, but did you love her? I missed her. I miss her still.

* * *

AND SO, YOU SEE, long before Lipschitz and La Dawidowicz, mysteriously interpreting the wishes of poor dead Sinsheimer, stripped me of the role of Ghost and assigned me that of Gravedigger, I had already had some practical experience in cemeteries. Nevertheless, the changes in roles seemed at first a demotion. I was thinking, naively, in sociological terms. A king and a gravedigger may both "crawl 'twixt earth and heaven," but the gravedigger, it goes without saying, has his belly in the dirt. Besides, I would lose considerable stage exposure in the first act, as well as all of the Ghost's long, magnificent speeches. My rendering of one line in particular—"O horrible! O horrible! Most horrible!"—I immodestly admit was especially effective; Sinsheimer had managed to get out of me the most soul-racking sob, a vocal tremor that shook the stage and hushed the watchers in the wings.

But I swallowed my disappointment. All through my convalescence I thought about the scene in the graveyard, trying to work my way into its meaning, digging "i' th' earth," so to speak. At last I have found it: viewed from the perspective of the Gravedigger—or Grave*maker,* as he terms himself and we had better term him—the play is transformed! *For the Gravemaker and the Prince are the two faces of a single coin.* I saw how Shakespeare insinuated this truth: the Gravemaker began to make graves on the day Hamlet was born; the skull, tossed casually out of the hole in the earth by the one, is picked up for contemplation by the other. Only after the encounter in the graveyard can Hamlet triumphantly assert, "This is I, Hamlet the Dane." May we not say, therefore, that it is the Gravemaker who leads Hamlet to his identity?

* * *

HAMBURGER AND HERMIONE PERLMUTTER were just going out for a stroll as I was returning from mine. We met at the corner of Broadway. She was holding him very possessively by the arm, laughing at something he was whispering into her ear. Well, well, well. (Watch out, Hamburger!)

I raised my hat.

When Hamburger saw me, his long face changed in an instant from gaiety to gloom.

"Have you seen the bulletin board?" he said.

"No, why?"

"Better take a look," he said darkly. "We'll talk later. See if you can find the Red Dwarf. I'll try to find the others."

The bulletin board is in the lobby, alongside the bulletproof glass window, behind which now sat Selma's temporary replacement. To it was pinned very prominently the following note:

!!! NEW AUDITIONS !!!

Hamlet

by

William Shakespeare

Directed

by

NAHUM LIPSCHITZ

A Lipschitz-Dawidowicz Production

Auditions Will Soon Be Held
For The Following Roles:

* *King Claudius*
* *The Ghost*
* *First Gravedigger*
* *Fortinbras*
* *Second Gravedigger*

* Costume Designer Also Wanted *
!!! No **Personalities** Need Apply !!!

Obviously Lipschitz had made his second move. It was a clean sweep. At the very moment when I have come to my new understanding of the Gravemaker's role, of its central importance, Lipschitz has kicked me out of the play!

But my attention was seized by another sheet of paper pinned alongside the Lipschitz salvo. It was a poem. My tormentor had struck again, perhaps now for the last time:

A SONNET TO YOU-KNOW-WHOM
When first I hinted at the culprit's name
And sought to point the hunter to his quarry,
I thought it fair to let him bag the game:
He was the victim. Now I think I'm sorry.
Why help a fool for whom all clues are cold?
Why make of such a simpleton my debtor?
The wolf had slyly crept into the fold;
The sheep with all my clues can't find his letter.
But still I think I'll grant him one last chance,
An opportunity to flush the vermin.
He'll take it or he'll simply stand askance,
Another stupid, bumble-headed German:
Look for the thief in Denmark's Elsinore;
He's in the play, and dallying with his whore.

I tore the sonnet from its restraining tack. I think I'm

going to have to take someone into my confidence. Probably Hamburger.

* * *

HAMBURGER IS A BITTER DISAPPOINTMENT to me. He is in the toils of a sudden passion that has crowded out any other concern. Friendship, for one example, is cavalierly brushed aside; for another, the Cause, worthy in concept if not in execution, is allowed to languish. And yet he was a founding member, his noble cry for justice drawing others, myself among them, into his doomed enterprise.

We met briefly just after dinner and discussed the situation. Our forces had suffered a total collapse. Salo Wittkower has already crawled back, sniveling and whining, to Lipschitz, and has been readmitted to the company. Blum has decided to "quit the theater" and rededicate himself to his sole area of expertise: he is going to set his cap for Mandy Dattner, the physical therapist—"Randy Mandy," he called her—a coup that, if he could pull it off, would be worth "all the bright lights of Broadway." Emma Rothschild is relieved to be able to return to chess: her game has been suffering, she said. As for the Red Dwarf, he is hors de combat for the time being, "drying out," according to Dr. Comyns, whom I met as he emerged from Poliakov's room to affix a Do Not Disturb sign to the door. "Two bottles of vodka in twenty-four hours. Some idiot must have started him off again, he's been off the sauce for years. That his liver functions at all confounds medical science. Mine, anyway. It's worth a letter to the journals."

"Will he be all right?"

"Probably," said Comyns cheerfully. "If the Feds don't get him first."

Through the door came the voice of the Red Dwarf, bravely singing between chattering teeth the "Song of the Volga Boatmen."

"Well, what are our plans now?" I asked Hamburger.

"Plans? Are you serious, Korner? Plans!" Then, in a more kindly tone, "There's nothing to be done right now, obviously. We'll talk about it again in a few days."

"So you are prepared to let Lipschitz just kick us out?

Hamburger drew himself up to his full height. (Even so, he was still a good three inches shorter than I.) "It pains me to have to remind you, Korner, that nobody kicked *me* out. I quit." He looked at his watch. "Meanwhile, if you will excuse me, I have plans of another sort for this evening."

"You can spare me half an hour, can't you? There is a personal matter—"

"Unfortunately, no." The Thalia Cinema, it appeared, was showing an old favorite of his, which coincidentally was also an old favorite of Hermione Perlmutter's: *Les Liaisons Dangereuses.* He must hurry, or he would be guilty of keeping a lady waiting. "You wouldn't care to join us?" he added dissuasively.

"Tomorrow, then?" I said. "I need your advice about something."

Alas, no. Hannah, Hermione—that is, Mrs. Perlmutter—had been kind enough to invite him to join her for the weekend at her daughter's "estate in the Hamptons." A limousine was to pick them up at eight in the morning. The foliage, he was given to understand, was quite magnificent at this time of the year. The daughter, by the way, I might have heard of, the famous neofeminist Lucille Morgenbesser? No? Pity. Her first book, *Re-Membering Freud: Toward a Feminist Psychology,* had been last year's sensation, a Book-of-the-Month Club choice. Her second, published only a week ago, was already on the *Times's* best-seller list: *Lesbos and Judaea: the Polarities of Commitment.* Clearly, he said, Lucille Morgenbesser took after her mother.

"Hermione Perlmutter is a lesbian?"

"Of course not," said Hamburger coldly. "What kind of shit is that? I meant as a writer." Not that La Perlmutter had published any of her work. No, not for her the descent into the "grimy commercial pit." But she had written over the years plays, poems, short stories, a "treasure trove in a trunk, a cornucopia of excellences." Hamburger was proud that she had shared some of her work with him, and he hoped he could persuade her to share some of it with me: as a man (like himself) trained in the Old School, a man, in short, with literary sensibilities, I would be well able to appreciate her talent. And now he must run.

At that point I said something shameful to his retreating back. It was a clear sign of my distress, certainly, but that is no excuse. "Blum failed to break that particular bank," I said. "And he had an ace hidden in *his* trouser pocket. Do you perhaps have a joker in yours?"

He turned slowly toward me. "What you imply about me, I choose to forget," he said. "We are old friends. But you have insulted a lady. That I can neither forget nor ignore. Hannah, Hermione, Mrs. Perlmutter, is a woman of impeccable honor and unassailable virtue. I think you want to apologize. Am I right?"

He was right. I apologized.

* * *

WHAT IS THE MATTER with these old men? I am reminded of Jumbo the Elephant. When he arrived in the England of Queen Victoria (a woman, as we know, of unbounded though scarcely acknowledged sexual energy), he was still quite young, and, vainly longing for union with a female of his species, he became unruly. He was treated as any English headmaster would have treated one of his charges caught in a like condition—that is to say, he was soundly thrashed and hosed down with icy water. For many years after that he could be relied on to give safe rides to children in the London Zoo. But after his acquisition by P. T. Barnum and his exhibition in Madison Square Garden, the aging Jumbo began to show ever-increasing signs of unruliness again. He fell into terrible rages. Some said these were caused by a kind of frenzy linked to the sexual cycle; others said they were caused by the shifting of giant molars. No one knew for sure.

Is the libido of old men an elephant, placid for years but always capable of sudden eruption? Is the only cure extraction, so to speak, or, as was the case with poor Jumbo, execution? I remember ruefully enough my own response to Mandy Dattner and Dr. Comyns as they rubbed against one another, ignorant of my abysmal voyeurism. But at least for me a sense of personal decorum intervened and prevailed. Blum, of course, is a special case: he is cursed with an unflagging libido. I suspect he suffers from what, as I recall my Krafft-Ebing, is known clinically as satyriasis, his *Kraft*—but here you must forgive the play on words—never ebbing. But is poor Hamburger, that gloomy and thin-faced pachyderm, a victim of Jumbo's disease? "My love is like a red, red rose," claimed the Scottish poet. *Hamburger, beware of thorns!*

And what is the matter with these old women? After Albert's death, the Prince being a short, stout, sexual popinjay in whom all Germany took a leering pride, Queen Victoria transmuted her misery in her lonely bed into spiritual exaltation and pneumatological longing. At teatime a place was always laid for the necessarily absent Albert. She taught all Europe how to mourn. But it is commonly believed nowadays that women's sexual desire increases at a rate inversely proportional to men's sexual ability—the rare example of a priapic Blum aside. The gods, we may suppose, are much amused. Of my own experience with the Contessa I have already written. What she needed, pour soul, according to the modern graphs, was a younger and less fastidious man.

But that Hamburger, for a woman, for *any* woman, and at his time of life, should refuse the request of a friend, should leave the battlefield at the first whiff of grapeshot; that he should abandon in exchange for a weekend in the country among the ephemeral literati what should be most important to him; that the autumn foliage—God save the mark!—should matter more to him than his integrity, I did not expect to learn.

18

AM NO STRANGER to betrayal.

Yes, yes, you may be sure I recognize the ambiguity of that sentence. Let it stand.

Lenin, you will recall, had pointed me to the Cabaret Voltaire. I entered and found myself in a dim, steaming room, red lamps here and there casting an unwholesome glow. To the left was the bar, zinc-covered, behind which stood the proprietor, wiping glasses. Business was good for so cold a night: most of the dozen or so tables scattered around the room were taken. To judge by all the tasseled caps and beer steins, the noisy chatter and wild laughter, this was a student nightspot. It had just the right degree of sleaziness to appeal to the sons of the Zurich bourgeoisie. The floor was covered with sawdust; the hot, damp air smelled sour. Barely visible in the far corner was an upright piano.

I doffed my coat and hat, for I was already sweating, and took a table against the wall. The girl who brought me my drink told me that if I liked, she would be pleased to sit at my table, but in that case she would have to get a drink for herself, a crème de menthe at least, or Herr Ephraim would be angry. She winked and indicated the proprietor, who was at that moment looking at me and nodding, as if he had overheard her words and was confirming their accuracy. She was a pretty, perspiring creature, with plump red cheeks, black Gypsy eyes, and a swelling bodice. Her name, she told me, was Minnie. Why did

I hesitate? I suppose because I was still smarting from Lenin's insult; certainly I was not going to put his advice into immediate practice. I thanked her but said I would not be staying long. Still, it would give me pleasure to furnish her with a crème de menthe if she would allow me to add an appropriate sum to my bill. Yes, she would certainly allow me, she said with a giggle. And off Minnie went, my money in her hand, her firm round rump undulating into the shadows. Sitting alone in the midst of revelry, I sipped my drink and tasted my idiocy.

Lights went on suddenly at the foot of the room, illuminating the far wall (on which had emerged from the shadows paintings of a bizarre and garish kind), the piano, and a floor space cleared of sawdust. A tubular young woman in a tubular black dress rose to her feet from a front table and walked slowly to the center of the "stage," her progress recorded by the tapping of a spoon on a tin pot. Sawdust adhered to her skirts like a furbelow. Her face was powdered dead-white, her eyes were enlarged by the application of kohl, and her mouth was a painted scarlet line. Accompanied by the pianist, she sang songs of the Belle Epoque in a clear albeit somewhat feverish voice. She kept her face entirely expressionless, with her lips moving mechanically, which added an unexpected element of irony to the songs of dark passion and lighthearted love.

It was late. I had an early-morning appointment with Professor Dr. Winkel-Ecke. It was my duty to support an heretical concept I had proposed: the absence of a relationship between the gathering of harvests and the declaration of wars. So far, the professor was letting me have my say before revealing my youthful errors: a meritorious endeavor undermined by meretricious ahistoricity. Eventually he would slap me heartily on the shoulder and urge me to cheer up: "All acknowledged truths must be examined from time to time. Occasionally we must even revise our thinking. If not this time, then perhaps the next."

At any rate, I had finished my drink and was thinking of leaving. Idly I watched the tubular chanteuse return to her table. A short, dark man got up there, but my attention was caught by a young woman whose back had been to me but who now turned her head to clap the performer to her seat. I could scarcely believe my eyes, but it was certainly she. I had found Magda Damrosch.

It is impossible to describe the emotions that swept through me then: joy, certainly, and relief, but terror also, as I might have ignored Lenin and hurried past the Cabaret Voltaire; wonder was there, and a fierce exultation, a mélange whose constituents I could not then and cannot now disentangle. I half rose to my feet, collapsed back into my chair, got to my feet again. There she was, not in my dreams but in the flesh, not two dozen paces from where I stood. Like a man in a fever, I stumbled over to her table.

"Fräulein Damrosch, I'm so happy to see you again!" She turned toward me and arched her left brow.

"Yes?" It was quite obvious she did not recognize me!

"I beg to remind you, we met on—"

"Ssh!" She frowned (beautifully!) and waved an admonitory finger. "Sit down and be quiet. Tzara is about to recite."

I had to endure the next performer, the short man with thick hair who had got up a moment before. He was neatly dressed in a dark velvet suit and wore a monocle that he could keep in place only by squinting angrily. I suppose you would call him good-looking. In one hand he held a cowbell, in the other a rubber ball, rather like an automobile klaxon without the metal horn. From the center of the stage he declaimed the most appalling nonsense in rapid French. I no longer remember what it was exactly—I was in any case scarcely in a condition to remember, with Magda Damrosch sitting no more than a hand-span from me—but it was something of this order: "When the pink crocodile saunters down Broadway, his straw hat atilt, then the houris of Lithuania ready themselves with coats of varnish." He went on and on in this vein, punctuating his recitation with clangs from the cowbell and crepitations from the rubber ball. Occasionally the pianist would throw in a chord or two. He finished to thunderous applause and threw out a generous hand to the pianist, who stood up to take deep bows.

"Now then. . . ."

"We met last September, Fräulein, on the train. My name is Otto Körner."

At last she remembered. "Ah, yes, the mama's boy." She thumped on the table. "Introductions, introductions," she announced. "Fräulein Emmy Hennings" (the *chanteuse*), "Herr Hugo Ball" (the pianist), "Herr Tristan Tzara" (the poet), "I wish to present to you Graf Otto von und zu Körner, a member of the Kaiser's Secret Service, here tonight in mufti. Thanks to his heroic efforts I was successfully smuggled into Switzerland. Applause, please." Each of them clapped, once.

Perhaps a look had passed among them. I do not know why otherwise they should have behaved in concert to exclude me. But they chattered and laughed among themselves, ignoring any comment of mine. "Waiter," they called, or "Waitress, more drinks here," or "Herr Ober, sausages, if you please," and grew more and more animated. It was humiliating. Even Magda seemed reluctant to be drawn from their circle, to talk to me. I was reduced to intermittent attempts to capture her attention, banal questions that she answered evasively. Where was she staying? Oh, with friends. Might I have the honor of escorting her home? No, her "friends" were picking her up. What had she been doing for the past six months? This and that. What *this,* what *that?* Oh, painting mostly: she wanted to become an artist. "Like those?" I said, indicating the grotesqueries that had merged once more with the shadows of the wall. "Ah, if only. . . ." (In time I would have to reassess the "grotesqueries": already on those walls in 1916 were van Rees, Arp, Picasso, Eggeling, Janco, Slodky, Selinger, Nadelman!) Would I see her again? Zurich was a hamlet. Yes, but would she come out with me, to dinner, perhaps? She supposed so. When? Sometime. Tomorrow? No, not tomorrow. The day after? She laughed at last with something of the delightful freshness and warmth she had shown months before on the train. "You win, *junger Mann,* you have worn me down. But there must be an exchange. If I *do* agree to go to dinner with you—I say *if*—will you promise to go home now and show me some mercy? Very well, one week from tonight. You may take me to the Restaurant Wallenstein."

Tzara had heard her. She had named the most famous and certainly the most expensive restaurant in Zurich, perhaps in all Switzerland. "Ow!" he said, shaking a hand limply as if he had burned it. "The Wallenstein! My God, Magda, what *is* this Graf von und zu, a munitions manufacturer?"

"At the moment I am a student."

Tzara screwed his monocle more firmly into his socket and grimaced horribly. "Ah, then I understand: you are *studying* to become a munitions manufacturer?"

The turn in the conversation had reminded me of tomorrow morning's appointment and thus of the lateness of the hour. I stood up.

"A speech!" cried Emmy Hennings, clapping her hands. Greasy sausages had smeared the scarlet line of her lips; perspiration had caused the kohl to run in driblets down her cheeks. Her features now seemed akilter, like one of *their* paintings.

"No," I said. "I am studying political economy." For some reason this answer seemed very comical to Ball and Tzara, and they burst out laughing. Tzara's monocle popped out of his socket and sank into his beer stein; Ball, with his pockmarked white face, looked like a paring of Swiss cheese shuddering in the wind.

Magda put a hand on my sleeve. "Never mind those idiots," she said. "Herr Körner is not only a student, Tristan. He is also a poet, a *published* poet." She turned to me, looking up with those wondrous eyes. "Herr Tzara might invite you to give a recitation."

Tzara had lost interest. He was peering into his beer. "Yes, by all means," he said, waving his hand dismissively. "Show me your work sometime."

"Remember," I said to Magda, "the Wallenstein, next week. Where may I call for you?"

"Ah, where, you are right, where? Right here, yes, why not? The Cabaret Voltaire, at eight o'clock."

Outside in the Spiegelgasse I wanted to leap and sing. I ran through the bitter streets, in love with life, in love with myself, in love with Magda Damrosch. Already I had excused her initial coldness. Perhaps I had caught her at an awkward moment; perhaps she had been embarrassed to be found in such company; perhaps because I had, like a fool, burst into an already established coterie, they had instinctively drawn together to expel a clumsy intruder. I heard only her warm laughter, saw only her eyes, her arched brow, felt only her charming hand on my sleeve. Fire ran through my veins. I leapt up the stairs to my room, threw myself fully clothed onto my bed, my "narrow cot," and fell immediately asleep.

My interview with Professor Dr. Winkel-Ecke went off more or less as I had anticipated. Somehow I got through the rest of the week. Work was impossible: I took icy showers, tramped for miles along the frozen margins of the lake, burned my energies in the raw air, fell exhausted upon my bed at night. I might have been Jumbo the Elephant. Slowly, all too slowly, creepingly, the week passed.

On the appointed evening I dressed myself, as you may imagine, with especial care. What a blessing that my mother had insisted on packing my formal evening clothes! ("He's going to be a student, Frieda, not a playboy," my father had grumbled. "A student may receive a dinner invitation," said my mother firmly.) I was smugly satisfied with the report my mirror gave me: my recent tramps along the lake had replaced my student pallor with a healthy, ruddy glow. I even winked at myself. The cab was already waiting downstairs.

At ten minutes to eight I entered the Cabaret Voltaire. An hour later I dismissed the chauffeur. An hour after that I walked disconsolately home.

Magda, of course, had not turned up.

19

ATURDAY MORNINGS ARE very quiet at the Emma Lazarus. The population thins out. The pious, at least those who are solo-ambulant, have gone to their several synagogues; aging children have come to take doddering parents away for the day or the weekend; the staff is reduced to an "essential services" skeleton. Ordinarily I enjoy the change of pace. For some of us who stay behind, Saturday morning is a time for quiet reflection.

You find me at the Emma Lazarus thanks to Hamburger. When the Contessa died he stayed by me, a firm friend, a rock. I learned then of his essential sweetness of soul. Every day he would come to West Eighty-second Street, unshaven, bringing with him a "little something" from Goldstein's, from Zabar's. He would stay late into the night.

The Contessa had been very fond of him, and he of her. "A true Continental," she had said, "cultured and refined. Like you, Otto." When he came to dinner, she would prepare his favorite dishes; he would always bring flowers and kiss her hand. Sometimes they played gin rummy together. Hamburger's grief, I often think, was deeper, more genuine, than my own.

On the eighth day he came and took down the sheets from the mirrors. He had shaved and once more looked spruce. "Come on," he said. "The sun is shining. We'll go to Goldstein's for breakfast and then take a little walk."

Later we sat on a bench in Central Park and watched the squirrels. The sun caressed us.

"It's time to think about your future," he said. "You're too old to live alone, you're not a squirrel. Listen to me, this is what I think: come to the Emma Lazarus. There we have first-class medical treatment, twenty-four hours; excellent kosher food; more activities than you'll live to enjoy. Every door has a mezuzah, except of course the toilets."

"I'm not such a fanatic, Benno. That was the Contessa, not me."

"We have an open-door policy: all Jews are welcome, you don't have to be religious, you don't even have to be Reform. Only the in-house rules are made by the rabbis. Apart from that you can live like a goy. It's like the State of Israel."

"But so many people under one roof."

"You can be as private or as sociable as you want. It's not an institution. Everyone decorates his own room, some even bring in professional decorators. We're not much on the outside, but inside is different. We're the Hotel Adlon, the Crillon, the Plaza of old-age homes. Believe me, I don't exaggerate."

"I'm not a Rothschild, Benno. I have only a small income."

"You don't know yet what the Contessa has left, may she rest in peace. Speak first to her attorneys, then decide."

She had left me everything: the condominium in Florida, the many canny investments made by the "Paganini of the Scalpel" in the days of his glory. I was amazed at how much there was. The attorneys would take care of everything, there were no problems, all I had to do was sign here, here, and here. A few weeks later I was able to tell Hamburger that money, at least, was no longer a problem.

"Then it's up to you," he said. "Come and take a look at us. I'll put your name up when next I see the secretary." He might have been a respected member of an exclusive British club.

"Perhaps it's for the best."

"That's the spirit!" he said, switching to the role of Marine Corps recruiting sergeant. "We can always use a few good men."

* * *

I FIRST MET BENNO HAMBURGER shortly after my retirement. It was in Goldstein's Dairy Restaurant, during a particularly crowded Sunday lunch hour. I told Goldstein I didn't mind sharing a table, and he took me over to Hamburger. There was the thin, sad face, now so familiar, the neatly cropped head that rests securely on a thick neck and portly torso. In sartorial elegance he can stand the test of comparison with Goldstein himself. The one, Hamburger, tends toward well-worn conservatism; the other, Goldstein, ever so slightly toward modish flamboyance.

Here I record the first exchange of words between us, as momentous in its way as the far better known exchange between Stanley and Livingstone:

"I'm almost finished."

"Take your time."

Joe shuffled over with a cup of black coffee for me and a check for Hamburger.

"I'll have the Walter Matthau," I said, "and perhaps a little extra sauce."

"You got it," said Joe, beginning a slow turn.

Hamburger had been examining his check with the scrupulosity of a government auditor. "You overcharged me a dollar-twenty on the Jack Klugman," he said.

Joe reversed his slow turn. "Goldstein put the prices up last week."

"A cup of coffee costs forty-five cents now?"

"It's a scandal," said Joe. "I wouldn't pay it."

"Goldstein is going to put himself out of business."

Hamburger took some bills out of his wallet and began to poke around in a change purse. He came up with a nickel and two pennies. " *'Poor in pocket,'* " he muttered to himself, quoting in German, " *'sick at heart'. . .*"

" *'I dragged my weary days along,'* " I said.

Hamburger looked up from his change purse, his eyes suddenly bright. " *'Poverty is the worst of plagues'. . . ,*" he said quickly.

" *'Riches are the highest good!'* "

"Goethe."

" 'The Treasure Seeker.' "

He sprang to his feet and extended his hand. I got to mine and took it.

"Hamburger, Benno."

"Korner, Otto."

We sat down again, and when Joe came back with my Walter Matthau, Hamburger ordered more coffee. We talked the afternoon away. There was only one awkward moment. "The name is familiar," he said. "I seem to remember it from the Bad Times. What were you then, a journalist?"

"Something like that," I said, and turned the conversation to safer topics.

It's hard to "get a handle" on Hamburger. Once, I asked him, as if I were seeking information, if he happened to know how the Dada Movement got its name. Since I propose to reveal in these pages the whole truth about the word's origin, a truth that has been suppressed for sixty years, Hamburger's immediate answer may amuse you:

"One day the infant Tzara was sitting on his potty in the nursery. In came his German nurse. 'Well, Tristan, little angel,' she said. 'Have you made a-a yet?' 'Yes,' said Baby Tzara. 'Made da-da, made da-da!' And there you have it: the Dada Movement."

Really, the man is impossible! On the other hand, I admit

that I have a personal weakness for this story. It has the ring of metaphorical truth.

Hamburger is like a picture made up from pieces of quite different jigsaw puzzles. Today he is a curious composite: gallant defender of a lady's honor, Jumbo the Elephant, literary critic with a taste for the sublime, advocate of women's rights and lesbian high jinks, and of course foliage fancier, nature's child.

Meanwhile, I sit here twiddling my thumbs.

20

O ONE AT THE CABARET VOLTAIRE admitted to knowing where Magda lived. "She'll be back," I was told. "She always comes back."

"But where does she go?"

"Vienna," said Tzara, enigmatically. "For instructions." Then he burst out laughing. I began to haunt Herr Ephraim's establishment, my studies forgotten or, if not forgotten, allowed to languish. Before long I had met most of the "gang": Marcel Janco, Hans Arp, Richard Huelsenbeck, Maja Kruscek (who was Tzara's girlfriend), Sophie Täuber (who would become Arp's wife), Max Oppenheimer, and others. They tolerated me but kept me on the fringes of their activities—unless they needed a living example of all that was wrong with the world, in which case "Graf von und zu" would be pulled into the center and asked to perform.

Much has been written about them; they have written much about themselves. We are told Dada was an "organized protest" by the middle-class young against the senseless slaughter of the war, a deliberate insulting of Western civilization, a concerted effort to thrust the stench of Europe's shame under her very nose. Or we are told it was a revolt against an intellectualism that had grown banal because it depended upon time-hallowed "truths" and not upon reason: the revolt had to embrace the alogical to protect itself from a takeover by the Philistines. And so on.

Well, it didn't look like that at the time. They were intelligent young people, certainly; sensitive, no doubt. And they were not lazy: they worked hard at their nonsense. But they were enjoying themselves immensely, too. Their delight was to shock for the pure pleasure of shock itself. What did Europe, what did "Western civilization," know of their revolt? Or care? It was enough for them if they could shake the fuddy-duddies of Zurich into tut-tutting alarm, disturb the comfort of the local bourgeoisie, tweak a few noses, pull a beard or two.

Like them, I was young. If they despised the war, I, by the time I met them, in 1916, had lost my naive faith in its glory, in the moral rightness of *our* cause as distinguished from the moral depravity of *theirs*, in Kaiser and *Vaterland*. Despite Huelsenbeck's mockery of me, I did not think that "everything has to be as it is." But I could not see why, in order to welcome a Nadelman, an Arp, or a Selinger, I had to kick out the German Romantics, whose serenity I loved and who had painted in a time when music and art and poetry came together in wonder-working harmony. They could not convince me that their *poèmes simultanés,* those meaningless chains of words and phrases brayed at an audience of beer-swilling students and punctuated by thumps on the table, clangs of the cowbell, gratings of ratchets, hiccups, bow-wows, and whatnot, were forging a new poetic language that would close forever the door on Goethe or, to step down but a rung, my beloved Rilke.

When Magda at last turned up at the Cabaret Voltaire, she was on the arm of Egon Selinger, the surrealist, the painter of eviscerated life-forms, with whom she was laughing and chattering away. They seemed to be on the most intimate terms. Well, they were a good-looking pair, I suppose. Selinger was an Adonis, tall and fair and gracefully muscled. Casual greetings were exchanged all around. No one got up; I, too, had learned to keep my place.

Magda paused by my seat, looked into my imploring eyes,

and pinched my cheek. "What," she said gaily, "are you still here?"

"For three weeks now, waiting to take you to dinner."

"Oh, that. I forgot. I had a headache."

"Which was it?"

"Both. I had a headache *and* I forgot. Besides, I saved you lots and lots of money."

There was no apology, not a hint of one. Nor would she pay attention to my complaints.

"Go away, *junger Mann,* I've had enough of you, you are boring me." She went and sat at the other side of the large round table where the "gang" held their conferences.

Meanwhile, Selinger had unwrapped a painting and was holding it up. "What do you think of it?"

It was a collage. An eviscerated fish reclined on the sports page of the *Neue Zürcher Zeitung.* The painting was in blood-red, violent greens, and bright orange, a typical Selinger of this period. The table wholeheartedly approved.

"What do you call it?" asked Arp, who in profile looked like a turtle: hair cut close to the scalp, no chin, hanging lower lip.

"*Primavera Four.*"

Thumps on the table, whoops, cries of "bravo!"

"Janco?" said Selinger, licking his lips nervously.

Marcel Janco, the dandy, with his perfectly regular features, his heavy-lidded eyes, his sensuous lips (the upper one a perfect bow), looked carefully at the painting again. He paused.

"It reminds me," he said, "that I've had no lunch today."

Anyway, it was midafternoon. The "gang" was discussing tonight's performance. They had already celebrated a French Night and an African Night. Their performances were growing wilder and wilder. They may not yet have known what to call themselves, but the sober citizens of Zurich already had a name for them: nihilists! Tonight was to be a Russian Night. Selinger could play the balalaika.

"Good," said Magda. "And I shall bring my scarlet tutu. I'll do the splits."

"Watch out for the suction, *Liebchen,*" said Selinger. "It can be painful."

Everyone laughed. I was ready to rise and defend Magda's honor, but she too was laughing, tickling Selinger in the ribs. "Pig," she said lovingly.

They were also planning a Gala Night, something Zurich would never forget, for some time in the future, and a magazine whose name, if they could find it, would also identify what they already felt to be a movement. *Omphalos, Priapus,* and *Prank* had been considered and rejected. *Cosmo-Chaos* was a strong contender, as was *Ka-Ka-Kunst.*

To an objective observer with a taste for farce, this was a moment not serious but hilarious. I stared at Magda with painful longing, she gazed at Selinger with hungry eyes, he watched Janco with evident ardor. As for Janco, he looked off into the distance with a mysterious smile. Who knew where his attention lay? His arm was around the neck of his current conquest, his hand resting comfortably on her bosom, his thumb idly flicking a nipple.

* * *

WELL, AT LEAST BLUM is making headway. I saw him and Mandy Dattner in jolly conversation in the fourth-floor hallway this morning, Sunday. She towers over him. He was making his point by poking her gently in the midriff, with each poke coming closer and closer to her breast. She was giggling. Who would think that fifty years—half a century!—separate them? The smart money bets on Blum!

* * *

I LOST MY SEXUAL INNOCENCE to Herr Ephraim's waitress Minnie.

We met by chance one Sunday afternoon in spring. The rain had stopped, the air was fresh and mild, and from the mountains came the distant rattle of thunder. The lake's surface rolled, a dirty olive-gray. It would certainly rain again. Meanwhile, like many of the town's inhabitants, we were out for a stroll. "How elegant you look, Minnie!" And indeed, she had contrived a pleasing flair and flounce to her poor costume. She beamed with pleasure at the compliment and impulsively took my arm. "Herr Körner! Such luck! Come, let's walk together." The truth is, I was grateful for the company. My mood was that of the lonely man in the tale by Poe who desperately seeks the meager companionship of crowds. Minnie lifted my spirits, her bubbling chatter chasing the cobwebs of melancholy from my brain. And besides, I was conscious of her bosom, to which she, nature's child, had drawn my arm.

And so on we walked, until the rain began once more to spatter the pavements. Gonfalon's Konditorei was across the street; we dashed there, laughing, seeking shelter. In those years Gonfalon's was a Zurich landmark, a rendezvous of quiet opulence. Minnie was at once awed and delighted to find herself in such surroundings. What a sweet tooth she had! The richest pastries were not too rich for her, and as for Gonfalon's specialty, hot chocolate topped with whipped cream and sprinkled with nutmeg, she drank down two with scarcely a pause between. I can even now see the tip of her tongue licking the cream from her upper lip! "Ah, sir," she said, closing her eyes in ecstasy, "that was delicious."

I suppose I thought of myself as an elderly uncle taking his little niece out for a special treat. In any case, suffused with good feeling, delighted that a few francs could purchase for Minnie such pleasure, I took her hand in mine. "You needn't call me 'sir,' not when we're out together as friends."

Softly, she pressed my hand. "What shall I call you, then?"

"Otto."

"All right, sir. Otto it is."

The afternoon was on the wane. We left Gonfalon's to find that the rain had abated. A blustery wind blew in from the lake. I was anxious now to return home, where the work I had earlier abandoned in lonely misery still waited. Minnie had served her turn. "Thank you for a most charming afternoon."

"Which way are you going, then?"

I pointed vaguely up the street.

"Ah, that's my way, too, we can go together, Otto. I've got an old auntie in that direction. I'll just pop in for a visit."

I was growing weary of her and, to be honest, already regretted having invited her to use my first name. She was, it must be admitted, common. (In those days one did not feel shame at such undemocratic sentiments.) She held my arm as before, chattering mindlessly on.

At length we reached the house where my landlady, a doctor's widow, eked out her pension by renting rooms to "young gentlemen with unimpeachable references." It was a solid, ample house in a solid, ample neighborhood. "And now, Minnie? . . ." I raised my hat.

"You live here, then?" I nodded. "How posh it is!"

I looked with her at the house. "It's adequate."

Suddenly her face creased with pain. "Ouch!"

"What's the matter?"

"I've twisted my ankle, that's what's the matter."

How had she done that, just standing there? "Here, lean on me. How can I help?"

"I'll be all right. All I need is a tiny sit-down." Her smile was mischievous. "You don't happen to have one, do you?"

I was, of course, the very soul of chivalry. Here was a Damsel in Distress! In such circumstances obvious differences in social standing and breeding counted for nothing. "If you think you can make it up the stairs, you can rest in my room. If not, perhaps my landlady . . ."

"I'll try."

In fact, she reached my room with admirable agility.

"Close the door, *Liebchen*, be so good. There's a horrible draft in here."

Scorning the easy chair and plump pouffe I showed her, Minnie made straight for my bed. She tried an experimental little bounce. "Ooh, *so* comfy!" She looked about her at the large room, the paneled walls, the ornate furnishings, the neat display of gentleman's toiletries. "You have this all to yourself, I bet." And when I nodded, she shook her head in wonder. "Some people are born lucky." With a gesture of dismissal she unpinned her hat and sent it skimming like a discus across the room.

I was rather at a loss as to what to do. I stood, therefore, leaning against the door as casually as I could, one hand behind me idly twitching the tails of my coat, the other smoothing my mustache. When the silence between us had grown embarrassingly lengthy, I asked her if she'd care for a brandy. She was eying me from top to toe, and she had a strange little smile on her lips. "A cognac, perhaps? Only as a restorative, I mean."

"Cognac makes me burp. You wouldn't have a nice crème de menthe? Well, never mind." She bent over to unlace her shoes, then took them off. "Here," she said, wiggling a foot at me. "Does it look swollen?" It did not, and I told her so. "Well, it hurts just the same. Come along, *Liebchen*, you're forgetting your manners. Take off that silly coat and help me off with mine. Then you can have a cognac if you like."

I silently cursed the mischance of our meeting. Now I would never be rid of her and her damned ankle. Nevertheless, I sprang to accommodate her.

"I need a tiny rub to fix me up—a massage, you know." She swung her legs up onto the bed and, using her elbows and rump, hitched herself back to a position of comfort, her head sinking into the soft pillows, her hair, unpinned with her hat, gloriously arrayed upon them. "Ah," she breathed, and turning to me, she spoke with unexpected formality. "Would you be so kind as to apply a tiny massage to the afflicted member?" She pointed to her ankle and patted the bed.

At long last I was beginning to get a glimmering of my situation. But nothing in my experience had prepared me for this moment. At the same time, I was beset by doubts. Plump Minnie was indeed an alluring, an arousing sight, stretched out at ease upon my bed. Her smile was welcoming, even eager. But what if my imaginings were false, were merely vile? She came from a class that lacked all subtlety, that would not recognize the indecorum of such a request from a relative stranger. And a worse thought yet: what if she supposed I expected payment for the treat at Gonfalon's?

"Wouldn't you rather I tried to find a doctor?"

She patted the bed again. "I want Dr. Otto."

I went and sat on the bed beside her. She lifted a knee to make the "afflicted member" more easily available to me. What I saw then of white thigh gleaming in the darkness beneath her skirt I pretended not to see, and I set about the massaging of her ankle.

"Ah," she said, and "ooh," she said, and then she said, "That's oh-so-much better, but the pain's moved a little higher up."

And so I massaged a little higher and then a little higher still, and soon I found myself at that place of which I had only dreamed. And it was warm and moist and, oh, so wonderful! And Minnie shifted and squirmed in harmony with the massage, and she moaned and said "ooh" and "ah."

She put her hand on me, she grasped me. "Now!" she said. "Please, now!" And she tore at cloth and buttons, and so did I. And "now!" she said again, and took me swollen within her, and wrapped her limbs about me and beat a wild tattoo on my back.

Korner, Korner, what are you writing! Remember, you are not Blum. Know when to draw a decent veil over your youthful raptures.

Yes, I lost my innocence to Herr Ephraim's Minnie. How utterly delightful she was, how healthy her appetite, how natural and uncomplicated our liaison! In Minnie I was fortunate indeed. Simple and forthright, she taught a bumbling boy how to be a man. She had formulated no philosophy but was by nature a hedonist. The body was designed to give and to receive sexual pleasure; all that was required of a man and a woman was mutual desire. Anything else—love, for example—was potentially perverse to the extent that it might distract from pleasure. Oh, love was all right if that was what you craved, but then, from that viewpoint, so were whips and chains. Her doctrine she expressed in her every bedroom act. I was for a happy while her eager disciple.

Lenin was only partly right. I had needed a pretty girl, and certainly I had found one in Minnie. With her I passed hours of delight. But the experience failed to free my energies for the serious endeavors of the great world. My thoughts now were wholly of the flesh. I longed with pain for the elusive Magda.

21

POLIAKOV IS BACK. The Red Dwarf put in a wan appearance at lunch today, walking slowly on weak legs and supported by a cane. There was not the hint of a jig in him. He joined me in the almost empty dining room, climbing onto his chair and propping his cane against the table. "So it goes, comrade," he said a little shamefacedly. Opposite us sat Señora Krauskopf y Guzman, her dark, deep eyes flashing, immersed in who knows what passionate Patagonian dialogue. A finger of buttered toast, already forgotten, stuck out like a limp cheroot from between her clenched teeth. At a table near the window Lipschitz held court, his lizard's head darting this way and that, bestowing his grace upon a half-dozen sycophants and toadies. Wittkower cut a bagel for him. La Grabscheidt smeared cream on it, Lustig poured him some apple juice from the pitcher.

The Red Dwarf sneered.

"You're feeling better?" I asked him.

"How much better can I feel? Comyns has put me on rice pudding, no raisins."

From the Lipschitz table came a sudden burst of laughter. "Oh, Nahum!" gasped La Grabscheidt, wiping her eyes as one overcome by merriment. Wittkower clapped his hands: "Oscar Wilde could take lessons," he said. The director licked his lips, tasting his bon mot.

From our table the Red Dwarf made an obscene gesture

with his right hand, discreetly masking it from the señora's demented gaze with his left.

"You've seen the notice?" I asked him.

"What did you expect, Lipschitz should sit around waiting for the bomb to blow up in his face? I won't say I told you so. I'll only say, didn't I tell you?"

"Hamburger's gone for the weekend. He says we'll talk after he gets back."

"Yes, talk. Go ahead, talk. Meanwhile, the Mad Monk over there, Rasputin—"

He put a warning finger to his lips. Eulalia was at his shoulder with his rice pudding. "Where's my raisins?"

"Dr. Comyns, he say you don't get no raisins."

The Red Dwarf sighed. "See what I mean?" he said.

Eulalia waddled around the table and gently removed the toast from the señora's mouth. "You want I pour tea now, Doña Isabella?"

Señora Krauskopf y Guzman looked up at her with impassioned eyes. "They called me the hollyhock girl." she said.

"They call you that again, you just tell me," said Eulalia. "Here your tea, Doña Isabella, honey."

The Red Dwarf waited until Eulalia disappeared behind the swinging doors into the kitchen. "The time for talk is over, finished. Now is the time for action."

"What sort of action?" I repeated.

The Lipschitz party got up from their lunch in a boisterous mood and left the dining room, the director in the van. Silently, we watched them go.

"What sort of action?" I repeated.

"Never mind what action. When I've acted, you'll know. Then will be the time for talk." He took a spoonful of rice pudding and held it in his mouth for a moment, savoring it. When he swallowed, his Adam's apple leapt two inches up his withered neck and then plunged to its place again. "Needs raisins," he said.

* * *

THE EMMA LAZARUS is filling up again; Sunday afternoon is on the wane. From my desk I can sense the renewal of stir and bustle: a hum of voices in the corridor, the whirr of the elevator going up and down, the strains of a Hoffmeister flute concerto from across the hall, the remote gurgle of a toilet flushing. From the kitchen the aroma that makes its way through the air ducts and into my room tells me that tonight we will have a beef-barley soup.

My room overlooks the street, not the avenue. At this time of year and at such an hour the location has a distinct advantage. While the sun, darkening the Palisades, prepares to set in New Jersey, the light that at the most acute of angles strikes my window has that wonderful pellucid yellow quality so beloved of the Dutch masters. One's fingers itch to hold a paintbrush. Meanwhile, from across the hall. Hoffmeister has given way, as well he might, to Mozart and *Le Nozze di Figaro*.

Ah, the vagaries of love! As I leaf through my manuscript, grown now to surprising length—my own modest effort *à la recherche du temps perdu*—I am struck by the number of pages that I, too, have devoted to this inexhaustible topic. "*Voi che sapete,*" sings Cherubino across the hall, "*che cosa e amor.*" Well, the vagaries of love are quite properly the stuff of comic opera. It is given to only a few, in art or in life, to pursue their amours on the grand scale. The rest of us must rely on these few to grant a kind of vicarious dignity to our petty liaisons. I say nothing of Blum, who is beneath our consideration and for whom love is little more than a viral infection, an itching beneath the skin that he seeks perpetually and vainly to scratch. But consider Hamburger, our own Jumbo, dashing off to the Hamptons, unable to admit even to himself his high hope to render peccable the impeccable honor, to assail the unassailable virtue, of Hermione Perlmutter, transformed in his amorous imagination into a Juliet.

What fools these mortals be! Even poor Sinsheimer, now resting permanently in Mineola, was not immune. I well remember one evening when we sat together in the resident's lounge, talking of *Troilus and Cressida,* a play in which Shakespeare at his most sardonic tells us the truth about this debilitating passion. Across the room sat three of our ladies (two of whom, incidentally, preceded Sinsheimer to Mineola), chattering and giggling together. His eyes misted over. "That's how it is," he said. And he began to sing, softly and achingly, "With what gladness have I the ladies kissed," as if recalling a time when he inhabited not the world of the Emma Lazarus but that of Lehar's *Paganini.*

And what of Otto Korner? Why should he be immune from this scrutiny? His love for Magda Damrosch may be excused on the grounds of his youth. However ridiculous, in youth love may be excused, even applauded, as a stage now reached in human development, a mark on the scale that denotes awareness of others outside of the self. It may even be beautiful: the toothless gums of the infant are far different from those of the dotard. Of Meta, his first wife, he still chooses not to speak. Of his second wife he has perhaps already said too much. But how does his Contessa, that good woman, may she rest in peace, measure up to the Contessa in the *Marriage of Figaro?*

Lorenzo da Ponte, Mozart's librettist, arrived in Vienna in 1783. Let us rejoice that he did so and grant to that inscrutable Purpose the awe it deserves. For without his arrival at that place and at that time we would have no *Figaro.* Let us therefore not regret his apostasy, this Venetian Jew who became a Catholic, a priest, and a poet. For the goyim he remains a Jew, of course; and for the Jews, in view of his success, he is still a Jew anyway.

The name da Ponte, I have always supposed, alludes to the bridge he so joyfully trod out of the Ghetto, but a bridge is not limited to one-way traffic. Certainly he was not a very good Catholic, let alone a good priest. He was kicked out of Venice, in part for political reasons but also for his embarrassing carnal indiscretions. Celibacy was not in his genes; he was something of a Blum, if not quite a Don Giovanni. His sexual scandals were such as to rock even that city of libertines and rakes. In Byron's day they were still talking of him. (They kicked him out of Europe too, eventually, all the way to the New World, where he became, of all things, a professor of Italian at Columbia College and initiated a certain faculty tradition in matters of the heart that, it is rumored, persists to this day.) At any rate, he arrived in Vienna as librettist with Salieri's Italian Opera Company, and Salieri found him a sinecure as court poet. But what matters to us are the librettos he wrote for Mozart, and in particular, in view of our present focus, the libretto for the *Marriage of Figaro*.

But Mozart himself was caught up at this time in love's vagaries, poor fellow, while scurrying about trying desperately to translate his genius into hard cash. Married to his inept Hausfrau, Constanze, he was nonetheless drawn to Anna Storace, the English soprano, the Susanna of his opera's first and inglorius performance at the Burgtheater in 1786, the Nancy who urged him in vain to join her in London. He botched it, of course. In music, a genius; in life, one of the rest of us.

Since, in the fields of Venus and her soft delights, Mozart and da Ponte were no more ennobled or ennobling than Hamburger or Korner or, yes, even Blum, to what may we attribute the grandeur of the *Marriage of Figaro*? To genius, of course, and to the happy conflux in time and place of two such sensibilities. But to say so much is to explain without explaining. What precisely did genius and conflux achieve? Into the familiar form of *opera buffa* and the earlier plot-stuff of *com-*

media dell'arte, with its lords who made sexual advances toward girls of humbler station, these two amorous klutzes—Mozart and da Ponte—injected the serum of recognizable human experience and emotion. The comic material is subordinated to sharply realized characters, defined in part by da Ponte and in part by the individual tone and richness of Mozart's music.

Here is the unexpected irony, the unfathomable paradox: *to achieve grandeur, art must descend to the level of palpitating humanity; obversely, to achieve grandeur, palpitating humanity must ascend to the level of art.*

* * *

I WAS RIGHT about the beef-barley soup.

The Red Dwarf is making a rapid recovery. Already he has discarded his cane. He paused beside my table in the dining room long enough to whisper, "Better we're not seen together for a while, comrade. Mum's the word." He put his finger to his lips, winked, and tottered off to sit in a corner by himself, leaving me with Blum and Señora Krauskopf y Guzman. Our table conversation was not memorable.

Hamburger and La Perlmutter have yet to sign in. Perhaps they have eloped.

* * *

THE EVENTS OF THIS MORNING have been so astonishing, so shocking, that I have not yet fully absorbed them. *The letter from Rilke is as good as in my hands!* I am dizzy with excitement. And of course my system is again in turmoil: a flutter about the heart, a feverish itch beneath the skin, loose bowels. Let me state at once that Hamburger has solved the riddle of the charades. He is a true friend. I am bitterly ashamed of my doubts about him, my ill thoughts. Granted his peculiar habit of mind, his—how might one put it?—his linguistic disposition, the solution was child's play for him. How can one hesitate to ascribe his predilection for the coprological image, his Swiftian wit, to that greater Purpose whose lineaments I have from time to time descried? But Purpose aside, to Hamburger belongs all due credit: his, the love of truth; his, the searching intellect; his, the lifetime of preparation for this moment of triumph. But my mind is awhirl.

The better to sort things out, for my sake as well as for yours, I shall start at the beginning, and as a kind of self-imposed penance, I shall omit nothing of my unutterable rudeness to him.

I knocked on his door before breakfast. He was in the midst of shaving and clearly in excellent spirits.

"Come in, Otto, old friend, come in. You've heard the news?"

"What news?"

He looked at me coyly, his eyes gleaming above the shaving lather. With his left hand held floppily aloft, he made a few fencing passes at me with the razor in his right. "*En garde!*"

I was in no mood for his japes. He tried again. "A little birdie didn't tell you something?"

"For God's sake, Hamburger, you're a grown man. Talk like one."

But he was not to be put down. "Never mind, in due course you'll know."

"You had a pleasant weekend among the Hamptons literati? The autumn foliage et cetera were to your liking?"

He was too far gone to notice my sarcasm.

"Pleasant?" he chortled. "Yes, you could say pleasant."

There he stood, wrapped in his elegant dressing gown of wine colored silk, his great girth shuddering with secret glee, the roguish expression on his thin face made all the more ridiculous by the globs of lather that still adhered to his cheeks.

"Finish shaving," I said. "We've much to talk about."

He waddled off to the bathroom, leaving its door open.

"We'll talk over breakfast," he called. "I'm starving. Country air, I suppose."

So that was it! No doubt after penetrating Hermione Perlmutter's final defenses, the old fool had proposed marriage. Ah, Hamburger, ah, Jumbo, Jumbo, so it was not the shifting of molars after all!

"Shave," I could not control my impatience. He turned on the hot water, and while he shaved, he sang the "Ah, how funny!" aria from *Die Fledermaus*. Then he gargled, long and loud, with a sound that rose and fell, recognizable after a while as the same aria transposed to a new medium.

He emerged from the bathroom clad only in his long johns. *"Ecce homo!"* he said.

Now it was my privilege to watch a Beau Brummel *de nos jours* prepare for the day. He stood at the open closet door, pondering. This? That? Perhaps this other?

"What do you think of this tie, Otto?"

I closed my eyes.

"A moment, my dear sir, patience, the blink of an eye." And he began bum-bum-bumming his bathroom aria.

At last he was ready, resplendent, refulgent. "What d'you say this morning we go out for breakfast, my treat? Not Goldstein's, of course. Wherever else you say. Who knows, perhaps over a second cup of coffee I might have something of interest to tell you."

This was too much. "*You* might have something of interest? Ha! About your indecent weekend I can already guess, spare me the details. What is it with you, Hamburger? For days now I keep telling you I've something of considerable personal concern to discuss with you, something that touches me dearly, something—I don't exaggerate—that has driven me to distraction, and all you offer me is evasions: 'Sorry, I'm off to the movies,' 'Too bad, I'm going to the Hampton's.' What is this? Perhaps it's time for Korner and his problems to go elsewhere." I had of course brought the charades with me, and now I shook them in his face. "Perhaps you haven't time to look at these. Of course not. Well, why should I be surprised? After all, you owe me nothing. Forget it, never mind, it doesn't matter. By the way, congratulations on your engagement."

Yes, to my eternal shame I went on at him like that. Poor Benno! I had pricked the bubble of his good cheer. Utterly bewildered by this unexpected and unfair assault, he dropped onto his bed—poof!—deflated, miserable.

"Forgive me, Otto, forgive me, old friend."

And so, having reduced him to sober and guilty attention, I told him about the stolen letter—at which news he took in sharply his breath—and handed him the charades.

As he read them, the color left his cheeks. His jaw dropped, and a haunted look came into his eyes. "Oh, my God!"

"Who is it?"

Hamburger passed his hand over his eyes, pinched the bridge of his nose, uttered a shuddering sigh.

"Benno, who is it?"

"Give me your hand." His own was trembling. "I want your word of honor you will leave this for me to take care of."

"First tell me who stole the letter."

"No, first your promise. If I tell you, you will *do* nothing, you will *say* nothing, you will leave it up to me. In twenty-four hours, thirty-six at the most, you will have your letter. But your word of honor, Otto."

What could I do? "You have it."

We shook hands solemnly.

Once he told me the name, of course, the charades proved embarrassingly simple:

Whoever tries to mouth the culprit's name
Must end in ordure to assign the blame.

Answer: *mouth-ordure-lip-shits.*

To *give* my first is sure to *give offense,*
But may *create a smile* (in other sense). (1)
Who *does* my second doubtless *finds his ease,*
But even if a czar *must bend his knees.* (2)

Answers: (1) *lip*; (2) *shits.* The third was the easiest of the three:

The gap that stands in view 'twixt *hip* and *tits*
Can soon be *closed in rhyme* by clever wits.

Answer: *hip-tits-lip-shits.* And of course the couplet of the
sonnet tells the same story:

Look for the thief in Denmark's Elsinore;
He's in the play, and dallying with his whore.

Answer: Lipschitz! Lipschitz!! Lipschitz!!!

Now, when more than ever I wanted to talk to him,
Hamburger was anxious to be rid of me. Gone was the promise
of a breakfast treat and a chat over a second cup of coffee.

"As you can imagine, Korner, I have much to do. And
before I act, I must think." He hurried me out of his room. At
the door he took my hand again, his expression woebegone.
"Remember, I have your word of honor. And remember this,
too: an accusation is no proof of guilt."

The door closed in my face before I could speak.

And so I sit here in tumult, waiting. And I am besieged by
questions. Why should Lipschitz have stolen my letter? Of
what value can it be to him? Can one suppose he has even heard
of Rilke? Can Tosca Dawidowicz have prompted him, that
harridan who rules him by a twitching of her skirts? Or was he

motivated quite simply by his own malice? And the old question: who pointed the finger at him, however enigmatically? What was *his* motive? Also malice? Toward Lipschitz? Yes, it seemed so. Toward me? Who can doubt it? And what of Benno Hamburger, my true friend, my pillar of integrity? How mysteriously he is behaving! What does he know about all this? How does he propose to go about recovering the letter? And so on and on and round and round, until my head spins and I cannot find my breath.

22

UR PORTRESS IS BACK: Selma sits once more be-
hind her bulletproof glass at the entrance to the Emma Lazarus.
She returned, apparently, this morning, unheralded, even as I
was conferring with Hamburger. I skipped breakfast and lunch,
not only because excitement destroyed my appetite but also
because it produced that looseness already alluded to. But by
midafternoon, having got (as Mandy Dattner might say) "my
act" somewhat more "together," longing for distraction and
unable longer to bear the vigil in my room, I descended to the
lobby. The sedentary occupied the comfortable chairs by the
potted palms. On seeing me, they sent up a twitter: "Hi, Otto,
going out?" "You need an umbrella." "You don't look so good."
(Here there were knowing winks and nudges.) "Chicken soup
with noodles tonight." And finally, "Selma's back." It was true:
there sat Selma at her proper station, visible behind the glass,
applying yet another coat of lipstick to her withered lips.
Braving certain dizziness, I bowed deeply before her and spoke
into the meshed mouthpiece embedded in the glass.

She buzzed me in.

Bernie, it appeared, had made a one-hundred-percent
recovery, touch wood, one hundred and ten percent, thank
God. He was better than ever. As for her, it had not been easy, as
(she ventured) I might well imagine, what with the initial
terrors of the hospital and then Bernie's long convalescence at
home. In her, Bernie had found, and used almost past bearing,

a nurse, a cook, and a bottle-washer. Of the bedpans she would say nothing, save that hauling him onto them and rolling him off had brought a return of her old back problems. Now, even to pick up a piece of paper—here she demonstrated, picking up the list of solo-ambulants: "oy!"—was agony. Now Bernie was talking of retirement; he liked the easy life. "Who ever heard of a C.P.A. retiring?" Well, if he thought she was going to hang about catering to his whims, he had better think again. It was a relief to be out of the house.

Meanwhile, she had already caught up on the gossip of our little community. There really was nothing of interest I could tell her, but that did not stop her from telling *me* the latest tidbits, among them two stunning items whose significance she was as ill equipped to recognize as I was almost afraid to contemplate. Nahum Lipschitz is in the infirmary with a broken hip, a severely sprained wrist, and numerous cuts and abrasions! It seems that just before lunchtime he fell down a flight of steps in the fire stairwell. What he was doing in the stairwell, when the elevator was at his disposal, he refuses to say, but he claims that the "accident" was engineered, that he was pushed. By whom? "By person or persons unknown." These are serious charges, and the Kommandant has been summoned home from Jerusalem, where he has been attending the annual International Conference of Jewish Old-Age Home Directors. The last thing he wanted, said Selma, hinting at certain "irregularities" that she was not at liberty to divulge, was to have the police and (worse!) the newspapers sniffing around. As for her, she did not believe that Lipschitz had been pushed. A momentary dizziness, and *voilà!* The man was eighty-one; at his age, such episodes were not unheard-of. And when had Nahum Lipschitz ever accepted the blame for anything? Meanwhile, he was lucky to be alive. His condition was grave: brittle bones, she explained.

The second item Selma had no reason to connect to the

first, and in fact she retailed it independently, while chatting about the warm reception she had received from residents and staff alike upon her return. It had done her heart good. Say what you like, there was still some good in the world. At any rate, shortly after one o'clock Benno Hamburger and Hermione Perlmutter had passed her window on their way to the front door, without even turning in her direction or pausing to check out. They had looked grim as death; he was holding her firmly by the upper arm, and they were walking at a determined clip. Selma had rapped on the glass, but they had ignored her. The nerve of some people. They knew the rules. She had tried to run after them, but what with her poor back and all, by the time she got to the front door, they were gone, and a long gray limousine was just pulling away from the curb. Imagine that, she sniffed. They didn't even know she was back.

An attempt on Lipschitz's life! Hamburger and his moll on the run!

O Jumbo, what have you done!

* * *

THE WORLD IS STILL FULL of surprises. The old analogies yet hold: "I am a little world made cunningly," said an English poet. Just so. And between the macrocosm and the microcosm stands the Emma Lazarus, racked by the same passions as heave the ocean on the shore, divide nations, and cause conflicts in the human soul. But surprise is merely the failure of perception, the myopia of a creature who, like Oedipus, runs from disaster only to encounter it, who sees his good turned to evil, his evil to good. In this sense, the figure for Purpose is less a ramifying tree than a spider's web of infinite complexity and total harmony, and in it we are caught, blinded from a vision of the whole by entanglement in a part. And the spider?

That, I suppose, is Time, which first traps us and then at length devours us.

These and such as these were my lugubrious thoughts during a sleepless night, with my foe struck down by my friend, and my friend fleeing the savage talons of the avenging Furies.

This morning the rains fell in torrents. On the bulletin board in the lobby was a terse notice: "Rehearsals canceled until further notice." When I entered the dining room for breakfast, it seemed to me that the voices hushed momentarily. I felt myself the cynosure of all eyes. La Dawidowicz ostentatiously cut me, turning her back. But soon the twittering resumed; the talk was all of Lipschitz and of the endangered play. At my table sat only Señora Krauskopf y Guzman. "*Buenos dias*, Doña Isabella," I said. She turned her magnificent, her passionate, black eyes up to me. "Twat twat twat," she said. "Jog jog jog, jog jog jog."

Eulalia brought me my modest breakfast: a bowl of porridge, a slice of dry toast, and a glass of tea. Scarcely had I begun on the porridge when I sensed a presence behind me. I turned. It was Hamburger—yes, yes, Hamburger! He was white-faced and grim, perhaps even angry. He still wore his overcoat, which glistened with raindrops, and under his arm he carried a slim rectangular parcel, in a neat wrapping of heavy, water-splotched brown paper. The shock almost killed me. Automatically I spooned some porridge into my mouth.

"Let's go," he said.

How could I get up? "I can't. I'm weak, I haven't eaten." My heart was thumping in its cavity. Surely he must have heard it.

He was pitiless. "Five minutes. Your room or mine?"

"Yours. No, mine. No, what does it matter? Sit down. Where have you been? What have you done?"

"My room. In five minutes." He turned on his heel and marched stiffly out.

I watched him go, my legs turned to water. As best I could, I fought the rising hysteria, the nausea, and tried to take some nourishment. It was no use. Making my apologies to the señora, I tottered from the table. Several times I had to pause and lean on the wall on my way to the elevator.

Hamburger's quarters are decorated in the manner of an English clubroom: polished wood, hunting prints, leather furniture, gleaming silver. He gestured impatiently to a chair, and I sat down. He went over to the window and stood for a moment with his back to me, looking down on West End Avenue. Suddenly he whirled.

"Nahum Lipschitz is in the infirmary," he barked.

"I know." I tried to keep the reproach out of my voice.

"Shit, shit, shit!"

To this triplicate of Hamburgeriana I could of course say nothing.

"He is innocent, completely innocent!"

"And what if he were guilty? Would *that* have justified violence?" I demanded.

"What pains me most, what I cannot forgive, is that you gave me your word."

I got up from the chair at this and stood before him. "He might have died; he might never recover. Do you know how serious this is? The Kommandant is on his way back from Jerusalem. 'Don't talk to him,' you said. I could have reasoned with him."

"Your word of honor, Korner. We shook hands."

"Ah, Benno, that you should think such an act would help me! Better I never saw the letter again."

"Too late for that now," he said bitterly. "At best it's a botched job. At worst . . . ? But don't worry, I'll not turn you in." There were tears in his eyes. "As for me, I must prepare to shoulder my burden of guilt, an accomplice after the fact. You must deal with your own conscience."

His words were beginning to penetrate my understanding. "*You* won't turn *me* in? But I thought it was *you, you* who pushed him."

"Me? Are you mad? I *knew* he was innocent. I as good as told you so yesterday morning."

"Then you didn't . . . ?"

"No, and you, *you* didn't . . . ?"

"No."

The emotions of the moment were too great. We fell into one another's arms, thumping each other on the back, sobbing, swaying, holding each other up.

"Hamburger, old fellow."

"Korner, my friend."

When at last we grew somewhat calmer, I said, "If it wasn't either of us, then who?"

Mutual enlightenment; we answered as one: "The Red Dwarf!"

Yes, had he not hinted to me over the weekend that he was up to something?

"We must, of course, denounce him to the authorities, Otto."

"Not so fast. Let me remind you of a great man's words: 'An accusation is no proof of guilt.' "

"We'll talk to him first."

There was more. Hamburger retrieved the parcel from his bureau and handed it to me. "This is yours."

I unwrapped it. It was my letter, elegantly framed. I could not hold back my tears. Silently we read it together.

Dear Mr. Korner,

I have read with great pleasure *Days of Darkness, Nights of Light* and congratulate you on a nicely turned-out little volume. One stands back in admiration of so precocious a talent, for an early spring promises an abundant harvest: "the roots dig deep."

> With fraternal good wishes,
> Rainer Maria Rilke

"In all these years, you've never told me about it," said Hamburger. "All right, you didn't want to talk about the past, that I could respect, I asked no questions. Some things it's better not to remember. But to say nothing about your poetry! Would it have hurt so much to tell an old friend about that, or to have shown him the letter?"

"How did you get it back? How long have you known it was stolen?"

"I knew nothing before yesterday morning, when you showed me the charades." Hamburger sighed and took a folded piece of paper from his wallet. "Look at this."

> My first for some's forbidden food,
> And, too, a ranting actor rude.
> My second will in town be found,
> With golden chain on belly round.
> My whole's imbued with passion's heat,
> In many senses good to eat.

"That's me," he said sheepishly. "*Ham, burgher.* Hamburger."

"Then you've been getting them, too?"

"No, just this one. And there was no mystery. It was handed to me." He rubbed the bridge of his nose. "The truth will out. I might as well tell you everything."

And so I learned about Hamburger's weekend in the Hamptons. It had been an idyllic time: a considerate hostess, cultured and congenial company, a sumptuous home, Edenic surroundings. Subsequent events, of course, had cast a retrospective pall, but at the time he had thought himself in heaven. At one point La Perlmutter had shown him her daughter's study. The wall above the couch was adorned with framed autographs: Kipling, Hemingway, James, Sartre, Weill, among others. His eye happened to catch Rilke's signature. "But I thought nothing of that. Why should I? Certainly I didn't stop to read the letter." They had gone into the study to enjoy a moment of privacy. "Hermione stood close; I drank in her perfume. My mind, I assure you, was on topics other than literary."

On Saturday evening, after dinner, La Perlmutter amused the company with charades. She had an extraordinary aptitude, creating them on the spot, viva voce. Each of the guests was gently mocked—"Tastefully, you understand. It was all done in the spirit of fun." Hamburger's name, she pretended, was particularly difficult. She would need time to think about it. The conversation in the drawing room moved on to other sprightly topics.

That night he achieved his heart's desire, reached an ecstasy beyond the power of words to describe. The next morning, at breakfast, she handed him the charade, the one he had just shown me. "For private consumption only," she had said demurely, at once alluding to and redoubling the risqué double entendre of the last line.

In the afternoon, during a walk on the grounds, with the brilliant foliage bathed in that extraordinary light I had observed from my windows at the Emma Lazarus, he had asked her to marry him, and she had accepted.

Hamburger held his head in his hands and rocked from side to side. He made a strong effort to pull himself together. "So now you know," he said, his voice trembling. "*She* stole your letter, *and* she sent you the charades."

"Your fiancée?"

"Not anymore. That's all over."

He had gone back with Hermione to the Hamptons to retrieve the letter. This morning he had returned alone.

"But why did she do it?"

"She wouldn't tell me. She cried and cried. '*He* knows,' she said. My heart was breaking, Otto. '*He* knows.' *Do* you?"

Did I? When a recent widower, I had rejected her advances. Since then our relationship, if that is the proper word, had been—what? cool? inimical? Was that it? A woman scorned? But who could have guessed that my slighting of her would have such calamitous consequences? Obviously I could say none of this to my poor friend. "I know nothing," I said. "Perhaps when she returns—"

"She'll never return."

"Never mind against me, what did she have against Lipschitz?"

"Who hasn't got something against Lipschitz?"

"Oh, Benno, I'm so sorry."

"It's finished, over and done with, all for the best."

What can one say in the face of such nobility, such grandeur of soul? Witness Hamburger, torn between loyalties, tumbled from felicity to misery, a Hercules at the Crossroads, and like Hercules choosing the heroic path!

* * *

THE RED DWARF claims innocence.

Hamburger and I confronted him this afternoon at two

o'clock, the beginning of the siesta hour, a time when the noisy engine of the Emma Lazarus idles at a gentle hum. He opened his door a crack and peered up at us suspiciously. Recognition dawned, and he flung the door wide. "Come in, comrades, come in!" We had got him up from bed: he wore only boxer shorts, voluminous, with blue polka dots on a dingy off-white background. What a hairy little fellow he is! The shades were drawn; the bed was rumpled. His room is appropriately Spartan: an iron bedstead, a small table, hard wooden chairs; on the walls, giant photographs of Marx, Lenin, Che Guevara, Marilyn Monroe. "Sit down, sit down," he said. The only object of interest in the place is a copper samovar gleaming on a small chest of drawers.

The Red Dwarf executed a little jig. "So, comrades, we've won the revolution without striking a single blow."

"Lipschitz says he was pushed," said Hamburger.

"Typical Zionist mystification. First they make the boo-boo, then they look around for someone to blame."

"A broken hip is more than a boo-boo," I said.

"Better a broken hip than a broken head."

"He may die, Poliakov," said Hamburger.

The Red Dwarf shrugged and held his hands apart in the manner of Michelangelo's *Pietà*. "And the rest of us?" he said.

The interrogation was not going the way we had expected. I tried another tack. "What was it you meant the other day? You told me it would be better if we weren't seen together for a while?"

He grinned, his gold tooth winking. From the pocket of a denim jacket hanging on the door, he took a key and held it triumphantly aloft. "The key to the costume closet! Poliakov reporting to the Central Committee: mission accomplished! But in the light of later developments, Comrade Director, it seems we had no need to liberate it." I suppose I blushed. "No need for modesty. You're the people's candidate."

"We'll see," I said dismissively.

"But what was Lipschitz doing in the stairwell?" Hamburger was not yet satisfied.

"That's easy," said the Red Dwarf. "He goes out there to pass wind. On this floor we all know it. Believe me, with that stink, no one could get near him. He must've blown himself off the landing, a self-propelled rocket."

Hamburger laughed. Such talk was, so to speak, right up his alley.

"Fundamentally," said the Red Dwarf, "he couldn't help himself."

"Not bad, Poliakov," said Hamburger. "Not bad. In such matters there is no motive: it was a case of fart for fart's sake."

* * *

I MUST SAY I miss Goldstein's. The brouhaha last week has rendered us all personae non gratae. One focus of the day has blurred. Hamburger agrees with me. It's not just a matter of the food, the denial of which is bad enough, it's also the absence of the total ambience, which offered some indefinable something that has all but disappeared from the Upper West Side. The smells, the sights, the very faces and accents were all deeply familiar, a goodfellowship that cannot be replaced. And Goldstein himself, his sensitive, florid mien, his portly, impeccably clad exterior, even his wretched jokes—all these I miss. Who sought this feud? Not I, not any of us. This morning, on my walk down Broadway, I happened to see through the glass Goldstein scratching his back against the central pillar in his customary fashion and Joe shuffling past on his poor bunions, a cup of coffee in his hand. Without even thinking, I waved. Goldstein turned away; Joe shrugged and shook his head.

Is there nothing to be done? Hamburger thinks not. "There you have an essential fact of life," he said. "Didn't you know? Can you have forgotten it? Good things come to an end, that's all there is to it. Best forget about it. Shit stinks; flush it away."

"After more than twenty years?"

"For me, longer."

Probably he's right. Even if we were admitted once again as customers, something would be different. What's happened has happened. Who knows better than I that the past cannot be changed?

23

HAT EVENING AFTER DINNER (grilled sole, honeyed carrots, a small boiled potato, fruit compote), Hamburger and I visited the infirmary, the least we could do. What a melancholy scene greeted us as we pushed through the swinging doors! Five hospital beds, only the middle one, dimly lighted by an overhead lamp, occupied: Lipschitz. At his bedside sat Tosca Dawidowicz, back bowed in sorrow, dabbing at her eyes with a lace handkerchief. Beside her stood Lottie Grabscheidt, holding a comforting, or restraining, hand on Tosca's shoulder. Lipschitz was stretched out like a corpse, his arms on top of the covers and resting along his sides, his fingers fumbling with the coverlet as if trying to pluck the little flowers printed on it. His eyes, sunk deep in his gaunt yellow face, were tightly shut; his tongue flicked out and licked his lips. In the dim light his skull gleamed dully.

With some trepidation, we drew near the bed.

"Green fields," said Lipschitz, his eyes still closed.

"What did he say?" whispered Hamburger.

"Green fields," said Lipschitz again.

"He's delirious, babbling," said Tosca Dawidowicz reproachfully, her voice choked with emotion.

"There used to be a tailor shop on Delancey Street," said Lottie Grabscheidt musingly, fingering her death's-head brooch. "Zalman Greenfield and Sons: 'What Suits You, Suits Us.' This was years ago."

"He maketh me to lie down in *green pastures?*" offered Hamburger.

Could that be it? "Yea, though I walk through the valley of the shadow of death . . . ," I went on, marveling.

Tosca Dawidowicz let out an anguished wail. Lipschitz licked his lips.

"Better take her out of here," Hamburger suggested to La Grabscheidt. "She's going to upset him."

"Come, Tosca, come, there's nothing more we can do. You'll make yourself—God forbid—ill!" And she helped her to her feet.

At the door La Dawidowicz flung aside Lottie's supportive arm, turned to face the bed, and struck that attitude from act 3, scene 1, that I well remember poor Sinsheimer coaching her in, her right leg bent, left leg trailing, the back of her left hand lightly touching the forehead of her upturned face:

"And I, of ladies most deject and wretched,
That sucked the honey of his music vows,
Now see that noble and most sovereign reason,
Like sweet bells jangled, out of tune and harsh."

She flung a kiss at the recumbent form, murmured "Good night, sweet prince!" then turned, distraught, and made her exit, followed by La Grabscheidt.

Hamburger, in spite of himself, applauded.

We turned back to the bed.

Lipschitz opened his eyes. "Are they gone?" he hissed.

I nodded.

"Thank God!" He was grinning.

The transformation was remarkable. But for the traction apparatus that kept his legs immobile, he was his former self. We congratulated him on his recovery.

"I'm finished with old women," Lipschitz said.

Hamburger winced.

"*That* one can suck a man dry. I had to insist, she wants to see me, she's got to bring with her a chaperone. Otherwise, give her five minutes, she'd be here in bed with me. A nympho, take my word for it."

Hamburger was anxious to change the subject ("Is there anything you need, something I can pick up from the library, a book, magazines?"), but Lipschitz was not yet finished.

"My own mother ran off with a presser from Bayonne. She was sixty-three, can you believe it? They used to call her the Belle of Pitkin Avenue. You can imagine why, so you know I'm not bragging. How d'you think it feels to have for a father a schlemiel? The life she'd led him, I told him he was better off without her. I myself was a laughingstock. 'What can she find in Bayonne,' he said, 'she couldn't find better on Pitkin?' This he said over and over again to whoever would listen to him. He never got over it, the old shmuck, may he rest in peace. So when I tell you, watch out for old women, I know what I'm talking."

"There've been rumors, Nahum, about your accident," said Hamburger.

"What rumors?" He looked at us sharply.

"Some people say you were pushed," I said.

"What people?"

"No one in particular. It's in the air. You know how it is around here. *Did* someone push you?"

"Maybe yes, maybe no. My lips are sealed. The truth's in here." He tapped his skull. "But this much I'll tell you, between me, you, and the lamppost. Not a word outside this room. This morning the Kommandant came to see me, and with him Rifkind, the shyster: How'm I feeling? I'm looking good. They taking care of me? He tells me he flew in from Jerusalem as soon as he heard the news. For Nahum Lipschitz, nothing but the best. He wanted personally to oversee my treatment.

"Meanwhile, I notice Rifkind taking some papers out of his briefcase. A formality, nothing to worry. All I had to do was sign a couple forms. The Kommandant was already unscrewing his fountain pen. Rifkind points with his finger, *here* and *here*. A detail, nothing: only I should sign I don't hold the Kommandant and the Emma Lazarus responsible for what happened." Lipschitz gave a dry chuckle. "Was I born yesterday? First, I told him, get rid of Rifkind, then we can talk. I had him by the balls, and he knew it. So the shyster puts back his papers in the briefcase and goes, a cholera should only catch him. A long story short, what it boils down to is this: on my part, I say nothing more about the accident; on his part, when Tuvye Bialkin dies, I have inside track to the penthouse. No papers, no signatures: a gentlemen's agreement."

Tuvye Bialkin is our second-oldest resident, a native of Odessa who made a fortune in Canada during Prohibition. The penthouse rooms are the plums of the Emma Lazarus, spacious, magnificent views of the Hudson, kitchenettes en suite.

"Is Tuvye ill?" Hamburger asked.

"He should only live to be a hundred and twenty," said Lipschitz piously, "but the Kommandant estimates about a week. Pleurisy, with complications." He licked his lips. "So everyone comes out a winner. You, Korner, you get to be Hamlet. Also the director."

"That isn't decided yet," I said.

"Yes, I've already given instructions. The Kommandant knows, also Tosca. But watch out, could be the production's jinxed. First Sinsheimer, then me."

Jinxed? I almost laughed out loud. What could a Lipschitz know about Purpose? "You'll be up and around yourself in no time," I said.

"Don't worry, it's yours in any case. You can do it, Korner. A piece of cake." And here he quoted the words that Hamlet, stoic in the face of death, utters to Horatio a little before his fatal duel: "The readiness is all."

Meanwhile, Lipschitz still held center stage. "To tell you

the truth, I did think for a while of reworking the play, making a few changes—Elsinore a veterans' hospital near Washington, for example. Then Hamlet could be a young lieutenant in a wheelchair, a World War Two hero, the Battle of the Bulge. And he'd have to find out who murdered his father, General Hamlet, also wounded, also a hero, but years before, maybe in Flanders, and also hospitalized. Ophelia could be a nurse; Claudius, chief medical officer at the hospital, the general's brother, now married to Gertrude, the murdered man's wife, and so on. Not bad, right? It has possibilities. Even burying Ophelia in Arlington: naturally the authorities would complain, and 'but that great command o'ersways the order, she should in ground unsanctified been lodg'd.' But the fact is, I've lost interest. And *that* you can blame on Tosca Dawidowicz." He licked his lips. "A Lilith, a succuba."

Fortunately, at that moment Dr. Comyns came in with Mandy Dattner. "Sorry to break things up, gentlemen, but before we tuck him in for the night, Miss Dattner wants to check the patient's muscle tone." He winked and showed his teeth. "I'm just here to protect her in case it's too good."

She smiled and raised her left brow. The effect is still devastating, still disorienting. Time and place instantly dissolved. I was thrust back sixty years to Zurich and stood trembling once more beneath Magda's scornful glance. Only Mandy's alarmed cry ("Mr. Korner, you okay?") returned me to the Emma Lazarus. She lurks within me yet, my Magda, like a bacillus in the bloodstream.

But Lipschitz merely closed his eyes and started picking at his coverlet. "Green fields," he said.

* * *

SINSHEIMER'S *HAMLET,* I am convinced, should form the basis of my own production. This is not simply a matter of piety. Sinsheimer knew what he was doing. The original text will be

154

restored; no more nonsense about Ophelia's burial in Mineola. If Tosca Dawidowicz is unwilling, even in dramatic representation, to be given a Christian burial, then she is free to leave the play. On this point I am adamant, no matter that I sometimes think I see in her the potential for dramatic excellence. There will in any case be a few cast changes. Hamburger is a natural for Horatio, the friend who remains loyal through all tribulations. And Wittkower's suggestion about musical accompaniment is still worth considering. But naturally I wish to put my personal stamp on *Hamlet,* and in this regard, my experience in different roles can be put to use. I have come to understand, for example, the Ghost's function as a foil for Claudius: "Look here upon this picture, and on this, the counterfeit presentment of two brothers." And I am prepared to give appropriate prominence to the Gravemaker, the philosophical significance of whose part I have unearthed, so to speak. But what of Hamlet himself, who challenges us to pluck out the heart of his mystery? No, I have not abandoned my belief that the Gravemaker does precisely that. But what he and the Prince learn of one another is known only to them. "This is I, Hamlet the Dane"—but what is this "I"? The enigma remains.

For me, it is a great temptation to conclude that there *is* no mystery at the heart. Hamlet shows us only a shell, an opaque and dazzling surface. What if within there is a void, a nothing? How hard Hamlet works to mask his inner being! But how can we recognize that inner being if we are denied an outward sign? Why should we not conclude, shown nothing within, that there is nothing there? Still, I recall an image I have already used of myself: a cave in which a bat with a broken wing flaps uselessly about. To succumb to such a reading of the Prince is to remold him, flatteringly—too flatteringly—into oneself, the very reverse of the actor's art.

Inspiration often comes to us from unexpected sources. The important thing is to be ever on the alert. Thus Lipschitz's gratuitous insulting of his parents has shown me the way. Here it is: *King Hamlet was a cuckold!*

"So what?" you will say. "That's a given. Everyone knows it." Yes, but it is a given that is largely overlooked in the pursuit of flashier game. The talk is all of Hamlet as Oedipus, of Hamlet vis-à-vis his mother. Thank Freud for that, of course. But what may we confidently assume Hamlet to have wanted of his mother? He had only a perfectly natural filial desire that she be chaste. We are presumptuous to assume anything more. All else is buried deep within his subconscious—the subconscious, let us not forget, of a dramatic construct. We cannot put the Prince on the couch at Berggasse 19; speculation about his Oedipal yearnings must remain futile, if not misleading. But a Hamlet sickened and, worse yet, *embarrassed* by his father's cuckoldry, him we can know something about.

It is the Ghost himself who first tells Hamlet (and us) about "that incestuous, that adulterate beast," his brother Claudius. Incest, yes; about this ugly and unsavory truth Hamlet already knows: in Shakespeare's day the marriage of a widow to her brother-in-law was incest enough. But now adultery as well! There must have been hanky-panky *before* his father's death! Things were not already bad enough? How this appalling news must devastate Hamlet! The need to avenge his father's murder, the honorable duty that he willingly, even eagerly accepts, must be undermined—how could it not be?—by the dolefully droll fact of his father's cuckoldry. What an exquisitely painful embarrassment! His father's virility called into question, and by his father himself. Like Lipschitz, Hamlet might well ask, "How d'you think it feels to have for a father a schlemiel?"

The Ghost, too, shows signs of embarrassment. No sooner does he raise the matter of Gertrude's infidelity than he drops it again, redirecting his son's attention to the incestuous marriage. The old king may wear horns, but he sees no need to draw the world's attention to them. He no more wants to punish Gertrude than the elder Lipschitz wanted to punish the Belle of Pitkin Avenue.

Hamlet himself praises his father as a gentle god, kind and loving—in short, anything but as a sexual being. Contrast this with his view of Claudius, whom he sees as a satyr, a kind of Freddy Blum, ugly, hairy, lustful. But Hamlet is not surprised that woman in her weakness should prefer the giant, untiring phallus to the impotent slumber of the marriage bed. "Alas, poor ghost," says Hamlet—not exactly the encomium a father wants from his son.

Who would have thought that Lipschitz, in his gross impropriety, should inadvertently give me the key with which I shall unlock the play?

24

TODAY OVER LUNCH (cheese casserole, steamed beets and cauliflower, apple cake and Viennese coffee) my thoughts turned anew to Magda and to Zurich, perhaps because last night at Nahum Lipschitz's bedside Mandy Dattner appeared and smiled. Thoughts are ever in such ways confluent.

By the beginning of 1917 I had given up any pretense of being a student and had dropped out of the university. Accordingly, I had instructed my bank to return to my father his generous letter of credit and had moved into squalid digs in Altneukirchengasse, not far from Lenin and the Cabaret Voltaire. Thanks to an acquaintance of my father's, I had found employment as a kind of sub–sub–literary editor of the *Zürcher Wochenblatt*, a job that paid my rent and made it possible for me to enjoy an occasional glass of wine with my regular dinner of bratwurst. My duties were simple: I passed on to the subeditor those recent publications that I thought he should bring to the attention of the editor, who in turn made a selection for submission to the *Wochenblatt*'s regular reviewers. Poverty, by that year, I had come to regard as a virtue. Moreover, still thinking of myself as a poet, one upon whom Rilke himself had put the stamp of approval, I found it amusing to hide *faute de mieux* beneath anonymity: in words rather like those that Brecht would one day give to Pirate Jenny, they had no idea with whom they were talking. In addition, it seemed to me that

I was living *la vie de bohème*, which could only appeal to Magda, the winning of whose heart was still my quest.

One day not long after my removal to Altneukirchengasse, Magda appeared at my door. She had never before visited my rooms, either here or earlier, in Oberstolzecke. You can imagine my excitement. She had a request, she said, one she could ask only of someone dear to her, someone she could trust absolutely. She had immediately thought of me.

Anything, anything. She had only to ask.

It seemed that she had some papers, family documents, matters of land transfer, estate taxes, that must be conveyed to relatives in Sweden. It was impossible in wartime to trust to the post. Would I be willing to take them for her?

"But Magda, surely you realize that the very war which makes the post unreliable also makes travel by private persons doubtful, difficult, even dangerous. I might be interned; I might never return."

"So that's how it is! My hero, the man who hints that he is in the Kaiser's service! Well, *junger Mann,* if you are afraid, there's nothing more to be said."

"I fear nothing. But surely you see . . ."

She pouted, on her an entrancing expression. " 'Yes, *but,'* always the *but.*" She dropped onto my bed, crossed her legs, and spread her skirt. "Your famous love of me is circumscribed by a *but.*"

"Nothing circumscribes my love for you. If I must go to Sweden to prove it, to Sweden I will go."

How my words made her smile, how she laughed! "Come, *Schätzl,* come to me." She opened her arms, and I sank into them. Our lips met in a prolonged, an exquisite, kiss. She let me explore her tongue with mine, an achingly erotic joy. Soon I sought to initiate those specialized mysteries through which Herr Ephraim's Minnie had been my guide. But Magda stayed my importunate hand, whispering in my ear, nipping gently the lobe, "Not now, *Schätzl,* my impatient hero, not now."

"Then when?"

"Soon. Later, this is not the time, Ah, how I want you! But first I must go to get the documents. So we must wait a little longer. For me, too, that's not easy. Ah, no, no." She squirmed from beneath me, got up from the bed, straightened her clothes. "But don't look so sad, poor sweetheart!" She would come again that night and give me the papers; we would dine together, and then . . .

She was to be mine at last! How bittersweet the agony of our parting! How fervent our kisses, how fervid our words of love! I burned with anticipation.

In fact, she didn't return. Instead, she disappeared from Zurich. Had she gone to Sweden herself? I was mad with worry, with disappointment, with longing, soon with rage. I pestered the woman who rented a room next to Magda's, above von Laban's dance school. "No, I haven't seen her. Why should I lie? But you know she often goes off like this. Be patient, she'll be back." All that was true enough. I resumed my vigils at the Cabaret Voltaire, haunted the other cafés favored by the Gang of Nihilists, paced the street in front of von Laban's. Ten days passed, fifteen, and then I heard that she was back. A light had been seen in Magda's room.

Breathless, heart thumping, I knocked on Magda's door. After a moment it opened a little. "Who is it? Oh, it's you. Go away, this isn't a good time." She was a mess. In the dim light at the top of the stairs I could see her forehead beaded with sweat, her cosmetics smeared on her face. A garish kimono was carelessly wrapped around her body.

"I must talk to you."

"Not now. Tomorrow."

She tried to close the door, but I thrust it open and pushed past her into the room. "How could you go off like that, without a word, and after what happened between us?"

"And what happened between you?" Sitting up stark naked on the disorderly bed, a cigarette held fastidiously between his thumb and second finger, its smoke curling up around his damnably handsome face, was Egon Selinger. He was utterly at ease, viewing with enjoyment the rubble that was left of my world.

"You'd better go," said Magda.

"Nonsense, Magda," said Selinger, patting the bed beside him. "Let him join us. It could be interesting."

25

HAVE CLIMBED TO THE TOP OF THE GREASY POLE"—
Benjamin Disraeli. The first meeting of the Emma Lazarus Old
Vic with Otto Korner as director went off I can't say entirely without a hitch. But on the whole it was, I think, a
success.

The staff, according to my instructions, had arranged the
chairs in a loose circle, with the high-backed one that will in
the actual performance double as the king's throne at the
circle's "head," directly beneath the St. Clair portrait of Emma
Lazarus. This was intended, obviously, to be the director's
chair.

Hamburger and I arrived precisely on time and found the
troupe already assembled. As we entered the library, the twittering stopped. It was a sobering moment. Hamburger must have
sensed my nervousness since he gave me an encouraging pat on
the shoulder. But to my consternation, the director's chair was
already occupied, and by a man altogether unknown to me, a
white-bearded fellow with glasses and wearing a sweater, cordu-
roy trousers, and loafers (no socks!). He was slouched cater-
corner into the throne, one leg draped casually over an armrest.
When he saw me looking at him, he smiled cheerily and gave a
little wave.

My first directorial crisis! The troupe was agog, waiting to
see how I would handle it. A false step now, I knew, could mean
a permanent loss of authority. I merely shrugged and walked

deliberately toward a vacant chair, one located, ironically, just beneath an early Selinger, an eviscerated purple cat on a green-splotched chrome-yellow background. "Wherever the director sits," announced Hamburger, acting in a kind of choral capacity, "*that's* the director's chair." The tension, at any rate, was eased.

Our newest resident, it turned out, was a certain Gerhardt Kunstler. He had arrived only this afternoon and was still finding his way around. (The ladies in the troupe were glancing at him speculatively.) He had dropped in, he explained, merely to get a sense of our activities, to meet a few new people, to see what sort of nonsense ("no offense intended") we were up to. We should just carry on and pay no attention to him. What he hoped to do was arrange a poker game, but that could wait.

I called the meeting to order, said a few flattering words about "our little family of thespians," explained that in my view a director should not be confused with a dictator, and then announced the cast changes: Hamburger would play Horatio, Pincus Pfaffenheim the Ghost, Salo Wittkower Polonius; the Red Dwarf would be promoted to First Gravedigger, and Freddy Blum had agreed to accept the role of Claudius. This last caused some grumbling (Blum, as we know, has his enemies), particularly from Salo Wittkower, who had survived two directors as the villainous king. Still, Wittkower was somewhat mollified when I told him that the use of musical motifs was still under consideration, and, in the event we determined to use them, "Pomp and Circumstance" would be equally appropriate for Polonius and would remain his. Then I turned to my conception of the play, which, I said, differed from Adolphe Sinsheimer's in only a few respects. La Dawidowicz, I could see, was becoming edgy, but she remained silent.

"I want to tilt the emphasis to bring out the important

theme of adultery," I began, and as simply as I could, I presented my arguments.

There was, I am happy to say, general assent, even admiration. For example, Lottie Grabscheidt said, "Wow!"

"That has real possibilities," said Wittkower generously.

"There *are* no possibilities," said Kunstler suddenly.

Obviously this fellow is a troublemaker. Watch out, Korner.

"Tell me, Mr. Kunstler," I said. "Is there some contribution that you might be able to make to our little production? We're always happy to welcome new talent."

"Funny you should ask." He had not noticed my sarcasm. "Years and years ago I worked the color wheel in summer rep. Boulder, to be exact; that's in Colorado. Three shows I've got to this day word-for-word." He counted them off on his fingers: "*Hamlet, Lizzie Borden,* and *Rose Marie.* 'Give me some men who are stout-hearted men.' That's how it went. 'Shoulder to shoulder and bolder and bolder': they loved that bit in Colorado. Well, I was young. I needed money for paints, for a hot dog, for beer. I hadn't had yet my big break, the mural in the mezzanine of the Exchange, downtown Topeka, *Fluctuations,* 1951. Could be you've seen it. The rest, as they say, is history. But acting, no, that's not my line. If you want, I could paint some scenery for you. Just give me the word."

"We already have beautiful scenery," said Minnie Helfinstein, at the moment a Lady-in-Waiting but in the event that Tosca Dawidowicz walks out, a shoo-in for Ophelia. "You should see the set for scene one, Mr. Kunstler. A person could count every brick on the battlements."

"Representational? That went out with the dinosaurs!" Kunstler laughed so hard he began to cough. "Cigars," he explained. "Don't worry, I can paint over it. What I see is a black background interrupted by a few asymmetrical shapes in muted colors."

"The scenery is not on this evening's agenda," I said. "We can take that up at another time."

"Mr. Director! Yoo-hoo, Mr. Director!" It was Tosca Dawidowicz, of course, making a great business of gaining my attention, waving her arms aloft in great sweeps, her fatty tissue jiggling. "I have a question, Mr. Director: what you going to do about (yecch!) Christian burial?" Her voice, I need hardly say, dripped acid.

The moment had arrived, as we had all known it would. Only Kunstler looked puzzled; the rest craned eagerly forward. There was utter silence.

"We are not going to tamper with Shakespeare's words, Tosca, apart, naturally, from the Sinsheimer cuts." (Sinsheimer had instituted certain judicious cuts in *Hamlet* because of its abnormal length and because of weak bladders on both sides of the proscenium. This is why we are also to have three intermissions.)

"In that case," she said, heaving herself to her feet, "some of us ain't going to stick around. For starters, you can find yourself a new Ophelia."

But I had had time to prepare for this challenge. Her gauntlet lay at my feet. I let it lie there.

"You are a person, Tosca, of extraordinary sensibility. Such people require special courage just to cope with the ordinary rotten facts of life." That held her. "But the fact here is, the people in this play are Christians, and Christians expect Christian burial. We can't do anything about that without doing unpardonable violence to the play."

"Hah!" She tossed her head and pounded her fists into her hips.

"But the good news for you personally, Tosca, is that Ophelia does *not* get Christian burial."

There was an excited murmur from the troupe.

"Remember, she gets only 'maimèd rites.' 'What ceremony else?' asks Laertes. None, says the priest. Only because orders have come down from the highest secular power does she get buried in that graveyard at all. So there's no possibility of Christian burial for Ophelia."

La Dawidowicz frowned and dropped her arms to her sides.

"Let us not forget what Sinsheimer, that great man of the theater, told us about the 'willing suspension of disbelief.' For the sake of the play the audience supposes you to be Ophelia, but that same audience also knows, and of course the printed program will make quite clear, that the part of Ophelia is merely *played* by Tosca Dawidowicz."

"Well, maybe." She sat down again.

"And when at the play's end you take your curtain call, when you blow your kisses to an ecstatic audience, it will be your name they'll be shouting, not hers: 'Tosca! Tosca!'"

"Please, Tosca," pleaded Lottie Grabscheidt. "I beg of you, listen to what he says."

She pouted. "I'll have to think about it."

"Never mind thinking," said the Red Dwarf disdainfully. "Yes or no?"

"Poliakov, please. Tosca knows we're working against time. She'll not keep us waiting long. Shall we say tomorrow morning, Tosca? Good. Meanwhile, ladies and gentlemen," I went on smoothly, "we must agree on a date for our performance. Thanksgiving is around the corner. I suggest we aim for the last night of Chanukah. Weekly rehearsal schedules and other pertinent matters will be posted on the bulletin board, as usual. One more thing: I assume you will empower me to send in the name of all of us a bouquet of flowers to our former director?"

From the troupe, murmurs of approval.

"Not from Pinsker on Broadway," said La Dawidowicz spitefully. "He carries only crap. For Nahum, money should be no object."

"You have only to say from where, Tosca."

"Okay, big shot, from Fratelli Fiorelli. On Madison and Sixty-fifth." She shot me a look of triumph.

"So be it," I said, pretending to jot down a note to myself. "Thank you, ladies and gentlemen."

Yes, I would say that all in all, I pulled it off. But my legs were trembling. Of my pounding head, I say nothing.

* * *

THAT NEW MAN, Kunstler, bothers me. There is something about him that tugs at my memory. I sense trouble. Before the group in the library broke up, he had already roped in Hamburger, Blum, Pfaffenheim, Wittkower, and La Helfinstein for a game of poker.

* * *

ONE OF MY FIRST ACTS as director was to send Goldstein a pair of complimentary passes to *Hamlet*. I enclosed them in a letter:

Dear Bruce,

Please accept these passes from Benno Hamburger and me as tokens of our continuing friendship and affection. We know that all concerned with the production will take heart from the thought that you and the companion of your choice are in the audience cheering us on. Meanwhile, I know that I can call on you and your considerable knowledge of the play should some directorial problem prove intractable.

> Cordially,
> Otto Korner
> Director, Emma Lazarus Old Vic

I showed the letter to Hamburger. He looked doubtful. "Go ahead, send it off. At worst, it can't hurt."

It didn't hurt. Today I received a reply:

Dear Otto,

Thanks for the passes. I'll be there. You want my help, you only got to ask.

Too bad about Nahum. I heard.

So how come you guys been giving me the cold shoulder? Coffee on the house next time you come in.

Sincerely,
Bruce Goldstein
Prop., Goldstein's Dairy Restaurant

I showed this letter, too, to Hamburger. "I believe it is peace for our time," I said.

Hamburger shrugged. "Let's hope you did better than Chamberlain."

* * *

SIMPLY TO KEEP YOU ABREAST of events, I should note that Blum reports success with Mandy Dattner. I was sitting in Goldstein's with the Red Dwarf this morning, enjoying a cup of coffee and a plate of fritters. Goldstein has proved as good as his word: the brouhaha is forgotten; we are on our old footing. In fact, Goldstein was sitting with us, a sure sign of special favor since this was the brunch hour, a busy period during which he ordinarily stands by his pillar directing traffic. Poor fellow, he had a cold, persistent; he couldn't shake it off. Misery had led to despair. "The neighborhood is changing," he said. "People come in nowadays, I don't know what to make of them. Ham and cheese on white toast, easy on the mayo, Pepsi on the side. I tell them this is a dairy restaurant, strictly kosher. Okay, they say, make it a burger, medium, and fries. I don't know should I look around for a buyer, sell the goodwill, or should I simply lock the doors and walk away, get out while I can still think straight." This is a familiar refrain, heard at intervals over the years as his lease comes up for renewal. I knew better than to comment. "Blaustein is bleeding me white. 'I'm a landlord, too,' I tell him. 'I know what the market can bear. The neighborhood's going downhill. We, at least, still bring in a good element, you should be grateful. Trumpeldor, for instance, still comes in, all the way from Hartsdale. You got a New York institution here. Don't squeeze the life out of it.' 'Business is good?' he says. 'Congratulations.' What's missing is compassion."

"Marx foresaw all this," said the Red Dwarf. "The bloodsuckers are sucking the blood of the bloodsuckers."

That was when Blum came in. Seeing us, he sat down at our table. "The world is still full of surprises," he said.

As you may imagine, this, coming from Blum, startled me.

"What'll it be?" said Goldstein.

"The Charlton Heston and a glass of tea with lemon. My stomach's acting up."

Goldstein signaled to Joe. "Did I ever tell you the one about the Jew, he's out traveling, and there's this storm: thunder, lightning, pelting rain?"

"Yes," I said.

"No, I don't think I've heard it," said the Red Dwarf.

"So he comes to this bridge, it's swaying in the wind, it can't hold out much longer."

"Yes, I remember now," said the Red Dwarf.

"No, go on," said Blum.

"The Jew has to get across. So he turns his face to heaven and he says, 'Lord, you get me safely to the other side and I'll give five hundred dollars to the UJA.' "

"Yes," said Blum, "I think I know it. To cut a long story short, it ends 'Lord, I was only kidding,' right?"

"Right," said Goldstein. He sighed.

Joe brought the Charlton Heston and the glass of tea.

"I've got another," said Goldstein. "A Jew is crawling across the desert, he's dying of thirst, and he meets a tie salesman. Wait, this one's fantastic."

"Now's the time to quit," said Blum. "While you're ahead. You want to talk fantastic? I'll tell you what's fantastic. Randy Mandy is fantastic. You get to our age, you forget what it can be like."

"For God's sake, Blum," I said.

"So you got into her pants?" said the Red Dwarf admiringly.

"What pants?" said Blum. "You kidding me? Nothing's hiding that honey pot. She tells me she's never had it off with an old guy before. I tell her she's in for a real treat. I ache just thinking about it."

The event had taken place, it appears, at about the time I was listening to the *Marriage of Figaro* playing on the phonograph across the hall and Hamburger was walking in amorous bliss around the grounds of the Hamptons estate with Hermione Perlmutter.

"Let me tell you, that girl's a quality gymnast," said Blum.

"Perhaps now you can give some attention to learning your part in the play," I said acidly.

"I've been meaning to talk to you about that," said Blum. "It's enough already with the play. I don't want to be in it anymore, it takes up too much sack time."

"I didn't hear that," said the Red Dwarf menacingly. "The

reason I didn't hear it is because I know you wouldn't want to make anyone angry. That's right, isn't it?"

Blum swallowed. "Right," he said.

(Ever since Lipschitz's accident, the Red Dwarf—quite unfairly, as I now know—has come to be seen as a man whom it is better not to tangle with.)

26

WO WEEKS HAVE PASSED since my assumption of control. For Lipschitz, of all people, I begin to have a certain respect. To take in hand the tiller of such an enterprise is to steer a course across a maelstrom, with trouble fore and aft, leaks beneath the waterline, faltering engines, a mutinous crew, the decks awash in details, details, details. My life, or what is left of it, is being consumed by the play, swallowed up. Waking and sleeping, it absorbs my energies. "The secret," says Hamburger, "is delegation. Find someone to take care of the shit." Yes, but whom? He himself is reluctant: "It's only a play, Korner. There's more to life than that. Look what it's doing to *you.*" But he, poor chap, still suffers love's torments. Although with noble courage he tore Cupid's dart from its lodgment in his breast, the poison yet rankles, yet festers. I observe him at rehearsals, absentminded, withdrawn into his sorrows. Meanwhile, the backbiting and petty rivalries persist. This one has a complaint against that one and whispers in my ear. Ruffled feathers must be smoothed, lumps of sugar thrust into vicious beaks. La Dawidowicz, who has "graciously" consented to remain in the play, is only too eager to assume with me the professional relationship she enjoyed with Lipschitz: A Korner-Dawidowicz Production! But I know that were I to let her hand wander too near the tiller, she would snatch it from my grasp.

The ancients comforted themselves upon a great man's

death by supposing him translated into a constellation. Sinsheimer is my polestar, by whose steadfast light I steer this ship. Lipschitz (who, by the way, is still in the infirmary and looks far from well) handed on to me a treasure the existence of which until last night I had no inkling, a thick manuscript, alas, never completed, but nonetheless breathtaking in its scope. The title-page alone tugged at my heart as it evoked poor Adolphe in all his admirable modesty: "*Notes on 'Hamlet': Prolegomenon to the Emma Lazarus Old Vic Production,* by A. Sinsheimer, Friend to Ronald Colman.*" Merely to riffle through the pages is to become aware of the man's meticulous concern for every aspect of the play, set down in notes that he continued to revise and augment until the day of his sudden death. Here are sections on Lighting, Costumes, Stage-Groupings, Color Symbolism, Voice Inflection, Scene Construction, and so on and on. The topics range from the historical to the speculative. There is, for example, a chapter of some thirty pages with the teasingly Freudian title "What Does Hamlet Want?" a chapter that leads him, as if by chance, to certain penetrating comments on Sarah Bernhardt's extraordinary re-creation of the role and to the remarkable affinities to be found between the wit of the Prince and that of Georges Sand.

Here, as another example, is a passage from the chapter entitled "The Duel, V.ii":

> . . . For Shakespeare's contemporaries the duel would have been a singular highlight of the play, an entertainment in itself, a match between near equals, whose passes and strategies the Elizabethan would have relished even as a modern American might appreciate the finer points of a football game on Rose Bowl Day. We may be sure that the Lord Chamberlain's Men would have been coached by fencing masters, that Hamlet and Laertes would have achieved a kind of figured ballet, *passes de deux,* as it were,

sufficient to cause the groundlings to quit their shuffling and pay their due of awed attention. . . . But what of us at the Emma Lazarus? In my youth I learned to wield an epée, albeit with only moderate skill. (Dear Ronnie once remarked, his eyes atwinkle, that I held my sword like a truncheon.) And what of our Laertes? [At that time played by Carlo Pflaumenbaum, now in Mineola, a man grossly overweight and by nature ludicrously clumsy.—*Korner*] Let us not forget last year's fiasco, in which Romeo preceded Tybalt to the grave. . . .

The duel remains a problem. And I do not think Sinsheimer's tentative solution is practicable: "A translucent screen, backlighted. The duelists seen only in silhouette. Professional dancers or members of a fencing club hired for the evening." The time grows short, and a solution must soon be found.

As you can see, *Notes on "Hamlet"* is a cornucopia. What hubris, what laughable ignorance was mine, when I sought to fill Sinsheimer's shoes! Without the *Notes* I would be lost.

A sheet of paper, obviously included in error in the manuscript, not only reminds us of the simple humanity of this fine man but also strikes an ironically poignant note:

> To purchase:
>   *Time* magazine
>   Sleep-Eze tablets
>   Cheese danish (or cherry tart)

Ah, that cheese danish (or cherry tart)! It was Sinsheimer's sweet tooth that took him from us, that caused his *Time* to run out, that gave him a Sleep of perpetual Eze.

* * *

THE EMMA LAZARUS is in the grip of poker fever, an epidemic that threatens the production itself. I was right that Gerhardt

Kunstler spelled trouble. Usually a new resident has the natural decency, the prudence, even, to keep himself in the background for a time, at least while he's learning the ropes. Not so Kunstler, who talks to everyone as if on terms of long-standing intimacy and, like a cynosure, draws the residents into a circle of which he is the center. The hearts of the ladies are all aflutter; one can see them blushing, dipping, dimpling in his presence. The gentlemen are no better, since he gives off an aura of dashing cosmopolitanism and masculine charm that seems to embrace them, too. From his table in the dining room comes the most boisterous laughter. None of this of course would matter were *Hamlet* not imperiled. I am *not*, for heaven's sake, in a popularity contest with the likes of Gerhardt Kunstler! But the game he arranged on his first evening has become a nightly entertainment, with Friday only, for obvious reasons, excepted. And the number of games has grown, until hardly a resident still capable of picking up cards is left out. Every table in the games room is taken. Large sums of money reportedly change hands.

But why should I care? you ask. Am I a latter-day Cato? The answer is very simple: actors who stay up all night feeding the kitty and puzzling over combinations of pasteboard symbols cannot give of their best during afternoon rehearsals. Salo Wittkower, for example, still does not know his new lines; Lottie Grabscheidt, in the scene in which I "talk daggers to her," fell asleep in her chair in the midst of my impassioned outburst; others walk about like zombies.

Hamburger, to my disappointment, has proved unhelpful. "You worry too much," he says. But he, of course, has a seat at the Big Table—that is, the one where Kunstler holds court, the principal game. (A regular there is able to sell his seat, I am told, for as much as a hundred dollars!) And when I wondered out loud whether perhaps I ought to go to the Kommandant, such nightly high-jinks being surely detrimental to the health of those under his care, Hamburger became quite huffy. "What are you, Korner, a tattletale? We are grown-up people here, we live in a democracy."

Meanwhile, I understand Kunstler has been asking questions about me. I pique his curiosity. Well, he piques mine. What is it about him that hovers in my memory just beyond the grasp of recall? At a convenient moment I shall launch some discreet inquiries. Selma in Personnel I can rely on.

27

AD NEWS TODAY. Nahum Lipschitz is dead. The shock of the fall, evidently, was too great. Only Lottie Grabscheidt was with him at the end. "He was raving, delirious," she reported, "making no sense at all. He was begging me to take off my brooch, it was killing him. Also, he was going on about 'green fields,' just like before. 'It's all right, Nahum,' I told him, 'the brooch is off.' But then he complained about the cold, how he would report Dr. Weisskopf for turning off the heat. I was sweating in there, but he was shivering like a piece of calf's-foot jelly. So I put some blankets on him from the next bed, and I felt his feet. They were stone-cold. 'I'm ready, Lottie,' he said, and he smiled like a baby. Then he was gone."

Tosca Dawidowicz is beside herself. Her screams could be heard on all floors. Out of respect for a former director, the Emma Lazarus Old Vic has voted to suspend all activities for a seven-day mourning period. I cannot pretend to have liked Lipschitz much, but I admit he used what small talent he had as actor and director to its uttermost.

Ironically, Tuvye Bialkin still occupies his penthouse suite. He seems to have recovered. At any rate, he was at breakfast this morning, his teeth in, chewing unconcernedly on a bagel and cream cheese.

* * *

MANDY DATTNER IS PREGNANT, or believes she is. "Not a whole lot," she said. "Only four weeks. But I know just the moment it happened. I could tell."

I had found her sitting on a bench on Riverside Drive, bundled up in a quilted jacket, staring through the trees, through "yellow leaves, or none, or few," at a lone barge making its serene progress up the silent Hudson. She was lost in moody thought and did not see me raise my hat. I sat beside her, supposing her melancholy brought on by Lipschitz's death. After all, her first failure.

"Life goes on," I said, or some such fatuous thing.

She looked at me, shocked. "Can you tell already?" she said. "Does it show?" And so I learned of her condition.

Miss Dattner was not inclined to draw a modest veil across the details. "We were going pretty good, you know, humping away, and like I had my legs up around his neck and all, so he was in pretty deep, and it was happening, you know." Her eyes became dreamy, lost focus. "He was getting into places I never knew I had in there, it was like fantastic, and like I was all hot syrup beginning to boil and then—boom!—we both popped together and I actually felt these great gushes just surging in—boffo!—and I was beginning to float way out, easy, just drifting, and then I felt it, you know, kind of like a cute little ping! sort of all by itself, like a soap bubble popping in the air, and I *knew*."

A seagull squawked overhead, then banked and swooped. We followed its flight to the river.

"The thing is, I'd been off the pill for days. Ralph had been kind of standoffish—nervous, you know—ever since Dr. Weisskopf had this talk with him. One of the old ladies must have complained or something. Anyway, Ralph told me his career was on the line and that we'd better cool it for a while. He was all antsy about something called 'immoral turpentine.' So anyway, I wasn't prepared, you know, I was like taken by surprise. Hey, I'm not complaining, it was great and all. But now I'm pregnant." She smiled. "Little Mandy, I'm gonna be a mommy." Then the tears began to fall.

"By Ralph you mean Dr. Comyns?"

"Yeah, Ralph," she sniffed.

"And have you told Dr. Comyns he's going to be a father?"

"Ralph? It wasn't him! I told you, we've been cooling it." She wiped the tears from her cheeks with the back of her hand. "Nobody ever listens."

As you can imagine, I was out of my depth. I wanted to put a comforting arm around her but was afraid to do so. Instead I draped it awkwardly behind her, along the back of the bench. "Whoever it was, will he marry you?"

"You crazy? He could be my grandfather!"

It *was* Freddy Blum!

To think that Blum should bring my analogy of the microcosm and the macrocosm, of the Emma Lazarus and the greater society beyond our walls, so much closer to completion! From this house of the dying was to spring forth new life. A seed had been planted and was even now ripening. I felt a tiny flutter of elation.

We walked back slowly together, arm in arm. How I had misjudged her! What has she, poor child, to do with Magda Damrosch, now spiraling for more than thirty years, a wisp of smoke in the air? She is a child of her own generation, decent after her fashion, abysmally ignorant, culturally vapid, but innocent all the same, however hedonistic. How young she is, how vulnerable! The nip in the air had brought a flush to her cheeks, and I suppose also to mine. I told her I would do whatever I could to help. She told me about Led Zeppelin.

* * *

THE DEATH OF LIPSCHITZ has given me a little breathing space. That puts the truth bluntly, but it remains the truth. The mourning period, for which I, too, of course voted, has granted all of us at the Emma Lazarus Old Vic the opportunity to disengage for a short while from a grueling rehearsal schedule and to relax somewhat the tension that finds outlet only in bickering. Like athletes preparing for an Olympic event, we, too, must pace ourselves, pause, and give to aching muscles a therapeutic respite.

At any rate, shortly after the siesta hour I went to visit Selma. I had the luxury of time on my hands. But I discovered that she already had a visitor: Gerhardt Kunstler was visible behind the bulletproof glass, slouched on a chair, his arms behind his head, his feet up on Selma's desk (a liberty I think not even the Kommandant would take!). Today he wore jeans, sneakers, and a sweatshirt. Does he own no socks? Selma, meanwhile, was primping, patting the declivities of her curiously colored hair, obviously enjoying herself. I had been anticipated!

He saw me and gave his familiar cheery wave. I pointed to the bulletin board as if to explain what I was doing in the lobby and pretended to read the notices. Out of the corner of my eye I saw him put a finger to his lips and then wave it warningly before his face. Selma nodded. I began to sense which way the wind was blowing. Selma, that most trusted of "agents," has been "turned."

* * *

I ENCOUNTERED THE KOMMANDANT in the lobby this morning. Lipschitz's death seems to have ruffled the surface of his calm. One might even describe him as skittish, wary, a trifle on edge. He strode toward me, a figure from the London edition of the *Gentlemen's Quarterly:* an elegant gray cheviot coat with a black velvet collar, a deep maroon tie with a muted design, in his hand a black bowler hat and a tightly rolled umbrella. His shoes gleamed. He stopped before me, barring my way. The sedentary, already in place, leaned toward us.

"Ah, yes, Korner, there you are. I was hoping to have a word with you."

"At your service."

"Quite. Play coming along all right, and so forth?"

"Well, in view of Lipschitz's sudden departure . . ."

"Of course, of course. Tragic loss. Er, they tell me, Korner, that you are writing an, er—now this is what I'm told, you understand—you're writing an exposé of the Emma Lazarus. Can that be true?"

"No."

"Well, then . . ." He crossed his legs and leaned casually on his umbrella.

"A kind of memoir, I suppose. A few incidents from my young-manhood. From time to time I refer to what's going on here now, more to clarify my own thoughts than for any other reason."

"Exactly." He smiled coldly. "Nothing libelous, I trust?"

"I have no intention of publication."

"Don't nitpick, man. What I want to know is, er—" He paused and tried again, this time striving for jocularity. "You treat us well, I hope?"

"Naturally."

"Good. I'd like to see it sometime."

I did not reply.

"So be it. A word to the wise, Korner: don't overdo."

His departure galvanized the sedentary: "Better watch it, Otto." "Say anything about me?" "Remember Lipschitz. None of us is safe."

28

ANDY DATTNER'S PREGNANCY put me in mind of
Meta this afternoon, Meta in 1925, just a little after her twentieth birthday. We had been married almost two years by then. I
see her on a sunny afternoon in May, sitting by the open
window, in her hand a book of poems that she puts aside as I
enter the room. A flush of genuine joy comes to her cheeks, this
beautiful young woman, this young woman who so loves me.
"Toto!" she exclaims, and she lifts her arms to me.

But I am in a foul mood—an argument with my father,
perhaps, or with our chief clerk, I no longer remember what. I
give her a perfunctory kiss on the brow and evade the arms that
would wrap around my neck. "My name is Otto. Oblige me by
using it. Let's have no more of this childishness."

"But you are my darling Toto. And besides, there's nothing wrong in being childish today." She giggles.

I sit in my chair, pick up the *Nürnberger Freie Presse*—
nothing there by Otto Körner, of course, the Wunderkind who
appeared and disappeared in 1914—and make a show of ignoring her.

"Mutti sent up champagne, which Käthi is putting on ice.
They're coming down later."

My parents live in the flat above ours. I rustle the paper.

"I saw Dr. Goldwasser today."

I do not look up. "Your famous migraines?"

"Toto, *look* at me. I have such *news!*"

Irritably I put down the *NFP*.

She looks down modestly at the hands folded in her lap but contrives to glance slyly at me from the sides of lowered lids. "Dr. Goldwasser says the stork is on its way." She looks up, her eyes shining, her cheeks aflame. "Oh, Toto, Toto, we're going to have a baby, a baby boy, I know it will be a little boy, I feel it!"

Who can express the happiness of that moment, the exaltation! I want to burst. I leap from my chair and gather her in my arms. . . .

* * *

BUT *WAS* THAT HOW IT WAS? Is it possible? The past we sometimes tend to see transfigured in a roseate glow. Memory is not to be trusted.

No, never mind: *that* is how I remember it.

29

AS THE WEEK OF MOURNING for Nahum Lipschitz draws to a close, and before the hectic busyness of rehearsals resumes, I should seize by the forelock this fleeting time of enforced idleness and, as I long ago promised, reveal the origin of the word *Dada*. In short, it is time to set the historical record straight; it is time for me to take my proper place, however foolish and comical, upon the world stage.

History, certainly, is a slippery business. For Carlyle it was a distillation of rumor; for Nietzsche it was nothing more than belief in falsehood; for Henry Ford it was bunk. But perhaps we should be satisfied with a remark of Voltaire, who could not have known that one day a cabaret would be named for him: "A fair-minded man, when reading history, is occupied almost entirely with refuting it."

Planted in the loamy soil of history, an untruth is almost ineradicable, like crabgrass. Thus, for example, in America we celebrate Independence Day on July 4 rather than (accurately) on July 2. It is possible to know and yet ignore the truth that Henry VIII of England beheaded only two of his six wives, and that Ladislaw XII of Lettow was a transvestite. Yes, we learn from history only that we learn nothing from it.

But now my task is great, and I confess that I quail before it. For the origin of the word *Dada* was from the first day deliberately obscured by the gang at the Cabaret Voltaire. And in the terrible and weary years that followed, even though they scattered to pursue their separate destinies, they remained united in their idiotic determination to suppress the truth. Huelsenbeck, for instance, claimed that he and Ball had come across the word "accidentally" in a French dictionary, where they found it meant hobbyhorse. Richter pretended that he had always supposed the word to be the joyous Slavonic affirmative "Da! Da!"—a "Yes! Yes!" to life. But Arp was the most cunning obscurantist of all. In *Dada au grand air* he succeeded in suggesting that anyone who sought the origin of the word was a dry pedant, the very sort of stupid bourgeois blockhead whom the Dadaists from the first had set out to mock. As for Tristan Tzara, he was unexpectedly modest: "A word was born, no one knows how." (In fact, apart from Otto Korner, no one knew better than Tzara himself how the word was born.)

When Magda Damrosch disappeared from Zurich, my heart stuffed carelessly among her belongings, I was plunged into a misery so profound that I thought I should never recover. At first, fearing that she had tried for Sweden on her own, I was lacerated by wild, romantic imaginings: I saw her traveling penniless according to her "principles," caught by fierce, sex-starved soldiers, interrogated as a spy, shot by a firing squad on a gray, bitter dawn. No doubt I derived some pleasure from my tears. What saved me was an ensuing anger—how could she treat me so!—that I sipped like cognac, a revivifying warmth with whose help I was able to lift up my ego from the rocks on which it lay broken. In brief, I washed, shaved, dressed in clean clothes, and left my room. Once more I began to haunt the Cabaret Voltaire, the Odeon, the Terrasse, the now familiar loci.

The Gang of Nihilists, meanwhile, were readying themselves for Gala Night, an "Extravaganza" (as Tzara called it) that was now a mere fortnight away and for which they had hired Waag Hall, their ambitions having grown beyond the seating capacity of the Cabaret Voltaire and their exhibitionism needing an audience more deliciously shockable than the rowdy students who nightly approved their antics. To me, listening to their gleeful plans and watching their frenetic preparations, it seemed that Gala Night would be little other than their ordinary entertainments writ large, nine parts bad taste and one part vacuity. Magda, for example, should she return in time, was slated to do the splits in an orange tutu and green leotards while Janco played an invisible violin and Tzara brayed one of his painful poems.

It was, in fact, the possibility of Magda's presence there that caused me to conceive my revenge. I would devise my own "skit" for Gala Night, one that would at once outdo the best that the Gang of Nihilists could come up with *and* prove to Magda that she could not with impunity trample upon my love. I would announce to the world, or to that part of it packed into Waag Hall, her cruelty to me. Whether I expected by such means to secure her love I am not sure. Certainly I did not want to lose her. In my emotional turmoil, logic played no part. Come what might, I should at the very least salve my bruised pride.

Tzara at first was cool to the idea of my participation. The volume of *Days of Darkness, Nights of Light*, which I had lent him some months before, he had not yet found time to glance at. But he could assure me that it served very efficiently as a handsome paperweight. "In a strong draft, however, well . . . I can make no promises." He spread his hands, popping his monocle into one of them.

I swallowed the insult and told him that I did not propose to recite my poems; poetry could safely be left to him.

He screwed the monocle back into his eye socket. "Well, then?"

I told him I had in mind a short "skit" with a wax display-window dummy. "I'm after something new," I said. "Concrete metaphor."

He looked doubtful. Janco wandered over, holding a *Weisswurst* to his lips like a cigar. I described my proposal to him, too.

"What's the point?" said Janco.

It was this question of Janco's, I am convinced, that decided Tzara. If there was no evident point, then ipso facto my concrete metaphor should be included. Nevertheless, I would not be allowed to perform alone. Tzara, and perhaps some others, would provide appropriate accompaniment.

Between that moment and Gala Night, Magda returned to Zurich, and with her Egon Selinger. My desire for revenge was then fueled by hate. I was seized by a recklessness that ripped in tatters my lingering decorum.

* * *

GALA NIGHT ARRIVED at last, warm and damp. A mist had seeped in off the lake. It lay low along the ground, shifting in eddies and swirls; it snaked in sudden leaps around corners. The Gang of Nihilists, many of them, had been in Waag Hall since midmorning, getting things in order. The stage was decorated with paintings, colored papers, balloons. At its rear, swaying with every passing air current, hung a full-size anatomist's skeleton in a rakish top hat, holding a clock whose hands were stopped at two minutes to midnight, or to noon: the viewer had his choice. (This was their trite comment on the state of Europe in the summer of 1916.) At stage left stood an upright piano festooned with ribbons and bespangled with glittering stars; at stage right was a low table in the center of which sat a huge papier-mâché wedding cake surmounted by a representation of Europa and the Bull (another political comment), flanked by Tzara's paraphernalia— cowbells, ratchets, klaxons, and so forth.

The citizenry of Zurich poured into Waag Hall, determined to be shocked, titillated, disgusted, confirmed in their solid and eternal values. They sat facing the drab curtain in good order, keeping their voices down, looking discreetly around for familiar faces, allowing themselves a quiet cough or two, rustling their chocolate boxes. Tzara peeked at them through a hole in the curtain and scurried back to the wings, a handsome little jackanapes, grinning with pleasure and rubbing his hands together. "*Avanti!*" he said.

The curtain opened on a darkened stage that was suddenly bathed in brilliant white light. Ball was discovered in blackface at the piano, playing "Tipperary." There was good-humored clapping, a few nervous giggles. I won't rehearse the sequence of "turns." It was the usual stuff from the Cabaret Voltaire, perhaps a little more elaborate, a little more brazen: the stage, after all, offered a larger area for their high-jinks. Magda was in the wings in leotards and tutu, sitting shamelessly on Selinger's lap. We contrived not to see one another. Meanwhile, the audience got its money's worth, saw what it had expected to see, was able to jeer, boo, clap derisively, and shout "nonsense!" and "imbeciles!"

No, never mind the first hour. I shall turn directly to my concrete metaphor, the climax and, as it turned out, the disastrous/triumphant finale to the evening.

My costume for the occasion was, thanks to my mother's foresight in 1915, the last word in elegance. You would have thought me on my way to lunch with the Kaiser at the very least. I wore an immaculate black coat of formal cut over gray-striped trousers. A silk cravat, precisely knotted and pierced by a pin of black onyx, disappeared into my dove-gray waistcoat. Spats, identical in hue and tone to the waistcoat, protected my sparkling black shoes. I had even acquired a monocle, and this was screwed firmly in place. Even Aunt Manya would have been awed, and my mother would have pinched my cheek in delight. And this aristocratic figure, as I supposed myself, walked on stage bearing an ordinary chair as if it were his sacred ancestral escutcheon.

The citizens grew quiet. Perhaps the civic authorities had in the interest of public order wisely decided to bring the "Extravaganza" to an end, and I was there to make the official announcement. A honking laugh from the back of the hall was met by an immediate and deferential "Ssh-ssh!" Ignoring the sensation I had already created, I went to the precise center of the stage and put down the chair, backed off and contemplated it for a moment, made a minute adjustment, and walked offstage. But before the wondering murmur could assert itself, I was back again, this time carrying in a fireman's lift a headless window dummy, a female mannequin. I lowered it to the chair. Anxious laughter from the citizens.

As I knelt to adjust the mannequin's position, the audience could now see that painted in neat black lettering over each wax breast was the syllable *Mag*, and that between these hillocks was a hyphen, thus: *Mag-Mag*. The nipples, in vivid carmine, peeped through the circles of the central *a*'s. The tension in the hall charged the silence. I glanced at the wings: Janco, grinning, gave me a thumbs-up sign; Huelsenbeck held his hand over his mouth; Tzara was hugging himself in ecstasy.

Onstage, I stood up and backed away from the chair. A single horrified gasp arose from the darkness, an intake of breath that united all elements of the audience. The legs of the mannequin were indecorously spread. But that was not all. (Even now I blush to record the rest; but the historian has his duty, and you may judge from what follows to what extremes the young Körner's passion and rage had led him.) In the area of the mons veneris and the sacrarium below it, I had painted a Venus flytrap in grasshopper green, its marginal thorns open to reveal the red blush within. The citizens were mesmerized. From my admirable black coat I removed with a magician's flourish a squat British toothbrush, and this prosaic item I placed in the mannequin's right hand. From my inner breast pocket I drew out a rubber douche complete with clyster pipes. *Voilà!* The mannequin's left hand received the douche, the rubber pipes snaking to the floor. I turned to the wings and snapped my fingers; on cue, Ball threw me a bouquet of paper flowers. I bowed politely to the mannequin and offered her the bouquet. That there was no response is not surprising, but at the moment, so convincing must have been my performance, the audience sighed as if in sympathy for me. For a moment, perplexed, I rubbed my chin, and then, inspired, I placed the bouquet in the headless neck-hole. That was it! That was precisely what the mannequin had lacked! Sterile Mag-Mag, cold and cruel, sprouted spring blooms gaily; nevertheless, the Venus flytrap threatened, and neither hand held out much hope. I strode from the stage.

The silence was at first absolute, thick, sepulchral. Into the silence, assaulting it, seeking to pierce it, break it into fragments, pranced the Gang of Nihilists, myself among them, at last a paid-up member. Ball thumped out Offenbach on the piano, Janco banged the drum, Huelsenbeck and I kicked out a cancan, Emmy Hennings did cartwheels, Magda did the splits, Tzara wiggled his rump like the stomach of a belly-dancer, everyone was occupied. Then we stood in line on either side of Mag-Mag and demanded the right to piss in various colors.

This was what the good citizens of Zurich had been waiting for. Here at last was the event against which they had been hoarding their fury. The storm broke, at first mildly, with boos and catcalls. But very soon there were more voices, angry voices: "Swine!" "Filth!" "Anarchists!" "Christ-killers!" The commotion in the auditorium of Waag Hall drowned us out. It was getting ugly. Janco said we should let down the curtain. Huelsenbeck agreed. But no, Tzara would have none of it. He exulted. The sweat glistened on his forehead. There was a sudden lull as the hall went quiet, as if gulping for fresh breath. Into the silence, Tzara bellowed, "And Calvin, too, if you think of it, was a shitless anal-retentive!" That was enough. That galvanized them. Pandemonium! There were scuffles, fights, the sounds of breaking glass, screams, police whistles. We brought down the curtain.

* * *

LATER WE SAT in the Café zum Weissen Bock and talked about the night's events. There had been some arrests, but of our number only Tauschnitz, like me a barely tolerated hanger-on, had been detained. He had been caught in a scuffle when some of the citizens tried to storm the stage. From the rest of us, the police had taken only names and addresses. Perhaps charges would be preferred, perhaps not: the sergeant was noncommittal. The manager of Waag Hall had been roused from his sleep to make an early assessment of the damages. Tsk-tsk. Profits would perhaps cover losses. "There you have the whole rotten system," said Tzara. Selinger, I was pleased to see, had a black eye, but as a consequence, with Magda draped over him all but swooning, was regarded as the hero of the hour, the only one of us tempered in the fire. Tauschnitz, needless to say, was forgotten. All pronounced the evening a thundering success. The Gang was now a force to be reckoned with.

I, however, was shunted to the sidelines. The table accommodated comfortably all chairs but mine, and so I sat outside the circle, behind and between Emmy Hennings and Richter, who made no attempt to let me in. Magda and I still contrived not to make eye contact. She was, in any case, fully occupied with her hero. I felt quite sick.

The Gang was trying to pinpoint the precise moment at which the citizens' hostility had first been provoked. Ball thought it was when Arp, in the costume of Wilhelm Tell, seemingly plucked an apple from the generous bottom of his "son," Sophie Täuber; Janco believed it was the scene in which he and Huelsenbeck, as a French and a German soldier, squatted, with trousers down, over a "field latrine" and discussed Swiss courage. But all agreed that the assertion of the "right to piss in various colors" had been the true turning point, and that Tzara's "brilliant" and "inspired" words on Calvin had capped the triumph. They laughed until they had tears in their eyes. And stupidly, I laughed with them. Ball, without embarrassment, loudly passed wind, a cause of fresh laughter. Hamburger would have felt right at home.

What utterly amazed me then, what amazes me still, was the fact that not one of them, not even the lady in question, recognized in the *Mag-Mag* painted over the bosom of the mannequin an allusion to Magda Damrosch. How could this be? I have long puzzled over it. The only explanation I can offer (and I confess that it does not wholly convince me) is that having been ideologically programmed to seek no meaning—the only significant point for them being pointlessness—they found none. My frustration was excruciating, my revenge a fiasco!

And now they set about stealing my coinage from me. "We are on the march," said Tzara, "and I am ready at this midnight hour to offer you, in all appropriate humility and solemnity, the long-looked-for name of our journal." He paused, tasting the moment. The monocle popped into his waiting hand. "*Mag-Mag!*" He looked around the table at the puzzled faces. "Wake up! Think of what we have here: *Magazin, Magie, mager!*"

What delight, then, what enthusiasm! These celebrators of unmeaning tumbled over themselves in the hunt for meaning. It became a game.

"*Magma!*"

"*Magnet!*"

"*Magnidicus! Magnus! Magnificat!*"

"*Magot!*"

"*Magic!*"

"Then we are agreed?" said Tzara.

It was intolerable. They had looked everywhere but at Magda Damrosch. What was I to do? My desire for revenge had turned sour in my stomach. To tell them now of my original intention, to explain what they should easily have understood, to spell it out now, with Magda openly caressing Egon Selinger, would be to reveal myself as the utter fool I undoubtedly was. I swallowed bile, but I could not remain silent. Perhaps obliquely the point could yet be made.

"*Mag-Mag* has a copyright," I said bitterly. "Try *Da-Da*."

There was an awed silence. They looked at one another. Tzara and Huelsenbeck screwed in their monocles in unison. Then Tzara lifted his glass of beer. "Little brothers and sisters," he said quietly, "we celebrate the absoluteness and purity of chaos cosmically ordered. I give you . . . *Dada*."

"Hurrah!" they cried. "Hip-hip-hooray!" They had caught not even a glimmering; to the contrary, in a fever of new excitement they began to discuss their first issue. I got up in disgust and left.

No one seemed to notice.

* * *

IN THE MONTHS that followed, Magda and I avoided one another. The hurt still rankled; my pride still burned. She seemed indifferent.

One bitter day in February 1917, however, I was walking in Niederdorf, on Spiegelgasse, to be precise. A light snow had begun falling the previous night, and now the streets were covered. In Niederdorf the houses huddled together like tramps in search of warmth. I was en route to a rendezvous with Herr Ephraim's Minnie, in whose ample and perspiring body I found some solace for my misery. Walking toward me through the falling snow was Magda. I crossed the street. She crossed it, too, and stood before me.

"Otto," she said, "let us be friends again."

She wore no hat upon her head, no scarf. The snowdrops glistened on her hair. The glove that held my arm was worn and split. She was a graced palace in whose purlieus no slime adheres. Selinger, I knew, was a rival no longer. He had absconded, it was rumored, to Lausanne, with the bootblack from the Pension Bel-Air, a pale and bony youth whose black hair stood up in frighted spikes. I was suffused at once and once more with love for her.

"Magda, dear Magda," I said, "we will forget what happened, we will start again where we left off. Come with me, live with me. Let me take care of you."

She hesitated not even a moment. "No," she said, and placed a finger to my lips. "No, *junger Mann,* you must never forget. But you must never go back, either. March always to the horizon, keep your eyes on the future."

"But Magda—"

"No." She was firm. "Friends?"

"Friends."

I turned and watched her make her way through the snow. She paused briefly before Spiegelgasse 14, opened the door, and disappeared.

I never saw Magda again. When next I heard of her, it was to learn that she had left Zurich for good.

* * *

MY OWN FIRST, MINUSCULE ROLE on the world-historical stage, *Days of Darkness, Nights of Light* and the article in the *NFP* had been quickly cut from the play in the interest of more dramatic events: the guns of Europe boomed. My second, as we have just seen, was farcical, and like Polonius, I was hastily buried. But at least both roles were relatively harmless: I alone was the victim. My third appearance was to be a catastrophe that reverberates still, that gives me no peace, that causes me endless pain.

What questions is Kunstler asking about me?

30

PERHAPS IT WAS A MISTAKE to cast Blum as the king. The man lacks the proper subtlety for the role, the ability to find the gesture, modulate the voice, control the play of facial muscles; in short, he cannot achieve the born actor's art, the means by which an audience might enter the mind of the murderer. For Claudius, despite his deed, is to my understanding fully human. Blum's acting style, I would guess, is that of the Yiddish Theater in its most primitive days. He struts about or stands on stage, gnashing his teeth and twirling his mustache. Today I lashed him with Hamlet's advice to the players: "Suit the action to the word, the word to the action; with this special observance, that you o'erstep not the modesty of nature."

"I should do it again?"

"Again."

"Have you heard the argument? Is there no offence in it?"

"*In't.* 'Is there no offence *in't?*'"

"'Is there no offence *in't?*' Okay now?"

"You're sawing the air, for pity's sake! You almost slapped Lottie in the face!"

"Oy, vey's mir. 'Is there no offence *in't?*'"

"*Offence* is the emphatic word, not *in't.* How many times, Blum, how many times?"

"A little patience, Korner. The man is doing his best." The voice from the pit was Kunstler's. (I have engaged him as prompter and thus can keep an eye on him, at least some of the time.) "Perhaps we should take a break."

"Thank you, Kunstler," I said icily. "When it's time to break, I'll know it."

"Fair's fair," he said.

"I've got to go to the little girls' room," whined La Dawidowicz. "You wouldn't want I should disgrace myself in front of everyone."

"Me too," said Wittkower.

"The little girls' room?" said Hamburger.

"You know what I mean, Benno," said Wittkower, aggrieved. "I've got to go real bad."

I threw up my hands.

* * *

During the break Kunstler came up to me.

"A man like Claudius deserves to my way of thinking a little understanding," he said.

"Please leave the actors to me."

"No, I don't mean Blum, I mean the real Claudius."

"That's what I've been trying to pound into Blum's thick head all morning."

"Of course, he *is* a murderer, there's no getting around *that.* But he's got to live with what he did, and naturally it's not easy for him. Probably he'd turn back the clock if he could, poor feller. Now he's trying to make the best of it. I guess we can't escape our past." He paused. "I like what you're trying to do here. You're serious, you show a good understanding."

Can one respond with rudeness to ostensible flattery? "Thank you," I said, and walked away.

Flattery, yes, but is there no offense in't? The man knows something.

* * *

I HAVE ADVISED MANDY DATTNER, I hope wisely, to say nothing to Blum about his paternity—not yet, at any rate. What good could it do her to tell him? He would crow like Chanticleer, parade before us all in that squat, distasteful way that thrusts his sexual equipment forward, encased, I am convinced, in some kind of metallic jockstrap, a codpiece, that grants it special prominence. Blum in leotards already crowds our rehearsals with a giggling audience of ladies. Besides, it's difficult enough to keep Blum's attention on the role; it would be sheer folly to invite distraction. Then, too, there are Miss Dattner's reputation and career to consider, at least in immediate prospect: I have not forgotten the suit that Hermione Perlmutter spoke of, which sparked her husband's rise from legal obscurity. The Kommandant is sensitive to publicity, especially since Lipschitz's mysterious accident and death. He is not above dismissing Miss Dattner for "immoral turpentine," for "interfering" with a resident, for who knows what, an innocent victim of sexual politics.

Needless to say, she is not anxious to tell her parents. "Oh, sure, they'd like that back in Shaker Heights, wouldn't they just. Like, come on home, Mandy, what's a little pregnancy? Mom would be real keen on filling in the girls at the temple, and as for Dad, jeez!"

"They might be more understanding than you think."

"You kidding me? Anyway, I wouldn't give them the satisfaction. Dad'd insist on an abortion for sure, probably in Siberia."

So that avenue is blocked, at least for the time being. If all else fails, Blum can be forced to make some kind of financial settlement. But that is for later. In the meantime, Mandy is calm, almost blithe, already suffused (or do I imagine it?) with a maternal glow, content to leave her problem in the hands of her "Grampus," as she has taken to calling me, a man who has failed miserably, again and again, to bring order to his own life.

31

DISASTER LOOMS! No more than a small cloud on the horizon this morning at breakfast when the first dismaying rumbles were sounded, it soon raced to fill the sky. Lottie Grabscheidt is ill, struck from the list of solo-ambulants, bedridden! The Kommandant is closemouthed, pursuing his policy of not alarming the residents. "Calm down, Korner," he said to me sternly, reaching for my pulse. "You're asking for it yourself."

"Asking for what?"

The eyes narrowed above the hawk nose. He adjusted the knot of his tie. "There's such a thing as medical ethics, you know." With spreading finger and thumb he smoothed his neat mustache. He got up and came out from behind his desk. "But I think I can tell you that basically she's sound as a dollar. A week in bed, at most two; she'll be up in good time for the performance."

"But that's the very last minute!"

"Yes, well." He put his arm around my shoulder and escorted me to the outer office. "Miss Kraus, have you informed the family yet?"

"The son is already on his way, Dr. Weisskopf." Herta Kraus basked in his brightness.

"Good. Now remember, Korner, *du calme, toujours du calme.*"

Dr. Comyns was only a little more helpful. The square

teeth shone between the fleshy lips. "If I were you, as a simple precaution, not to admit to more than I know, but I can guess your reason for concern, and that's why I'm prepared to advise you, since it can't hurt one way or the other, to think about, at least theoretically, the possibility of beginning to work, for a while anyway—you know, a word to the wise—with, in theatrical parlance, one of her understudies."

One of her understudies indeed! Lottie Grabscheidt has only one understudy: Hermione Perlmutter. It's too late to train anyone else.

After some huffing and puffing, Hamburger admitted that he had the Manhattan telephone number of Hermione's daughter. He brought his address book to my room and stood by me anxiously while I phoned.

"Ms. Morgenbesser's residence."

"I'd like to speak to Mrs. Perlmutter, please."

"One moment, sir."

"She's there," I mouthed to Hamburger, who looked faint.

A different voice: "My mother's resting right now, but I can give her a message. Who'll I say is calling?"

I told her.

There was a pause. "All right, I knew it was only a matter of time. Listen, I've already spoken to my lawyers. You creeps haven't got a case, so why don't you just piss off and give my mother some peace?"

"But Mrs. Morgenbesser—"

"*Ms.* Got that, asshole?"

"Ms. Morgenbesser—"

"You've got your autograph back, right? So why don't you just take a flying fuck?"

"But all that's forgotten. It never happened. A mistake on my part. We want your mother to come back to the Emma Lazarus."

A pause; then, quietly, "Oh."

"The Old Vic depends on her. We want her to play Gertrude."

"Oh."

"It's an understudy's dream."

"Perhaps I was a little hasty. You have to understand, she's very upset. I can't bear that."

"Naturally, naturally. You're her daughter, after all. Perfectly understandable."

"Look, I can't promise anything. I'll talk to her."

"That's all I ask." Hamburger was tugging at my sleeve and whispering in my ear. "And tell her Benno sends his best." Another tug: "His *very* best."

"*Ciao.*"

"*Ciao.*" I hung up.

Hamburger looked sheepish. "If you can make such a sacrifice, Korner," he said, "I can swallow my pride. Your need is greater than mine."

So now we wait. The mood in the company is glum. As for me, I call upon my depleted reserves of stoicism. In all this, there is Purpose.

* * *

A TOUCHING SCENE in the lobby this morning. Hamburger and I were standing by the bulletin board; he was trying to dissuade me from canceling the production. The notice was in my hand.

"You mustn't do it, Korner."

"What do you want from me? Osric can go. The Assistant Gravedigger we can do without. But *Hamlet* without Gertrude is an impossibility."

We were whispering. The lobby's sedentary leaned toward us.

"But after all the work—the weeks, the months, your own high hopes?"

"You think I *want* to cancel? Perhaps we can manage some sort of program, recitations, excerpts from a few scenes. I Solisti can help out in the intervals."

"Wonderful. A regular Flo Ziegfeld. Maybe the Red Dwarf could juggle a few plates. You I wouldn't have put down for a quitter. In those lonely days, Korner, when I championed you for the directorship, little did I think it would mean the dissolution of the company."

"Not the company, the production. Besides, why should you care so much? You were never the keenest member. 'It's only a play, Otto': how many times have you said that to me?"

"It's you I'm thinking of, and the others."

From the sedentary there was a sudden stillness, an almost palpable quietude, as if they were sitting on the brink of the extraordinary. We stopped our bickering and turned.

Through the open portal, accompanied by a younger woman of Wagnerian massiveness, a woman swathed in an ankle-length mink coat, came Hermione Perlmutter. She was back!

As soon as she saw us she stopped, confused, timorous, a little round figure in a jaunty naval officer's overcoat cut modishly short and adorned with shiny brass buttons. Tilted back on her head, roundness upon roundness, was a flat flying saucer of a hat, rather like those worn by Italian priests, navy blue, from which a ribbon of the same hue depended. Eyes abased, she took a shy, a tiny, step forward.

The play of emotions on Hamburger's face was something to see. He, too, took a step forward. From his throat issued a small cry.

"Benno!"

"Hannah!"

Suddenly they were running to one another. He caught her in his arms, leaning forward over their stomachs. There in the lobby they kissed and embraced. When such a mutual pair and such a twain can do't, they stand up peerless.

"Oh, Hannah!"

"Oh, Benno!"

The sedentary were all atwitter: "Worth the price of admission"; "Better than a movie"; "A person with a heart of stone would melt."

Hamburger shook hands with Lucille Morgenbesser and relieved her of her mother's overnight bag. The daughter is a formidable woman whose gums figure prominently when she smiles. Hamburger brought mother and daughter over and introduced Ms. Morgenbesser to me.

"Mr. Korner," said La Perlmutter, "I am quite overcome with embarrassment. What can I possibly say?"

"You can say you're ready to take on a starring role in *Hamlet!*"

Hamburger, almost bursting with happiness, gave me a playful punch on the shoulder. "But first, champagne! I'll ask one of the porters to go out."

For the benefit of the sedentary, I raised my voice. "When you offered to have my Rilke letter framed, Mrs. Perlmutter, I didn't expect such elegance. I must reimburse you."

She thought at first that I was mocking her. Her little hands flew up to cover her eyes. "Oh, oh."

"No, I insist."

She peeked at me between her fingers, was reassured, blushed, smiled. "Not at all, it's a present."

Lucille Morgenbesser glanced at her watch. "If you don't need me anymore, Mother, I'd better run."

"But what about the champagne?" said Hamburger.

"Another time."

"She's lecturing at the New School," said La Perlmutter proudly. " 'Sappho, Leviticus, and the Limits of Faith.' Run, darling, run."

I tore up the notice canceling the performance and put the pieces in my pocket.

* * *

THE RETURN OF HERMIONE PERLMUTTER has given new life to the company, a shot of adrenaline that today carried us through rehearsals like seasoned actors. We were running through act 4, scene 5, 215 lines packed with dramatic tension and the most subtle interplay of individual emotions. From the opening line, Gertrude's "I will not speak with her," it was impossible not to sense the electricity in the air. La Perlmutter, in a quilted red dressing gown, might have been preparing for the role all her life. Freddy Blum abandoned his histrionics, his melodramatic posturings, and caught the very life of a king at bay, found out, inwardly squirming, but through sheer force of will putting up a facade of imperturbability. Even Milos Pasternak, the Messenger, who hitherto had delivered his dozen lines in monotone and in the disquieting accents of the Lower East Side circa 1910, conveyed convincing alarm—"Save yourself, my lord!"—as he fell upon one knee before the king, pointing to the wings as if the Furies, not merely Laertes, were about to issue from them.

But of Tosca Dawidowicz I lack words to praise. Her talent, dormant until this afternoon, burst into sudden blaze. Since the Prince does not appear in this scene, I was able to watch her performance from the third row center. And I confess that I was entranced, transported to that unhappy court at Elsinore, the Emma Lazarus forgotten.

Tosca Dawidowicz *was* Ophelia. One did not see an obese, embittered old woman in a gray sweatsuit, her face in profile like a heavy crescent moon, nor yet the large pink curlers marching like a plastic army in tight ranks across her head. One saw instead the poor demented girl, Hamlet's "most beautified Ophelia," bereft of her sanity by blows too powerful for her gentle spirit to withstand: "There's fennel for you, and columbines. There's rue for you, and here's some for me. . . . There's a daisy. I would give you some violets, but they withered all when my father died." That look of tender bewilderment as she distributed the flowers, that hesitant gesture as if she half feared a blow in return, that exquisite shudder, as if for a second she had been granted respite from madness and insight into the bitter truth, these were moments to treasure. Not Sinsheimer, not Lipschitz, not I, no one but Tosca Dawidowicz could claim credit for this triumph. The spell was broken only when the scene came to an end. "My bladder's about to burst! Me first for the little girl's room." The whole company applauded her as she ran for the wings.

Yes, this was a moment to savor, and I am proud of our little troupe. Still, the excitement threatened to get out of hand, with Hamburger, whose drinking perhaps bears watching, even calling again for champagne. I was forced to remind them that much hard work still lay ahead, with little enough time left in which to complete it. "Just the same, ladies and gentlemen," I added, "I think we have here a winner!" Shouts of jubilation and raucous back-slappings.

* * *

THINKING OVER the scene later, and remembering mad Ophelia's wistful songs, I was put in mind of Mandy Dattner:

> By Gis and by Saint Charity,
> Alack and fie for shame,
> Young men will do't if they come to't—
> By Cock, they are to blame.

Precisely so: by "cock" they *are* to blame. And if Freddy Blum cannot qualify as a young man, Ralph Comyns can. I determined then and there to have a few exploratory words with the reluctant doctor.

I found him in his office, a bottle of Dr. Pepper in his hand and his feet upon the desk. He was leafing through a copy of *Geriatrics Today*.

"You guys give me a pain in the neck," he said genially, putting his feet down. "To what do I owe what, knowing you, you probably think I should regard as this honor?" He gestured at me with one ear of his stethoscope, a visible question mark, a concrete metaphor. "If you want me for the play, you'll have to see my agent."

I pretended to a slight sore throat.

He took a look. "Seems fine to me, you old goldbricker, pink as a baby's bottom. Beautiful tonsillectomy, they really knew their business in those days. Suck a lemon drop."

"How's Lottie Grabscheidt?"

"Coming along nicely. Tomorrow she can have visitors. You can toddle along there and bother her instead of me."

"But she'll be well enough to take part in the play?" In fact, given today's wonderful teamwork on stage, it occurred to me that we would be better off without her. La Perlmutter, excellent in herself, has proved a catalyst to excellence in others. (Of course, I wish La Grabscheidt no harm.)

"That I wouldn't count on," he said. "Patience is the operable word." He winked and narrowed his eyes. "No pun intended." He squinted at me. "You look a bit gray, now that I look at you. As long as you're here consuming my valuable time, I might as well give a listen." He adjusted his stethoscope. "Strip to the waist."

I began to undress. "You should take a look at Miss Dattner when you get a chance."

"Why, you old goat, whatever are you suggesting?"

" 'She has of late, but wherefore I know not, lost all her mirth.' The effervescence is gone. She sighs a lot and seems sometimes on the brink of tears. As a layman, I would diagnose a case of unhappiness in love, a broken heart. But a doctor might think differently. It might be something truly organic, maybe a virus, a low-grade fever."

He looked thoughtful.

"She's a beautiful girl, a good family, too, pillars of the community, Shaker Heights. But she's all alone here in New York. I worry about her."

He seemed distracted.

"The stethoscope, Doctor."

"What? Oh, yes." He listened back and front while I coughed. He went through the familiar routine twice. "Take my advice and ease up some, get out more, walking's good for you. And make proper use of the siesta hour. I'm going to give you a Valium, but I want to see you again in three days. You can get dressed now." He helped me on with my undershirt.

"You're not married, Doctor?"

"You know I'm not."

"A doctor should always be married. It's an old truth still valid today. It prevents loose talk."

"Talk?" He looked at me sharply.

"Well, in the course of his work a doctor has to examine his female patients, some of them cursed with active imaginations. He has to probe all their hidden secrets; their very sacraria must yield to his careful scrutiny."

He laughed. "If *my* female patients are concerned about their sacraria, as you put it, they have more to fear from Freddy Blum than from me."

"One reads such odd things in the papers."

"Sacraria! Boy-o-boy!"

"The trouble is, the gossip is all in the other direction."

"What does that mean?"

I shrugged. "You're the doctor."

The blood drained from his face, and the hand on his stethoscope trembled. "They think I'm gay, is that it?"

"In a place like this, naturally tongues wag. For some it is their only exercise."

"They think I'm a homo, a queer!"

"Please, Doctor, calm yourself, the last thing I wanted was to upset you. Only, a word to the wise." I buttoned my jacket and left him standing there, rooted to the spot but shaken, I think it fair to say, out of his complacency.

Another seed is planted. May it find fertile soil.

32

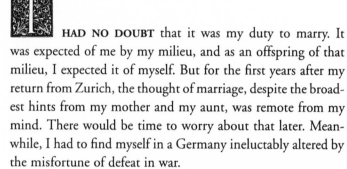 HAD NO DOUBT that it was my duty to marry. It was expected of me by my milieu, and as an offspring of that milieu, I expected it of myself. But for the first years after my return from Zurich, the thought of marriage, despite the broadest hints from my mother and my aunt, was remote from my mind. There would be time to worry about that later. Meanwhile, I had to find myself in a Germany ineluctably altered by the misfortune of defeat in war.

I returned to Berlin at the end of 1918, a time of revolution. Snipers were on the rooftops, and there was firing in the streets. The imperial stables were under siege: troops loyal to the Kaiser fought troops who were not. Skirmishes erupted in Charlottenburg, bullets flew in the Anhalterbahnhof, armed violence broke out in the Belle-Alliance-Platz. In some places one had to keep his head down and scuttle crabwise across the street simply to buy an ounce of tobacco, a kilo of sausage. Those were bodies down there, human bodies, pumping their lifeblood onto the cobblestones. Elsewhere the stench of slaughtered horses poisoned the air. The civil police ran in circles, blew their whistles, were powerless. Into the vacuum of a disintegrating kingdom rushed a myriad of political malcontents, with meetings, rallies, marches, protests everywhere, here a soldiers' council, there a workers' council, unionists, loyalists, anarchists, communists, a city on the brink of chaos.

Here was soil fertile for Dada, and in fact Huelsenbeck,

our old acquaintance from Zurich days, had returned to Berlin at the beginning of 1917, where he took over the reins of an incipient Dada "government." The "Dada bomb," as Arp was later to call it, had already exploded by the time I arrived, penniless, my flirtation at the skirts of Swiss literary journalism ignominiously over, my tail between my legs, obedient to my father's summons and my mother's importunings.

With Dada in Berlin I, of course, had nothing whatever to do. In any case, the tone of Dada here had a stridency that cast the Dada of Zurich into a tame, almost cozy light. If in Zurich Dada had merely toyed childishly with politics, in Berlin it embraced politics with lascivious intent, it swallowed politics, it spewed politics. In Zurich Dada had scarcely shaken Order from its foundations; in Berlin the foundations of Order were gone. From all this I was by temperament and circumstances aloof.

After the jubilation attending the return of the prodigal, my father took me into his study for a "serious talk, a man-to-man exchange of ideas." It was time, he said, for me to take the future into my own hands. The nation faced stern times ahead, times that would demand of its sons the uttermost of their courage, more perhaps than in the war itself. Today the battleground was outside our windows. "Discordant elements" strove to tear the beloved Fatherland asunder. They must not succeed. And they would not, if only young men like me, "true patriots," would roll up our sleeves and from the fallen masonry, the rubble, of the old order build the firm foundations of the new, learning from past mistakes but always cleaving to past achievements. In my case, this noble mission required me to enter the family firm. In fact, he said, that had always been his hope, that a new generation would prepare to take over the helm. My future career, it seemed, was decided.

Father embraced me. "Come, Otto," he said kindly, "let us seal your determination, our agreement, like gentlemen: a handshake and a thimbleful of cognac." We shook hands. The decanter stood ready, glinting on the sideboard. He poured; we drank. The ladies waited for us anxiously in the drawing room. "It's settled," said my father. "He's joining me in the office on Monday morning." My mother and my aunt clapped their hands, delighted; Lola hung adoringly on my arm.

And so I entered the Körner Office Equipment and Stationery Company, moving steadily through the various departments until my father was confident I had a "firm grasp of affairs." In time I traveled abroad on the firm's business, mostly to England but also to Austria, Hungary, Czechoslovakia, the fragments of the old empire. Despite the treacherous economic currents of those times, Körner's prospered.

When I left for Switzerland in 1915, my cousin Meta had been a child, only ten years old, a little girl in pigtails and dirndl. When next I saw her, in 1922, what a transformation! She had blossomed into a beauty, tall, slender, with dark tresses, a creature to inspire the Pre-Raphaelites. The blush came easily to her cheeks, the smile to her lips. At once she became for me the image of maidenly purity, the obverse of Magda Damrosch, whom now I could remember only disheveled, sweating, in her kimono, Egon Selinger naked on her bed. I was ashamed of the comparison, which was, I thought, an insult to my cousin, but it came unbidden to my mind, the two young women side by side. It marked perhaps the beginning of my healing.

We met again during a family holiday in Berchtesgaden. Only my sister and her husband were missing; the newlyweds were in Venice. I had at first been reluctant to go. Having myself ignominiously sat out the war, I was ashamed to face Meta's brother Joachim, a wounded and decorated hero. He put me at my ease at once. "As you see, Otto, like you I am beginning to lose parts of myself." He had been in the mountain sunshine for a week or more by the time I arrived and was already deeply tanned. He wore the patch over his missing eye with a certain dash, his badge of honor, and despite his wooden leg and cane he got about nimbly enough, masking his pain, the wince that occasionally transfigured his handsome face, as best he could. Of the bitterness that was in later years to overwhelm him there was as yet no sign.

The three of us—Meta, Joachim, and I—got along famously. It was a halcyon time. Joachim had a powerful open touring car, specially equipped for his needs, in which he drove us at reckless speed through the mountains, scattering dust and chickens in the hamlets, the dogs barking, the peasants shaking their fists, the wind whipping Meta's hair, our laughter carried away behind us by the wind. We swam in cool, clear lakes, picnicked on their margins, talked endlessly of books, of music, of the future of the world.

Sometimes in the evenings, the family gathered around, Meta would play the piano for us. She played well, a delightful frown of concentration on her face. My mother transferred her Schiller-reading evenings to Berchtesgaden. We all took turns with the well-loved passages, discussed the works. Once Meta embarrassed me by taking out a copy of *Days of Darkness, Nights of Light* and insisting on reading from it: "There are other poets, after all." My father snored gently through the recitation, a handkerchief over his face, but the applause at the end woke him up: "What? What?" Afterward Meta brought the book over to me, where I sat withdrawn in the shadows. She held it to her heart. "Inscribe it for me."

"What shall I write?"

She thought for a moment. " 'To my beautiful cousin Meta, Fondly, Toto.' "

"What vanity! Here," I said, scribbling. " 'To my mischievous cousin Meta, With much love, Otto.' "

She bent and kissed me gently, a feather touch, on the cheek, snatched the book from my hands, and ran from the room. My mother and Meta's mother nodded at one another, smiling. They knew what they knew, but for my part I believed my feelings merely cousinly.

Nevertheless, Meta and I were married on July 16, 1923. She was eighteen; I was twenty-seven.

Did I love her? I was proud of her beauty, of her purity, of her culture. I was comfortable with her. It was plain that she adored me, incomprehensibly but certainly. At times her ardor embarrassed me. But as for love—well, I suspect that in such matters the balance is seldom even.

* * *

KUNSTLER KNOWS everything!

This morning I had an appointment with Dr. Comyns. Nothing alarming, the usual thing: constipation, headaches, and so on. The pendulum has swung back all the way. Occasionally he prescribes something that works, it's worth a try; but "fundamentally," as Hamburger says, Comyns believes in stewed fruit. The waiting room outside the office is tiny, claustrophobic. Kunstler was there before me, reading a magazine, his legs stretched out, filling the space.

"Come in," he said, as if he had sent for me. "Sit down. The doctor's backed up, a new girl, a fresh morsel for Blum." Already he has an insider's knowing breeziness of tone. "Beautiful day, not too cold."

"I haven't been out yet," I said.

"Perhaps when you're finished here. We could go for a walk in the park."

"Unfortunately, I have many things to do."

We sat in silence for a while, listening to the muffled murmur of Dr. Comyns's voice well launched upon a flood tide of tangled sentences.

"Have you been back?" he said.

There could be only one meaning. "Never."

"They have a program there, you know, to bring back

Berliners for a visit, the refugees from Hitler's time, all expenses paid."

"Very decent of them."

"I went last year. It was something."

I said nothing.

"I was lucky, I got out just under the wire, in April 1939." He sighed. "Those were terrible times, terrible. Sometimes I think it couldn't have happened, I must have dreamed it, a nightmare. I had a cousin, on my mother's side, Sonya, my only relative. She got out herself in 'thirty-eight, right after *Kristallnacht*. Sonya sent for me from Mexico City. By then she was living with a Mexican film producer, Iago Colon, perhaps you've heard of him? No? In any case, we didn't stay there long. She married a Texan from Amarillo, a salesman in automobile accessories. He had one fabulous asset: he was an American citizen. People were desperate in those days, I don't have to tell you. Just the same, he got a bargain, she stuck it out with him. Sonya was a real beauty, easygoing, a wonderful cook. She sang, too, a soprano, could have become a professional. So that's how I came to America.

"I've painted my pictures in every one of the states except Hawaii and Alaska, can you beat that? Of course, I didn't set out to make a record, but I traveled around a lot, mostly New Mexico and New York, the Taos–Greenwich Village axis, in the old heroic days. But also Colorado, Oregon, Louisiana. After I'd racked up about fourteen states, I thought what the heck, I'll try for the whole shebang. Some places—Nebraska, for example, or Georgia—I stayed maybe only a weekend. In New Mexico I owned a burro, two dogs, and a cat. Also I had a wife, but that's another story. Seen any of my work?"

"I think not. But I can't pretend to know anything of modern art."

He grinned. "But I bet you know what you like."

"I am not a Philistine, Mr. Kunstler."

"Poker not your game?"

"No."

"Pinochle?"

"An occasional hand of bridge."

"Everyone's got a story to tell, I guess."

To this, of course, I made no reply.

"There used to be a Körner Stationery Company on the Wilhelmine Platz, an old, old firm, from the nineteenth century at least, a giant of a place, 'By Appointment,' even. Any relation?"

"It was my family's. My father ran it until they took it away from him. I, too, worked there."

"So that's it! And do you by any chance remember a Klaus Kunstler, a chief clerk? He died in 1932."

"Of course."

"That was my father."

So here it was at last, the past, sitting sprawled before me. In Gerhardt Kunstler I could now see the lineaments of the father. But Old Kunstler had been an erect, a punctilious man, formal in bearing and utterance, my father's highly respected right-hand man, kindly but firm in business matters, his advice—and surely correctly—always outweighing my own. And now I remembered him earlier, too, when I was a child, and his miraculous waistcoat that always had a boiled sweet in it for me.

"Well, well, well," said Kunstler. "I know all about you. The grand doings of the Family Körner were the staple of dinner conversation in our more humble home. Your father had promised mine that there would be a place for me at Körner's. That's what my father wanted, our own family tradition of service. But I had other notions. Eight-thirty to six-thirty and nine to one on Saturdays was not my idea of how to live. 'Thank you, madam,' 'At your service, sir.' "

"Your father was very kind to me."

"He didn't have much choice, I would say."

"Nevertheless, I remember him fondly."

"Fondly, yes, and with good reason. He made millionaires of you! But no, I don't really mean that. Old resentments, I suppose. I'm amazed at myself. All that is long over and done with. Forget what I said. You're not to blame for society's ills. And besides, you lost everything. . . . But you wrote, too, didn't you? After Hitler came into power? You were something of a journalist, that's right, isn't it? Every other week, I seem to remember, there was another Körner article."

The door to Dr. Comyns' office opened. The "new girl" was as thin and bent as a twig. She wore a blond Afro-wig over her parrot's face. Dr. Comyns made the introductions, but I paid no attention to her name. It took all the strength I had simply to stand on my trembling legs.

"Which of you fakers is next? Mr. Kunstler?"

"Go ahead," Kunstler said to me. "I'm in no hurry."

"Perhaps you'd better, at that," said Comyns in alarm. "Your color is far from good." He helped me into his office.

* * *

MY TROUBLES, it seems, may be solved by a Valium, a muscle relaxant, and, inevitably, stewed fruit.

* * *

WHY DID THE MUSE no longer whisper in my ear? How was it that the flame of inspiration had died so utterly in me? The forge at which, while still a boy, I had hammered out my verse, the bellows blasting, the coal white-hot, now stood long idle, long neglected. Yes, I could with effort still shape a poem, but it was a dead thing, lacking lively heat. I turned to prose, short stories, began a novel. No use, no use. In my frustration I threw myself into my work at the Körner Company, turned my energies into ringing coin, grew thick in the middle, witnessed the shrinking of my soul, became what I most despised. Within, I wept. My youth was gone; I was now married, had a child. Responsibilities mounted. With a sour and envious spirit I read the publications of my friends, my heart leaping at a bad review.

Meta knew what was wrong with me, but her early efforts to ease my inner misery served only to increase it. "Why don't you write anymore, Toto?"

I was sitting in my study, angrily leafing through a sheaf of papers I had brought home from the office.

She stood before my desk humbly, like a schoolgirl awaiting reprimand. "Please, Toto."

Still I ignored her.

"Why won't you write a little poem for me?"

I tasted the bile on my lips and at last looked up at her. "Because, my pet, I do not write my 'little poems,' as you justly call them, on demand."

Her cheeks reddened. She turned from me and silently left the room. How could I have treated her so! My eyes smarted, and I longed to call her back, to run after her, to fall on my knees before her. Instead, I savored the bile.

Otto Körner in marriage was that ugliest of monsters, a sadomasochist. His wife's natural joy he perceived as a deliberate reproach to him. He began to treat her, this intelligent and blooming woman, this loving wife, as if she were a naughty and irritating child. "Really, Meta, for heaven's sake!" (tone: mild exasperation); "You will permit me to remark, Meta, that that was not exactly the wisest choice" (tone: icy politeness); "How extraordinarily witty, Meta!" (tone: sarcastic scorn). She would flinch, turn away, blush, sometimes even cry.

My pleasure at her anguish caused me an anguish that gave me pleasure. I was, I suppose, testing her. How far could I go before she ceased to love me? Far, very far. But over time I killed something in her. No longer did she smile when I appeared; no longer did she seek to wrap her arms around my neck. I became Otto; Toto vanished. Decorum entered our household, at least in my presence. With her friends, with our families, signs of the old spontaneous joy could still appear, splashes of bright sunlight against the enveloping gloom. With little Hugo in particular, the bubbles of happy laughter burst forth.

The child became a battleground between us. Meta was, I told her, making Hugo effeminate; he clung too much to his mother's skirts, we would have to send him to boarding school.

"No, no, Otto! He would be so afraid. I could not bear it!" She held Hugo to her, kissed his curly head.

"Your brother, Joachim, went to boarding school. He came to no harm."

"That was different. He was older."

"Well, we shall see."

Pure torture, nothing but torture. I did not dream of sending Hugo away; I, too, could not have borne it. Jealously, I tried to win him from her. In vain. They had a secret understanding, the two of them, a bond unspoken, almost palpable. I could not penetrate it. Hugo grew quiet in my presence.

In time I stopped sleeping with Meta. It began as an experiment, another test. I started to stay late at the office, feigned tiredness, feigned indifference to the demands of the libido. How would she react? At first with understanding, then with tears, at last with resignation. Another turn of the screw: I began to sleep in the guestroom. She said nothing. After a while she moved my clothing there.

In my lonely bed I relived again and again the moments of our first rapture. Meta had a strong libido; it had been her thrust on me that tore the stubborn hymen, a wild, an exultant frenzy. She had lain then beneath me, gazing into my eyes with an intensity of adoration reserved by a medieval martyr saint for a vision of the New Jerusalem. She had loved me utterly and unreservedly. All this I had thrown away. No matter that by then what I wanted most was to hold her once more, undo what I had done; our estrangement had gone too far.

I managed in my madness to convince myself that she was to blame for the indifference I had carefully cultivated in her. We spoke to one another finally with distant politeness only. Before family and friends we still contrived a show of marital contentedness; alone, there was only the foul odor of our mutual irritation. She no longer loved me, but the vacuum the departure of love had left within her was not, I think, yet filled with hate. That would come later, when the musicians of the New Order began to tune their instruments for the saraband of death, when it became evident to her that I was prepared to sacrifice wife and child to the demands of my ego, the sick appetite of my pride.

How can I convey to you the living woman? It is an impossible task. She is beyond my grasp, where I thrust her. How could such innocent Beauty have loved so guilty a Beast? Desire needs food, like anything that lives. I had fed on Meta but offered her only poisoned scraps.

33

HERE IS NOTHING either good or bad," says Hamlet, "but thinking makes it so." Why he says it is an open question. Sinsheimer's note on the line is unhelpful: "A common reflection." Hamlet knows well enough what is bad: fratricide is bad, incest and adultery are bad. It is curious, however, how easily he moves from the particular to the general when the subject is evil. He openly admires Horatio, but Horatio's fine qualities teach him nothing about the nature of man. And yet if his apparent moral relativism does not ring completely true, it does not ring completely false, either. Still, I would be happier if Claudius had said those words, or even Polonius.

I was moved to these reflections by an encounter that took place yesterday morning. Then I was reluctant to record it, but today, and in the interest of completeness, I set it down. I was sitting in the library reading the newspaper, or rather, attempting to read it, my powers of concentration being somewhat impaired by an indefinable physical malaise, Dr. Comyns' regimen otherwise already benefiting me. It was as if the body were girding itself in response to an apprehensiveness engendered in the mind, an unmotivated anxiety. There were things to be done, and not merely the assimilation of printed disasters, which task I undertake daily not only out of habit or to stay *au courant* but as an exercise to stimulate a sluggish brain; no, I also had a list of small tasks to be taken care of before the principal business of the morning, the going over of my notes for the afternoon's rehearsal, the arrival of the players at Elsinore.

Leonard Sweetchild, the First Player, is giving me trouble. The role demands a subtlety beyond his grasp. The First Player, after all, has to deliver his lines and control his gestures in two distinct styles. On the one hand, he has to speak as a professional actor responding to the warm hospitality offered him and his fellows by his princely patron; on the other, he has to speak as an actor "in character," first in the Hecuba passage in act 2, scene 2, where Hamlet requests a sample of his thespian skill, and later, of course, as the Player King. Shakespeare distinguishes the two language modes clearly enough for any ordinary understanding, but Sweetchild, unfortunately, has a tin ear. Worse, if he has an iota of acting talent in him, I have yet to see it. Worst, he has a dismaying and highly visible habit of taking steps as if every inch of his shoe sole were required to make contact with the stage in a deliberate and slowly rolling gait. To this comical rhythm he recites his lines. There is no discernible distinction whatever in the two aspects of his part.

He remains in the play for historical and sentimental reasons. Unlikely as it must seem, Sinsheimer was very fond of him. They sang the songs of the old operettas together, the sentimental *Schmalz* of Kalman, Lehar, Fall, arm in arm beside the piano. Sweetchild took the death of Sinsheimer very hard; not even Lipschitz had the heart to oust him after that, and now I have inherited him. Well, somehow I must penetrate his denseness.

Meanwhile, I was sitting in the library, as I have said, my own denseness such that the newspaper paragraphs failed to penetrate it, my hand trembling rather more than usual. The day was severely overcast, with a grim, darkly smudged sky. Not much light entered the windows; all the lamps were lit. It might have been late on a winter's afternoon. Impatient with myself, I was on the point of abandoning the paper unread when Kunstler and Hamburger came in.

"God save you, sir," said Hamburger.

"My honored lord," said Kunstler.

"Good lads, how do you both?" I said.

They were in a jocular mood. I tried my best to match them, if only for Hamburger's sake. They got on well together.

"We've been looking for you, Gerhardt and I," said Hamburger. "Guess who were last night's big winners? You wouldn't believe how much."

That Hamburger, who knows well enough my attitude toward these nightly debauches that sap our players of their energy, should thrust his glee under my nose, I looked not to find. "Congratulations," I said, in as even a voice as I could muster.

"So, Otto," said Kunstler, "you, too, are in luck. We're going to treat you to breakfast at Goldstein's. Whatever you want, you order. The sky's the limit."

"Actually, Lottie Grabscheidt is treating, in case you don't want to spend our money. Can you imagine? She's holding three aces and a king, and she loses the pot." Thus Hamburger.

"And she folds with a full house," said Kunstler. "Don't forget that."

" 'Better we were playing strip poker,' she tells us."

" 'Do me a favor,' says Blum—he's also losing heavily—'don't strip.' "

"So, old friend," said Hamburger, "we're taking you to breakfast."

"Unfortunately, I've already had breakfast. Besides, Comyns has put me on a regimen."

"Well, coffee, then, Otto," said Kunstler. "Come and have coffee. You can watch us eat."

"Many thanks, good of you. But alas, I have a full schedule this morning. And rehearsals, as always, this afternoon." I shook the newspaper and lifted it, dismissing them. "You find me trying to catch up with the news before getting to work."

"Half an hour you can spare," said Hamburger, his disappointment, like a child's, painted on his face.

"Sorry. A rain check."

"Listen, Benno," said Kunstler, "if he can't, he can't. Do me a favor, go over to Goldstein's and get us a table. I'll be along in a minute. I want to have a private word with Otto."

The last thing I wanted was a private word with Kunstler! I rustled the newspaper impatiently. Kunstler, meanwhile, waited until Hamburger had disappeared and then sat down on the chair opposite. I lowered the paper and made a show of disgruntled resignation.

"So, Otto, we can talk."

"The library is not the place for a conversation." I pointed to the sign: Silence Pleases; Please, Silence.

"It's no secret you don't like me."

"Mr. Kunstler, I scarcely know you."

"I get on with most people."

"I've observed."

"Take just now, for example: all I wanted was to be sociable, treat you to breakfast. Was that so terrible?"

"Very kind of you. But as I said, I'm on a regimen."

"So what is it? What's bugging you? Get it onto the table, clear the air, talk turkey."

"Your command of idiom is exemplary."

"Is that what you do to the hand of friendship? Spit on it?"

"Very well, Mr. Kunstler, since you ask. You've been making secret inquiries about me. That, as you can imagine, I don't like."

He seemed genuinely puzzled. "What d'you mean?"

"You want I should spell it out? All right. I saw you in

Selma Gross's office. No doubt you remember the day. When you spotted me outside, you put your finger to your lips, and Selma nodded."

"But that had nothing to do with you! It was a private matter—Selma's. You got it back to front: she asked *me* to keep quiet."

"Of course."

"I swear it." He put up a hand as if about to take the Oath of Allegiance. "Look, I can even tell you about it now, if you want. The rumor's already circulating, the blabbermouth must've told one person too many. Selma's leaving Bernie, that's all. She says that since his operation he's a changed person, wants to be waited on hand and foot, even refuses his Friday-night duties. He's afraid of the strain, a relapse. She's going to take him for a bundle; then she's going to quit work and become a resident here. She says it's a lively place, the Emma Lazarus."

And Selma had said not a word about it to me!

"You believe me now?"

How could I not? A pause. "I apologize, Mr. Kunstler."

He grinned and waved my apology aside. "Never mind the 'Mr. Kunstler.' You can call me Gerry. But you see how it helps to clear the air? Okay, another thing." He grew serious. "Benno tells me you don't like to talk about the old days. Of course, I understand. Perfectly. You'll excuse me, I've seen the number on your wrist. But in Dr. Comyns' office I scraped a raw nerve, I could see, and that had nothing to do with the war years; the subject was your writing. Yet you clammed up. Why?"

"A man does not bare his soul to the first stranger who comes along."

"Who asked you to bare your soul? We were only chatting, that's all. But you looked as if I'd pulled your trousers down. Why should you be ashamed?"

"Because I've much to be ashamed of. And I still don't want to talk about it, not to you, not to anybody. You want to be friendly? Be friendly: drop the subject. You don't know what you're putting your nose into." I was trembling, whether from anger or terror I cannot say.

"But you're wrong just the same. First, you were not the only one. Second, you may even have done some good, particularly in the early days. Third, what counts is motivation and intent. You did what you did for the good of all. What more could you do? No one could have imagined what was coming."

I said nothing.

"Think about what I've said. If you want to talk later, we'll talk. If not, not." He got up and put out his hand. "Friends?"

Well, I took his hand, of course. What choice did I have? Kunstler, who knows everything, knows nothing! But in his ignorant wisdom he put his finger very precisely on my shame.

* * *

THE PROBLEM as I came to see it in the camps was not the terror or the physical deprivation or the pain or even the utter lack of hope, the gray misery of squatting in filth for weeks and months and years while the mad dance of death went on all around. The problem was how in such circumstances to retain the merest shred of human dignity. The signposts of civilization, the countless unrecognized details of ordinary life through which we find our bearings, gain our sense of time and place and personhood—these were gone, vanished forever. Beyond the barbed wire was a scarcely imaginable Paradise, peopled with golden gods and goddesses. Yes, the world at war was Paradise! Within the compound was Hell. We were creatures of nightmare, ugly, stinking, subhuman. You see, it was getting harder and harder not to believe the propaganda. I was beginning to assume that they were right, that *I was where I belonged.* That was the danger.

My solution was simple: I reentered the past. Time, of course, does not exist in Hell, but before the camps there had been time. I dived into the ocean of time, and when I surfaced, lungs bursting, gasping for air, I held in my hands nuggets of memory. I dived again and again, returning always with treasure. Eventually I underwent a metamorphosis, reversing the process of evolution. Gills appeared, a tail, fins. I became a fish and stayed in the ocean.

Well, I grow fanciful, and I blush to think of you smiling at me. "Speak plainly, Otto," my father would say. "Spare us the poetry." Meta would have understood, though. She could trade me metaphor for metaphor.

To put it plainly, then, I chose a day from the past and relived it. At first it wasn't easy. The memories were fragmentary, brittle, evanescent, and the brutal facts of the camp were insistent. But little by little I gained in skill, recalled details I had thought gone forever, joined shard to shard. I relived whole days, then weeks. It was important not to cheat: it was tempting to reshape the past. But all I wanted was to become a human being again, and life for human beings, after all, is not unalloyed bliss. I relived sorrow as well as joy, and more often than either I relived perfectly ordinary, utterly humdrum days.

It was like learning to ride a bicycle. The child falls off, rubs his bruises, perhaps cries a little, and tries again; at length he can wobble along, he has the hang of it; at last he flies like the wind. It was just a matter of balance, after all. Yes, but that was the tricky part: one could not sit idly by, mouth agape, immersed in fantasy. The routine of the camp had to be fulfilled, the formations, the work details, the attempts to avoid the notice of our capricious dance masters in their polished boots. One had to maintain a pious subservience to the transient hierarchy of doomed souls within the compound, pay careful attention to the shifts in faction and power. One had to give such care as was possible to the minimal imperatives of the body, to the bestial scramble for a rotted turnip-top or scrap of rancid fat, to evacuation, ablutions, rags stolen for warmth, to sleep.

What was required to balance the bicycle was a radical shift in temporal perception. The stuff of memory became my everyday reality; everyday reality became a figment of my mind. I negotiated the routines of the camp with the same degree of involved disengagement that you yourself grant yesterday's incidents remembered today. Think about yesterday: you see yourself, don't you? You know what you did, what you said, what you felt. You might even "relive" some of yesterday's emotions, embarrassment, exultation, anger. But of course where you are today is in fact . . . where you are. That is perfectly normal. For me, however, the normal relationship between yesterday and today was reversed. Where I *was* was the past; what I seemed only to "remember" was the present. It was a deliberate effort of the will, and it saved my life.

Here is how I did it. I would select a date—for example, July 17, 1914. I was with the Infelds, on holiday in Baden-Baden. My aunt and uncle had kindly invited me to keep Joachim company. Neither the "old people" nor his little sister were much fun for him. It was a particularly happy time. My book had just been published. The juices of youth were flowing. Baden-Baden was in bloom with pretty young ladies—all chaperoned, of course, but that only added an exquisite spice to our enjoyment. The fun was in the stolen moment, the covert glance, the blushes, the sighs. We were young, very young, with straw hats on our heads, boutonnieres in our lapels.

We had lunch that day at a restaurant in the Black Forest, the Blue Trout. The room was cool and timbered. The fish swam lazily in the tank. The diner would tell the waiter which one he wanted, and within twenty minutes it would appear on a plate before him, cooked to perfection. What was astonishing was the resignation with which the fish met their fate: they seemed to know when their number was up. Down would go the net into the tank. All the fish but the chosen one would scatter in alarm. But the chosen fish, *your* fish, would make only the most desultory effort to escape, a minimal motion of the tail, a shudder, and hoopla! it was caught.

I can still ride the bicycle.

* * *

IT IS NOT TRUE that I retain nothing of the past but my letter from Rilke, and of course my memories. I have some photographs that once belonged to Lola, which Kenneth Himmelfarb thrust on me, along with a few family odds and ends, when Lola died. Some of the furniture, the paintings, the books that made their way from Nuremberg to Central Park West to West Eighty-second Street are still to be found here in my room in the Emma Lazarus. The photographs, generations of them, some brought by Lola to New York, many sent to her from Germany in the few years after she left us, are collected in an old shirt box that sits on a shelf in the closet, here as on Eighty-second Street. When Lola died, I got off the bicycle, packed up my memories, and put them out of reach, in a closet of the mind. Until today I have never wanted to look at the photographs, frozen warrants of life, of happiness, of belief in continuity that could show me only the dead. But today, impelled by I know not what, I took them out, sifted through them, grouped them. How they skew the past! Well, no one reaches for his camera, after all, to take a snapshot of family misery. There they were, all my dead, not knowing they are dead. Why describe them? All families have such photographs. I was able to look at them without emotion. Then I put them back on the shelf.

You know now that I had a son, Hugo. He was named after Meta's maternal grandfather. He was a splendid little boy, you must take my word for it, born with a sense of humor. Of course, his smile tended to fade in my presence. But I've told you about that. He got his looks from Meta. Today he would have been in his early fifties; that's hard to grasp, impossible to understand. But of course he is long since dead.

* * *

I AM ON THE BICYCLE AGAIN, but I have lost my sense of balance. I am dizzy, both literally and figuratively. What is happening to me?

For the last thirty years I have existed in the present, disposing of my life a day at a time. Only, unlike most people, I had no past. My first fifty years, at any rate, were high on the shelf, behind the closet door. I began these memoirs "to set the historical record straight," to leave a written record of the origin of the word *Dada*. Prompted by the seemingly purposeful arrival of Mandy Dattner in our midst, that became important to me.

Accordingly, I went to the closet of the mind and removed a few items for display, a carefully controlled "retrospective," so to speak, of the Zurich years of Otto Körner. But once the box was opened, the contents tumbled out, uncontrolled, uncontrollable, revealing folly upon folly. The last pitiful truths demand to be told.

* * *

THE BICYCLE races downhill, and I cannot control it.

* * *

THIS TIME I do not choose the day. This time the day chooses me. It is April 3, 1933. The Nazis have been in power for a little over two months. The Jews are in shock. Waves of violence have swept over Germany, and not against the Jews alone: the Brownshirts are settling old grudges. The New Order has begun in high gear. There is nothing to restrain the hooligans

229

now; the mobs are in the streets. Today is the third day of a state-sponsored boycott of Jewish businesses. Coincidentally, Körner's has been closed for "inventory and reorganization."

We are in my parents' living room, where we are having tea and those delicious pastries that my mother knows Hugo is so fond of. The spring sunshine pierces the curtains; the ormolu clock ticks away on the mantel shelf. There is a fire in the hearth, for despite the sunshine, the day is chill. I see it all so clearly.

Meta sits straight-backed, as always, holding little Hugo to her as if to protect him from immediate attack. She is clearly agitated. She bites her finger, breathes with effort. I imagine that my first duty is to calm her. Hysterics, I feel, cannot help. She is alarming Hugo: seven years old and he is wetting his bed again. This is how I react to the beginning of the end: it is a matter of family decorum.

My father sits in his stuffed chair by the fire. His hand trembles, his cup and saucer clink against his watch chain. He is sixty-eight now, but you would suppose him much older. In the new era he has lost his robustness, his air of decisiveness. He, too, is adrift, bewildered by the events that have overtaken his beloved Fatherland. Meanwhile, my mother is at the table selecting a cream puff for Hugo: "Let me see. . . . Which one will make him grow the fastest?" She deals with the looming disaster by ignoring it. Politics, phooey!

And where in this domestic scene is Otto Körner? He leans against the bookcase, a study in nonchalance, one hand in his pocket, the other resting lightly on a leather-bound volume of Goethe's collected works.

Meta can restrain herself no longer. She appeals to my father. "Tell him we must all leave—you and Mutti, too. Lola and Kurt, Joachim, my parents, we must all get out!"

"Really, Meta, leave Father alone, he has enough to worry about." In my voice I express a hint of indulgent exasperation.

"We can't simply drop everything and run for the border because a few idiotic louts get out of hand, now can we?"

My father rallies. "Before there were Germans in Germany, there were Jews."

"As soon as there were Germans, there were anti-Semites."

"But there, you have said it yourself." I speak as if she has handed me a trump card. "Anti-Semitism is nothing new in Germany. Fortunately, today we have laws against that sort of thing."

"Laws? What laws? Hitler is the law. Streicher is the law. Jewish judges are being publicly humiliated. They're stringing us up in the streets." We have heard this morning of a Jewish lawyer lynched by a mob in Kiel. She turns back to my father. "Did Otto tell you? Three days ago Hugo had to sit on the Jews' bench in school. They measured his head with calipers, a demonstration of Jew-filthy inferiority."

She must have been holding Hugo too tightly, for he squirms, and she releases him, kissing him on the temple. His grandmother lures him to the table. She is holding up a plate with a cream puff. "Why are they making such a fuss, Grandma?" She ties a napkin around his neck. "Pay no attention, grown-ups like to exercise their jaws *before* they eat."

"It won't go on like this," says my father. "It cannot. Hindenburg—"

"Hindenburg can do nothing!"

"Personally . . ." I take a sip of tea and smack my lips together. "Ah, excellent! Darjeeling?" I put the cup and saucer down and pick up the volume of Goethe. "Personally, I expect any day to hear a public announcement over the radio: General von Such-and-such or von So-and-so has taken over the reins of government. It's only a matter of time." I leaf through the book as though looking for a pertinent passage.

From Meta, a look of open scorn. But she says nothing more.

How could I have been so blind, so insanely smug? Well, of course, I knew my Germans. One had to adjust his perspective to the larger view. Sporadic acts of anti-Semitism were no more than the initial exuberance of the Nazi triumph, a passing phase of the new Reich. Things were bound to get better, settle down. What were we if not Germans? We sprang from the German soil; we were Germans in our innermost souls. One could not, in any case, give in to female vapors. One had responsibilities. No doubt I believed all that.

But I had other, more pressing, imperatives. A week before Meta's unseemly outburst in my parents' living room, I had received an urgent call from an old school chum, at that time an editor on the *Israelitische Rundschau*. As the wave of panic swept over the Jewish community, an effort was already under way to draw together the various Jewish organizations and form a common front against the terror. I was associated with no faction; indeed, I was an unknown. My friend wanted from me a series of articles on the current crisis. On the third day of the boycott I dropped the first of my articles into the postbox. More were to follow. Before the end I was also to appear in the *Jüdische Volkszeitung*, the *CV-Wochenende*, the *Monatschaft der deutschen Zionisten*, the *Hebräische Welt*, and others whose names I forget, the whole spectrum of Jewish publications. Again and again I was to urge the Jews of Germany to stand fast. It was cowardly to flee the homeland only because a few months or even years of hardship lay ahead. "The history of German Jewry teaches that we must wait, and we are capable of waiting," I wrote. We had reason for pride in our dual heritage. No one and nothing could strip us of our essential German identity. We were bound by history and fate to our beloved Fatherland. "As a matter of right—legal, moral, and religious—we belong on German soil": this was the poisonous nonsense I spewed forth. And why? Because once more I had a readership. Because thousands all over Germany were drinking down the honeyed palliative of my words. I received hundreds of letters from my fans expressing gratitude for my forthright stand.

Leaning casually against the bookcase that day, a series of articles already bubbling away in my head, I could scarcely pander to my wife's panic. "It will all blow over," I said. And I delivered myself of those fatuous paragraphs already en route to the *Israelitische Rundschau*.

How many besides my own flesh and blood have I on my conscience? I should have screamed from the rooftops, "Jews, run for your lives!"

* * *

OLD AS I AM, I am still pedaling, zooming downhill, my heart bursting. The fact is, I cannot stop, and I am afraid to jump off.

* * *

SHE ASKED ME again, did Meta. Asked me? She begged me, implored me. "We must get out now. Now, Otto. Soon it will be too late." Terrified, she plucked at my sleeve, her eyes deep-sunk. "Lola and Kurt will vouch for us, we must go to them, to New York."

This was in 1935, shortly after our countrymen had stripped us of our citizenship. A new outbreak of violence and intimidation was sweeping across the land. Meta and Hugo scarcely went out anymore. Hugo had a tutor at home, a meticulous man, formerly of the Royal College, now dismissed from his post and cast out of his home by his gentile wife. The tutor was a hapless wanderer to whom we were giving temporary shelter.

"Please, Otto!"

But I was deep in a new scheme. "Symbiosis" was its grand name. The idea was to create some kind of state-within-the-state, its citizens known from the word *Jude* to be imprinted on an identifying document, but otherwise self-governing and working for the mutual benefit of both entities. How mad we all were! We refused to recognize that they saw us as maleficent bacteria in the bloodstream of an otherwise healthy body politic. There was only one solution, of course. The bacterium having been identified, it must be eliminated, annihilated. Meanwhile, stupidly, some of the bacteria created committees, held meetings, drew up resolutions, produced draft constitutions, fought over words and phrases, grew passionate, toiled long into the night. How could I, a possible future minister of a possible state-within-the-state, my shoulders already bowed with the anticipated burden of office, the fate of German Jewry in my hands—how could I cave in to the hysterical and defeatist ravings of my wife? And how would it look if I, the spokesman for symbiosis, allowed my wife and child to flee while urging others to stand fast? It was out of the question.

It was then, I believe, that Meta began to hate me in earnest. She never asked me again. I cannot remember that she ever again spoke to me, no, not even after *Kristallnacht*, when my parents retired one night to swallow Veronal, obtained who knows where. They left a note, of course, in my father's neat handwriting: "We execute upon ourselves the judgment of our Fatherland."

So you see, by the time of Lola's suicide, I was already an old hand. In November 1938, however, I was still green. Meta's reaction was maniacal laughter that went on and on until her voice gave out and she lapsed from croaking into silence. She was never quite in her right mind after that. Hugo looked after her. Poor boy, what a world he found himself in!

* * *

AND SHE LAUGHED AGAIN when, three years later, they loaded us into the train. By now her flesh had shrunk to the bone. She might have been Hugo's grandmother, an old madwoman, a crone, pale and ill smelling. A doctor, a fellow "passenger," slapped her sharply across the cheek, a kindly blow, carefully calculated; her pitifully thin face scarcely shifted on its stalk. By the time we arrived at the camp, she was already dead.

Hugo would not leave his mother's body. I had to pry his fingers from her arm. Then I pushed him out of the train and sent him sprawling onto the platform. A blow on his temple from a guard's casual rifle butt, and he joined his mother.

How can a man with such crimes on his conscience go on living? Only by dropping a portcullis before the horror, digging a moat around it, locking it away immured in stone. The heart cannot otherwise endure such grief. But why, he must ask himself, should he live at all? He creates a theory of Purpose.

34

WHEN THE BICYCLE STOPPED, I fell off—which is to say, I fainted. That is, at any rate, what seems to have happened. Imagine the consternation in the library, where my little drama took place! There was Korner, shortly after a light breakfast of tea and toast, having picked up the *Times* from the rack and about to sit down, suddenly on the floor. The Red Dwarf, who witnessed my performance from the door, tells me I put a hand to my forehead as if perplexed and then sank slowly onto the carpet. Two of the ladies screamed. From the lobby, the proximate sedentary hobbled in to see what was what. The Red Dwarf ran for Dr. Comyns, who came at a gallop, shooed the curious from the room, loosened my collar and tie, thrust smelling salts beneath my nostrils, and so urged me back, coughing, to the Emma Lazarus.

Here I still am, ladies and gentlemen, two days later. All that remains of what the genial doctor calls my "episode" is a small bandage on my right temple—that and a strange mood, a heady mélange of calm and good cheer. Dr. Comyns racked his brains, tested me with every suitable test known to him, and drew a blank. Finally he delivered himself of an opinion: "These things," he said, "happen." Nevertheless, I am temporarily off the list of solo-ambulants, barred from rehearsals, and "under modified observation." With the Kommandant not yet back from a seminar in Washington, Dr. Comyns is naturally reluctant to take chances. As for my starring role in *Hamlet*—

now only three days away!—well, he says, *if* I don't excite myself, *if* nothing further "happens," why, he ventures to suppose I'll be able to perform.

In my present mood I seem unable to worry. First, I had a word with La Dawidowicz. The entire company, of course, by now knew of my indisposition. Spirits were low. As for La Dawidowicz, she was already in mourning. Her hair in frizzled disarray, her eyes red and moist, a black dressing gown wrapped around her loose rotundity, she opened her door to me as one gazing into the pit itself. "You too," she moaned. Her teeth were not yet in. "First Adolphe, then my sweet Nahum, now you."

"Come now, Tosca, don't be foolish. Here I am, you see me. I'm fit as a fiddle."

"The Angel of Death points a finger, and you tell me I shouldn't be foolish. I should be happy, maybe?"

"How would you like to be codirector?"

"Codirector of what? A funeral service? That's what you're offering me, big shot? Nahum was right, he should rest in peace: the play's jinxed."

"The play will go on as planned."

"You're a solo-ambulant all of a sudden? You believe in fairies?"

"I ate something that disagreed with me, that's all. I need someone to take over rehearsals, to solve the last-minute problems, someone with intelligence and understanding, someone who can shoulder the responsibility. Now, whom here in the Emma Lazarus could I come to but you? Still, if you're not interested—"

"Codirector?"

"I need someone to rally the ranks, someone with experience, a strong personality."

"The programs have already been printed."

"The Kommandant will make an announcement from the

stage: 'We are fortunate to have as codirector the beautiful Tosca Dawidowicz, our wonderful Ophelia.' "

"Not, you should know, that *that* matters."

"Of course not. The play's the thing."

To my intense displeasure, she kissed me, a slobbering toothless kiss, on the cheek. "You got yourself a codirector!"

"Work around me as best you can. Kunstler can read my lines, no need to have him act. And Tosca"—I pointed to her black dressing gown—"put on something gay this morning, something to lift the company's morale. You have an eye for such things."

* * *

THE SEED has put down roots. Today I spotted a green shoot.

Sitting in the waiting room a few minutes before the hour of this morning's "observation," I supposed I heard the doctor calling me to come in. I opened the door and surprised Mandy Dattner and Dr. Comyns in an embrace of the most extraordinary passion. They were, I am relieved to say, fully clothed. Nevertheless, he stood there in the cold winter sunlight that streamed through his window, his hands supporting and savagely kneading her buttocks, his legs slightly bent to withstand the strain, while she, her legs wrapped around his midriff, rubbed herself up and down against him. One of her arms was flung around his neck; with the other she had contrived to reach behind her and beneath his bruising fingers to cup and manipulate the bulge at his crotch. Meanwhile, their mouths sought one another with such eager suckings and smackings that the click of their teeth was audible above their moans.

"Excuse me," I said.

For a moment they froze in place; then they leapt apart, Mandy landing neatly with a practiced bounce on the balls of her feet. Hoopla!

"Grampus!" she exclaimed, and burst into laughter.

Dr. Comyns reached for his stethoscope and straightened his tie. "That will be all, Miss Dattner, thank you." He stroked his beard between forefinger and thumb with the air of a philosopher pondering a problem in metaphysics.

"Yes, Doctor," she said with a wink to me. And she left, pausing only to blow an impudent kiss to him from the door.

His aplomb was masterly, I must grant him that. By not so much as an "ahem" did he acknowledge that I might have seen anything untoward. He examined me with his customary thoroughness, remarked once more on the grayness of my color, put that down to a lack of fresh air and exercise, and sent me on my way.

*　*　*

IN THE AFTERNOON Mandy visited me in my room.

"The thing is," she said, frowning, "Ralph thinks it's like *his.*"

"Perhaps it is."

She sat cross-legged on the floor, oblivious of the white lacy strip flanked by rich tendrils of hair that she presented to my view. "I told you, I *know* when it happened."

I looked deliberately elsewhere. "Freddy Blum can't make babies."

"I never said it was Mr. Blum."

"Your discretion does you credit. Blum it certainly was not. If not Dr. Comyns either, then someone else. About that possibility I neither know nor want to know."

"But I felt a ping."

"A ping is no proof of paternity. Blum is sterile. I tell you this only because you need to know it. Obviously it is not the sort of information to be bandied about."

"O wow, gee, you're *sure* about Mr. Blum? He's, you know, like what you said?" Up went a tentative eyebrow. She hovered on a smile.

"Sterility," I said pompously, "is a frequent concomitant of priapism; the two go, as it were, hand in hand. Read your Krafft-Ebing, your Havelock Ellis."

"Gee, I dunno."

"Trust me, I do."

"Wee-urd!" She squirmed on her bottom, the white strip shimmering in the darkness. "Then it'd have to be Ralph! Oh, Grampus!" She leapt to her feet in a single motion, my little gymnast, and flung her arms around me. "Then it's all okay!"

"But now things are serious, Mandy. You're practically a fiancée, and soon you'll be a mother. It's time to impart a measure of decorum to your life."

"You mean I gotta redo my pad?"

Was she mocking me? "I mean it's time to stop fooling around."

She kissed me, delighted. "Fuddy-duddy!"

* * *

As for Blum, perhaps he *is* sterile. At the least I spoke a metaphorical truth.

* * *

For the last forty years I have toyed with the idea of Purpose, have tossed it like a ball into the air, have apprehended pattern, movement, meaning, an ineluctable goal, a striving toward *somewhere* in the restless chaos of existence. These foolish pages bear witness to the lasting witlessness of my endeavor, a vain defense against the terror of the void. For what "purpose" can any rational being find in my life? No longer can I delude myself that *because* I cannot see order, ipso facto, it exists. To be sure, every present moment is the pinnacle of all that has gone before. To that extent, all my past was prologue to this now. But Purpose? How laughable! Have I been spared when better than I—much better—were not, in order that I might tread the boards of the Emma Lazarus in the company of others as decrepit as myself? We, like Dr. Johnson's lady preachers, may justly be compared to dogs trained to walk on their hind legs. The wonder is not that we do what we do well, but that we can do it at all.

No, there is only the present. This was the truth I recognized when Lola died, her poor body hanging grotesquely from the water pipe, her husband crouched in torment on the kitchen floor. But I was wrong to sever the present from the past, for the past has no imperatives that the present cannot refuse. What can we do but grasp the fleeting moment? For me, in this now, that moment is our play. I want to be Hamlet. And I care not a whit for the comical figure I shall cut.

As for Purpose, that comes not from without but from within. The Contessa's lawyers have proved as efficient as ever. Hipsy-pipsy, the papers have been drawn up; pipsy-hipsy, they have been signed and witnessed. When I leave the ever-present now and enter the eternal then, Mandy Dattner will receive in trust for her child that estate which was mine, thanks to the generosity of Kenneth Himmelfarb and the wonderful cunning of the Contessa's saintly Meurice. There's Purpose for you.

35

HE EXCITEMENT at the Emma Lazarus is everywhere apparent. La Dawidowicz has reported that all's well
with the play. Kunstler has been reading my lines. "A good-
looking feller," she said. "A ladykiller. A pity he wasn't with us
sooner, a feller like that we could always have used. It's a waste,
him sitting in the prompter's box. No disrespect to you, Otto,
believe me. Kunstler also would make a fine Hamlet. And how
about you, incidentally? You okay?"

Tomorrow is our big day. The ladies are flushed and
chatter like nervous magpies. Wittkower paces, mumbling his
lines. Pfaffenheim stands before the long mirror in the second-
floor corridor and practices his gestures. The stage manager
cannot find the goblet from which Gertrude is supposed to
toast her son, and Leopold Nordheim II, who ten years ago
donated to our community a sixteenth-century silver Cup of
Elijah, once in the household of the Sage of Prague, refuses to
release it as a substitute. And so it goes. Through all this
madness I retain my strange mood of calm cum good cheer.

Starting at noon tomorrow, we are having an Open House.
Relatives and other guests will be free to wander through the
communal rooms, where our residents are even now setting up
little booths to display their "arts and crafts." Coffee and tea urns
will bubble all afternoon; all afternoon heaping platters of minia-
ture doughnuts will emerge from the kitchen. In the library, I
Solisti will entertain the musically disposed. In the lobby

Kunstler is mounting an exhibition of recent (relatively speaking) paintings. The penthouse lecture room is being readied for a feminist symposium to be led by none other than Lucille Morgenbesser, Hermione's daughter, who is donating her time without remuneration, on the topic "Maccabean Women: Keeping the Lamp Alight." The members of the board, the Kommandant, the staff, resident and nonresident alike, will mingle with the visitors. In short, this is to be a gala occasion.

* * *

THE GREEN LIGHT this morning from Dr. Comyns. I emerged from his office into the corridor to find an anxious group waiting for me. "So?" said the Red Dwarf. I gave them the thumbs-up sign. La Dawidowicz pinched my cheek. "You should only break a leg," she said. "What kind of talk is that?" said Pfaffenheim. "Theatrical talk. It's a way of saying *mazel tov* without exciting the evil eye," explained Wittkower. "Such superstitious crap from a boss-coddled elite has always ground the workers down," complained the Red Dwarf. "Good friends, my thanks to all," I said. There were cheers, an unseemly rowdiness. Nevertheless, they meant well, and so I did not rebuke them.

To be honest, I was surprised to have passed the doctor's examination. Earlier I had experienced what I might call a "near episode"—that is to say, a dizziness. Luckily I was sitting on my bed at the time, still in my pajamas, and I waited until it passed over. It left me with a certain queasiness that makes the thought of food repellant. Some nourishment I must take, but common sense dictates that I avoid the seasonal and well-loved potato pancakes, especially this evening.

* * *

LIKE DR. COMYNS, Hamburger is not pleased with my color. "What you need is a little sunshine, some warm air, you look like shit. Hannah and I are going to the Bahamas once the play is over. Why don't you come with us?"

"On your honeymoon you won't need me."

"Not exactly a honeymoon." He looked a trifle embarrassed. "Lucille, the daughter, she's got a tax expert, a brilliant woman, Harvard Business School graduate, highest honors. She's explained we're better off single, taxwise, you understand." A pause. "You think I'm an old fool, Otto?"

"Mrs. Perlmutter is an extraordinary woman."

"Exactly, you've said it yourself." He shied away from that topic and returned to the matter of my health. "But seriously, why don't you join us?"

"First of all, I like my winters cold. There is a decorum even to the seasons. As for my color, it says nothing about how well I am. Dr. Comyns thinks I'm fine. To be honest, I've never felt better. A few episodes of dizziness don't deserve a trip to the Bahamas."

"A *few* episodes? There have been more than one?"

My tongue was ripe for biting. "And what if there have? Passing phenomena, nothing more."

"How do you know that? You're a doctor, maybe? Such things are warnings. They tell you to slow down."

"Not a whit. We defy augury."

"It's only a play, Otto. It can be postponed."

"No, it *can't* be postponed, it's tonight. I'm an old man, Benno, eighty-three last birthday, older even than you. I've been old for a very long time. When I was young I thought I had a role to play on the world-historical stage. No, don't laugh, that's what I once thought. The stage has shrunk with my flesh. What is left for me? Here is my stage, here at the Emma Lazarus. Tonight I am to be Hamlet. You must be my Horatio in deed, my constant friend. This is no time to let me down. You must promise not to interfere. Promise me, Benno."

Sadly he shook my hand.

"Cheer up, for heaven's sake! Look at me, *I'm* cheerful. In a week you'll send me a postcard: 'Having a wonderful time. Glad you're not here.' "

* * *

MY SUIT OF SOLEMN BLACK lies on the bed, ready for the donning. From downstairs I hear the laughter, the lively chatter, the stir and bustle that tell me the hour is nigh. When darkness fell, residents, staff, and guests, too, crowded into the library, where we witnessed the lighting of eight candles, Tuvye Bialkin holding the *shamash*, the serving candle; we heard from him the three blessings, our expressions of gratitude for the candles, for the great miracle granted us so very long ago, and for having been brought to this day. Amen. Amen. Amen. I have decided to skip the evening meal. The latest "near episode," scarcely noticeable, has passed, and I again feel calm and strong. Only, it is peaceful here in my room, here at my desk, beneath my Rilke letter in its fine new frame. To hand is a small glass of cognac, a sip of which will cause the blood to race and wash the last of the cobwebs from my brain. I am content.

I riffle through the pages of this manuscript, the mountain heaped upon my desk, and I see that I have not always been kind to you, Benno, for in truth I did not know till now to whom these writings were addressed. But if not you, my dear Horatio, then who should be the repository of my story? You will in friendship forgive me this as you have already forgiven me so much more.

A knock at the door: La Grabscheidt in full evening dress—black, of course—her curious grinning pin upon her bosom, a tiara tilted quaintly on her head, recovered, I am happy to say, a little excited, perhaps, perhaps a little tipsy, able at least to swell the stage as a Lady-in-Waiting. She reports that the audience is making its way to the auditorium, the actors are assembling. La Dawidowicz, faithful to her pledge, is in command. It is the moment to put on my costume. But I, the "star," have still a time of grace. The Kommandant has yet to make his unctuous speech of welcome—there are big donors out there in the audience, to say nothing of a representative of the British consulate in New York, whose acceptance of our invitation surprised us all, and of the arts editor of the *Jewish Charivari*, who has already devoted three days to interviewing the company. How very proud Sinsheimer would have been! After the Kommandant's speech comes the singing of the Hatikvah, insisted upon, against the Red Dwarf's strong objection, by the late Nahum Lipschitz and retained in his memory. (The evening will end with a singing of the "Star-Spangled Banner," led by the Ladies' Glee Club, which depends for its success on the number of bladders able to hold their own.) And after the Hatikvah the battlements of Elsinore, starkly thrusting against a black sky and battered by thunder and lightning. Hamlet does not appear before scene two: "A little more than kin, and less than kind." La Grabscheidt has promised to give me ten minutes' warning.

I am confident of our triumph tonight. The dizziness is quite gone. The bat sees at last the exit from the cave and summons its strength. The trout essays a desultory twitching of the tail. In a minute I shall place this manuscript with the shirt box upon the closet shelf. And there will yet be time to sit awhile before La Grabscheidt's summons.

* * *

THE READINESS is all.